THE LAST TRUMPET

THE LAST TRUMPET

A HUGH RENNERT MYSTERY

TODD DOWNING

COACHWHIP PUBLICATIONS

Landisville, Pennsylvania

The Last Trumpet by Todd Downing
Copyright © 2012 Coachwhip Publications
Introduction © 2012 Curtis Evans
No claim made on public domain material.

ISBN 1-61646-152-7
ISBN-13 978-1-61646-152-2

Cover Image: Bull (cc) VectorPortal; Background © Llaszlo

CoachwhipBooks.com

CONTENTS

INTRODUCTION
CURTIS EVANS

"Mr. Downing is a born detective story writer."
—Edward Powys Mathers ("Torquemada"),
review of Todd Downing, *Vultures in the Sky* (1935)

THE RICHNESS AND DIVERSITY of American genre writing during the Golden Age of mystery fiction (c. 1920 to 1939) is much under-appreciated today. Golden Age mystery readers could choose from a wide variety of literary dishes, be it the tough stuff of the hard-boiled boys (most famously Dashiell Hammett, Raymond Chandler and James M. Cain), which has long received the lion's share of the attention that scholars have granted American Golden Age crime writers; the psychological suspense (or HIBK—Had I But Known—as it was once disparaged) of Elisabeth Sanxay Holding, Mary Roberts Rinehart, Mignon Eberhart and Leslie Ford; the urban sophistication of Rex Stout, Patrick Quentin and Rufus King; the madcap humor of Phoebe Atwood Taylor and Craig Rice (the latter making the tail end of the Golden Age); the eccentric extra-vaganzas of Harry Stephen Keeler; the police procedurals of Helen Reilly; the courtroom dramas of Erle Stanley Gardner; or the magnificent baroque puzzles of S. S. Van Dine, Ellery Queen, Anthony Abbot, John Dickson Carr, C. Daly King and Clyde B. Clason.

This listing of authors just scratches the surface of American mystery writing in the years between the two world wars. So many accomplished mystery writers from the period have undeservingly fallen into obscurity. One such individual is Todd Downing, the Golden Age chronicler of fictional murders in Mexico.

Todd Downing was born in 1902 in the town of Atoka, Choctaw Nation, Indian Territory (soon to be Oklahoma). Though one-eighth Choctaw and, like his father Samuel (Sam), an enrolled member of the Choctaw Nation, Todd Downing had what in many ways was a traditional, early twentieth century small town American upbringing. Both Todd's father Sam and his mother Maud were staunch churchgoing Presbyterians and Republicans and Todd was brought up according to the proper precepts of these two orthodoxies.

Yet the Downing family of Atoka was unusual in its great love of reading. From an early age Todd Downing could be found in nooks and corners of the family's two-story foursquare house with his nose buried in books. He particularly loved romantic tales of adventure, played out in settings around the globe. Beginning with Sir Walter Scott's and H. Rider Haggard's colorful sagas of derring-do, Todd moved on, in his teenage years, to crime and mystery, in the form of the short story collections of Arthur B. Reeve, creator of the virtuous scientific detective Dr. Craig Kennedy, and the novels of Sax Rohmer, creator of the diabolical criminal mastermind Dr. Fu Manchu.

After Todd became a student at the University of Oklahoma in 1920, he soon discovered Edgar Wallace, the awesomely prolific English king of the thriller. Todd devoured Wallace shockers at a prodigious rate. (His library of books, bequeathed at his death in 1974 to Southeastern Oklahoma State University, included sixty-five Wallace novels and short story collections, as well as Wallace's autobiography and biography.) Yet as the 1920s progressed, Todd, like many bright people in his day, became increasingly interested in fair play detective fiction, where the point is not emotional jolts but cerebration: the reader tries to solve the mystery for her/himself through clues provided within the text by the author. Over the decade of the twenties Todd purchased detective novels and short story collections by Anthony Berkeley, Earl Derr Biggers, Lynn Brock, G. K. Chesterton, Mignon Eberhart, Rufus King, Marie

Belloc Lowndes, Baroness Orczy, Mary Roberts Rinehart, T. S. Stribling and S. S. Van Dine.

Between mysteries Todd managed to find time to qualify for his B.A. and M.A at the University of Oklahoma, as well as to take classes in Spanish, French and anthropology during summers spent at the National University of Mexico. In 1928 OU hired the young Atokan as an instructor in Spanish. (Todd was fluent in five languages: English, Choctaw, Spanish, French and Italian.) In addition to teaching his OU classes and conducting summer tour groups in Mexico, Todd continued voraciously reading both detective novels and crime thrillers; and in 1930 he began reviewing mysteries of all sorts in the literary pages of Oklahoma City's *Daily Oklahoman*. Especial favorites of Todd's in the mystery line were Agatha Christie, Dorothy L. Sayers, Ellery Queen, John Dickson Carr, Dashiell Hammett, Mary Roberts Rinehart, Mignon Eberhart and additional worthy writers who likely are less familiar to many today: Anthony Abbot, Rufus King, H. C. Bailey, Eden Phillpotts and Anthony Wynne (for more on Todd Downing's mystery fiction reviews see my book *Clues and Corpses: The Detective Fiction and Mystery Criticism of Todd Downing*).

Encouraged by an older colleague at the University of Oklahoma, Professor Kenneth C. Kaufman, Todd Downing wrote his first detective novel in 1931, not long after he had begun contributing mystery fiction reviews to the *Daily Oklahoman*. Eventually published in 1933, *Murder on Tour* introduced Todd's most important series detective, United States Customs Service agent Hugh Rennert, who would appear in seven detective novels between 1933 and 1937. (A Hugh Rennert novella, probably written by Todd in 1932, was published in 1945.) Besides *Murder on Tour* these are: *The Cat Screams* (1934), *Vultures in the Sky* (1935), *Murder on the Tropic* (1935), *The Case of the Unconquered Sisters* (1936), *The Last Trumpet* (1937) and *Night over Mexico* (1937). All six of these later novels now have been reprinted by Coachwhip Publications.

The Hugh Rennert detective novels are primarily set in Mexico (the one exception being *The Last Trumpet*, where the action

ranges from Cameron County, Texas to the Mexican state of
Tamaulipas). Todd Downing's authoritative and fascinating use of
Mexico as a setting in his detective novels makes him one of the
most important regionalist mystery writers of the Golden Age and
is his most significant contribution to the genre. Additionally, the
Rennert novels are graced with teasing fair play puzzle plots, styl-
ish writing and interesting characterizations. Hugh Rennert himself is a notable detective, modest, middle-aged, self-reflective and
somewhat melancholy, yet resolute and determined. ("A good kind
man," one character calls him in *Night over Mexico*, and he is.)
Hugh Rennert is fascinated with Mexico and *vacilada*, the mirth-
fully stoic attitude of the country's people toward life and death;
and over the course of the series Todd Downing explores what
might be termed the metaphysical relationship of Rennert and
Mexico in interesting ways. We learn a lot about both a man and a
country.

After 1937 Todd Downing wrote two more detective novels,
both with a different series detective (Texas sheriff Peter Bounty,
introduced in *The Last Trumpet*): *Death under the Moonflower*
(1938) and *The Lazy Lawrence Murders* (1941). He also published
the work which he considered his crowning achievement as a
writer, a non-fictional study of Mexico, *The Mexican Earth* (1940;
reprinted by the University of Oklahoma Press in 1996). Sadly,
Todd's attempt in the 1940s to write a mainstream historical novel
about Mexico came to naught. Todd had resigned as an instructor
at the University of Oklahoma in 1935 in order to devote himself
professionally to writing, but after 1941 he would never publish
another novel—indeed, after 1945 he never published any fiction
of any kind again. In the 1940s Todd found employment as an
advertising copy writer in Philadelphia. One of his ads, the tongue-
in-cheek mystery homage "The Case of the Crumpled Letter," was
chosen in 1959 as one of the 100 greatest advertisements.

In the 1950s Todd returned to the teaching profession, taking
posts at schools in Maryland and Virginia, but after the death of
his father in 1954 he returned to Atoka to live with his octogenar-
ian mother and teach Spanish and French at Atoka High School,

from where he had graduated thirty-five years earlier. After the death of Todd's mother in 1965, Todd lived on alone in the old family home until his own demise in 1974. The professional highlight of his later years was his appointment as Emeritus Professor of Choctaw Language and Choctaw Heritage at Southeastern Oklahoma State University (then Southeastern State College). Reflecting Todd's continued interest in his Choctaw heritage were his series of lessons in the Choctaw language, *Chahta Anampa: An Introduction to Choctaw Grammar*, and his historical pageant play about the Choctaw Nation, *Journey's End*, both of which were published in 1971, forty years after he penned his first detective novel.

Todd Downing is buried beneath a simple headstone in Atoka, the place of his birth. Fittingly, his writing lives after him.

1
BLOOD AND SAND

I

IN SPITE OF her resolve not to make a fool of herself at her first bull-fight, Janell Lincoln began to tremble when the trumpet-call ended on a shrill brassy note and the crowded amphitheatre became quiet and tense.

The trumpeter looked exactly like a vain little monkey decked out in rose and gold as he took the instrument from his lips and bowed. Then, unperturbed by the fact that no ovation was forth-coming, he smiled proudly and canted his head to listen to the echo.

The echo took a long, long time to die in the crooked shimmer of heat which rose from the arena toward the hard blue sky and the dazzling white clouds wandering in from the Gulf of Mexico. It rang in the girl's ears, and she thought: *It's a tiny live thing that wants to escape, but can't!* She had a momentary nightmarish sen-sation of being trapped there too—in an inverted glass bowl which was lined by tier upon tier of dark, strange faces and clamped down tightly upon a round floor of yellow sand. Sand that was furrowed deeply and splotched by damp red stains.

She slid a hand over the hot concrete and felt her father's fin-gers close over it. They were strong and gentle surgeon's fingers whose touch always carried reassurance.

"Feel all right?" he asked. "If you want to go—"

"No, no." She shook her head firmly. It had been her sugges-tion that they should come across the Rio Grande to this dedica-tion of Matamoros' new arena. He had agreed reluctantly. She had noticed his effort to detain her as long as possible outside, dispatching post cards to school friends up north. "Christmas Day, and I'm on my way to a bullfight!"

His luminous grey eyes were regarding her keenly, and there was an anxious look on his face. She hadn't become accustomed yet to the rich, even coat of tan which he had been acquiring, or to the flesh which had rounded out his cheeks, softening the old angularity of his profile. With his broad shoulders stretching the cloth of his white tropical worsted coat and the sun glinting upon the grey hairs at his temples, he was, she decided again, a distinguished and handsome man. He held his Panama hat upside down between his knees, lest it serve as a target for an orange peel or worse.

She moved closer to the loop of iron which separated their seats. "Really, I'm thrilled by it. What happens now?"

"The *banderillas*—the darts."

Her eyes followed his to the arena, where the bull stood, his attention fixed on something which was hidden from her sight by the red wooden fence. A massive coal-black creature with long symmetrical horns, he was motionless save for an occasional twitch of the tail and an impatient pawing of the sand. They were on the east side, close down in the sun, so that his shadow loomed hugely toward them.

A ripple of applause went over the stands, and her father said: "Carlos Campos. Evidently he's going to place the darts. Usually the *matador* lets someone else do it."

She leaned forward to get an uninterrupted view of the young man who had stepped out from the shade, brandishing in each hand a barbed stick from which dangled strips of coloured paper. He was taller than most Mexicans, and his skin-tight green-and-silver trousers and jacket set off to advantage the contours of a sinewy body. He held his head high, to smile at the crowd, and the sun played upon his dark-olive mobile face.

"So that's Carlos Campos!" she murmured.

"Yes." Dr. Lincoln watched the *matador* move with graceful springing steps over the sand. "I'm glad his father can't see him now."

"You told me that he wouldn't let Carlos go into the ring, didn't you?"

"Yes. He always opposed it. But Carlos had the fever, the *afición* the Mexicans call it, and practiced with young bulls on the *hacienda*. He got quite a local reputation. Partly because he's left-handed, and that's a novelty. But he waited until his father's death before he appeared in public."

Campos had stopped within six yards of the bull and was rising lightly on his toes, lifting one dart and then the other to arm's length. Like a man going tentatively through setting-up exercises.

Suddenly he advanced, with a swift circular movement, and drove the barbs into the animal's neck, close together, directly behind the head. The bull gave a low, angry bellow, but seemed too surprised to attack. The *banderillas* fell forward, aslant on either side of his face, and began to drip. The blood glistened brightly in the sun.

In front of them a Mexican in a tight black suit and little straw hat was consuming a cigarette with quick, nervous puffs, never taking the tube from his lies. Wisps of smoke floated back into Janell's face with a sickening, sweet odour like cheap incense.

She turned her head away and glanced over the stands. When her father began to fan her gently with his hat she managed another smile. "I'm all right. It's just the sun and the crowd and—and people staring at me."

"Staring is as much a part of the entertainment as the bulls. It's not considered rude in Mexico. And"—he patted her hand—"you can't blame them when such a good-looking girl sits here with an old fossil like me."

She noticed, however, that he raised his eyes and scanned the near-by rows. "Up in that box," she told him, "a man's been staring at me through field-glasses."

He looked up at the row of *palcos* high up on the south side, his smile broadened, and he waved a hand in greeting. "They're friends," he said in a relieved tone. "The young fellow with the glasses is Kent Distant. The other is Hugh Rennert. You haven't met either of them, have you?"

"No. Who's Hugh Rennert?"

"A newcomer to our neighbourhood. He's building that house a couple of miles east of us."

"Oh, yes. That brick bungalow." The neighbourhood, she knew, meant that little community a few miles outside of Brownsville which combined so happily the advantages of city, suburbs and country.

"Rennert used to be with the United States Customs Service. His father died recently and left him some money, I understand, so he resigned and came to Cameron County to grow citrus fruit." She realized that her father's purpose was to give her an opportunity to disregard what was happening below. "Kent Distant is the son of an acquaintance of mine—David Distant. You may have heard me speak of him."

"The Oklahoma Indian?"

"Yes. David is supposed to spend Christmas in Brownsville. Kent came down from Washington to meet him. He's studying for the Foreign Service there. He's staying at the Jester Hotel, on the highway above our place, you know. I've been intending to ask him over for dinner."

"Well, why don't you?"

His eyes had a twinkle, but behind that, she saw, they had become thoughtful. "You'd like me to?"

"Why, yes. It'd be fun to meet an Oklahoma Indian."

"Kent's half Indian. A fine young man."

There was a moment of silence. Janell said to him sternly: "I believe, my dear, you have that look in your eyes. Turn your head this way. Yes, you have."

"Mind telling me what you mean?"

"It's that predatory look mothers get when an unmarried male comes within range of a daughter who's been left on their hands. You're forgetting that I'm going to be an old maid and keep house for you."

"I thought you might have changed your mind since last summer."

"Of course not."

He astonished her by dropping his bantering tone and saying: "You don't want to take that resolution seriously, Janell."

She was vaguely uncomfortable and didn't respond.

"Something might happen to me, you know," he went on gravely. "That would leave you very much alone in the world."

"Don't say that!" She gripped his arm tightly. "Why, nothing could possibly happen."

His mood changed again, he laughed and glanced upward. "All right. Sorry. I think Kent's on his way down here. Want this?" He held out the purse which she had put into his pocket for safe keeping.

She took it absently, located mirror and lipstick. She was surprised to see the paleness of her face, the nervous brightness of the deep-set eyes which were so much like her father's. Strands of ash-blonde hair which should have been fluffy clung damply to her forehead, under the brim of her navy-blue straw hat.

But her thoughts were on her father. She had had no idea that he could still slip so easily into the dark apprehensive mood which used to worry her so. True, this had been a calamitous winter for communities like his at the southernmost tip of Texas. Early in the fall the tropical hurricane had swept in from the Gulf, raking the Magic Valley with its fury. There had been enormous damages to the citrus fruit orchards upon which everyone depended, directly or indirectly, for a livelihood. She knew from his letters that the suffering which he had witnessed then had left its trace upon him. And it was such a few years before that he had seen her mother's body brought mangled from the wreckage of a train.

A deafening roar of applause went up from the lower rows, and she hastily replaced the contents of the purse and slipped it into her father's pocket again.

The *matador* had affixed his third pair of darts and was disappearing beneath the fence.

A shadow fell across them and a soft, pleasant voice said: "Hello, Doctor. Enjoying the fight?"

Dr. Lincoln looked up and smiled at the tall young man in whites who stood in the aisle. "Hello, Kent. Yes, we're determined to enjoy it."

The newcomer removed his hat and leaned over, with one hand upon the iron loop at Lincoln's shoulder. As he did so his eyes (of such a dark brown that they appeared black) rested on Janell, and he smiled. She was a bit disappointed that he wasn't markedly different from the young men she knew in college. Many of them had hair just as black and straight, cheek-bones and noses no more prominent than his. He was good-looking, self-confident, but that was all. She knew from her father's expression that he was going to try to be humorous.

"Have you heard from your father yet, Kent?"

"No." Distant looked at Janell again. "Not a word. I thought he'd be here in time to join me this afternoon. So I got a box with two seats. When he didn't show up I persuaded Mr. Rennert to come along."

"I didn't know Rennert was a bullfight fan."

"He's not. But he had an errand in Matamoros, so I talked him into coming with me." He cleared his throat. "We thought you folks might like to trade seats with us. You'd be more comfortable in the shade."

"Why—watch out!"

Distant ducked his head just in time to escape an orange peel.

Dr. Lincoln laughed. "Lucky that wasn't a beer bottle, Kent." He looked rather sharply at the young man, who was glaring back at the packed rows. "Pretend you didn't notice it. Otherwise you'll have a whole crate of fruit sailing down here. Oh, excuse me!" he said, with an elaborate note of apology. "I was forgetting about you, Janell. This is Kent Distant, whom we were just discussing. My daughter Janell, Kent."

They acknowledged the introductions, and she said: "Thank you, Mr. Distant, but we couldn't deprive you of your seats."

"Oh, that's all right. We won't mind the sun. Mr. Rennert sent a message to you, Doctor. If you've had enough of the fight, he'll buy you a beer outside."

"Well, well, tell him I accept with pleasure. You take Janell with you. Have Rennert join me here. As soon as this bull is killed we'll leave. Meet you by the exit."

"Well—" Distant hesitated. "If you're quite sure—"

"Quite all right, my boy. Take good care of the little girl."

Janell felt a big hand close about her elbow, assisting her up the concrete steps. All along the aisle heads turned in her direction, and she was aware of the intense direct gaze of black jewel-like eyes. She couldn't understand why she felt so terribly embarrassed, why she felt impelled to smooth down the skirt of her linen suit. One was stared at when leaving a football game, of course. But this was different. . . .

"You mustn't pay any attention to what Father said. He was trying to have some fun out of me. We weren't really discussing you. I just happened to see you looking at me through those glasses."

"Oh, that!" Distant chuckled. "We were studying the facial expressions of the crowd. Mr. Rennert says that's more interesting than what happens in the arena." They crossed the ramp and started up another flight of steps. It was shaded, however, and cooler. "We turn to the right here."

He guided her along another narrower ramp, near the top of the amphitheatre, and into a small cubby-hole open on the side which faced towards the ring.

A middle-aged man in the inevitable white lightweight clothing rose as they entered.

"Miss Lincoln," Distant said, "this is Mr. Rennert. Janell Lincoln, Mr. Rennert."

"I'm glad to know you, Mr. Rennert. Father says you're to be a neighbour of ours."

"Yes, as soon as my house is finished." He was tanned, as she had come to expect all men to be in this land of year-round sunshine. She liked his ready smile and the friendly look in his dark-brown, grey-flecked eyes. "What did Dr. Lincoln say to my offer of a beer?"

"He agreed at once." She sat in the chair which Kent drew back for her. "Poor Father, he's perfectly miserable. He only came because I wanted him to. He said to join him and he'd have a beer with you after this bull is killed."

"I'll be going then. There's the last trumpet."

"The last one?"

"Yes. The signal for the kill."

II

"Nice fellow, isn't he? I got acquainted with him at the hotel."
Kent pulled his chair forward so that he could gaze over the ledge.
"The *matador* is going to give his toast to the mayor now. Want to
use these glasses?"

"Thanks. You've seen bullfights before?"

"No, but I've read about them." He laughed. "Mr. Rennert says
that's the only way to get a great emotional experience out of a
bullfight. To stay at home and read about it."

The height and the lenses put a different aspect on the scene.
The heat waves fused the sand into a lake of molten gold, in which
the bloodstains and filthiness were dissolved from view. Campos,
too, looked more impressive as he walked across the arena, holding the folds of his gold-embroidered cape in his right hand. It
passed round his body in the opposite of the accustomed fashion,
so that his left arm was free.

The Spanish say that the heart of a bullfight crowd is a woman's
heart, captivated by colour and pomp and more than all else by
blatant maleness. Campos must have known this, for he moved his
legs so that the sunlight played upon his thighs and loins and revealed the rippling of the muscles under the tight trousers. The
amphitheatre grew still again, filled with the orgiastic tremor of
heavy breathing and hot, tense bodies perspiring under the sun.

Janell felt a return of the anticipatory excitement with which
she had entered the place.

"Enjoying it, isn't he?" Distant commented. "This is his first
appearance, they say."

"In public, yes. He used to fight bulls on the family *hacienda*
south-west of here."

"That's right. Dad visited there three or four years ago." He
turned to her. "That's where he met your father, wasn't it? And—
oh, I'm terribly sorry!"

She kept the glasses to her eyes. "Yes, that was when Mother
was killed in a train wreck. Is that why your father is coming down—
to testify for Dr. Torday?"

"Torday? The man who had his neck broken but lived?"

"Yes. The Mexican National Railways are trying to break their indemnity agreement with him. He owns a radio station here in Matamoros. And a sanatorium down on the Gulf. Father's on the staff there. Tonatiuh, they call it, the Aztec name for the sun."

"Testifying is only incidental with Dad. But Torday heard that he was coming and asked him to be ready to if it was necessary."

"This Carlos Campus is to be one of the witnesses, too. It was on his father's *hacienda* that the accident took place."

"There's another man here who was on the same trip. Mr. Bettis. He manages the Jester Hotel, where Mr. Rennert and I are staying. We were watching his face a few minutes ago. He's in the same section you were in—F."

"Let's see what people look like from up here." She surveyed the east side of the amphitheatre.

"There's Bettis. On the first row of the *tendidos*."

"The *tendidos*?"

"Yes. The first row of seats, just behind the *callejón*, or runway, is called the *barrera*. The next is the *contrabarrera*. Then come the *tendidos*, the twelve rows in front of the gallery. Locate Bettis? Three seats from the right aisle."

"Oh, yes."

She focused the glasses upon a short fleshy man, probably in his early forties, the vacuity of whose face might have been due partially to huge tortoiseshell spectacles. He had thin corn-coloured hair plastered down so that it almost, but not quite, concealed the bald spot on the top of his head. He was leaning forward, as if in the grip of excitement, and his knees seemed to be crushing the crown of his straw hat. As she watched he drew from his pocket a flat silver case and extracted a cigarette.

"He didn't bat an eye when the horses were gored," Distant said. "Quite a contrast to that other American a few seats farther on in the same row. I've forgotten his name, but Mr. Rennert knows him."

"Why, that's Professor Radisson. We didn't know he was coming or we'd have brought him with us. He has an apartment in the old carriage house back of us."

"What's he professor of?"

"He isn't really a professor any more, but everyone calls him that. He's making a study of Indian languages in Northern Mexico. Been at it for years. He makes his headquarters in Brownsville part of the time."

There was a woodenness about Radisson's posture, as if his head were held in position by an old-fashioned photographer's clamp. There was a woodenness, too, about his face, which was burnt by the sun to such a deep mahogany that it had the impassivity of a Mexican's. He looked about the same height as Bettis, but older. In contrast one got the impression that his tan-coloured suit of tropical worsted covered a wiry body of solid bone and muscle. He had close-cropped, dark brown hair, worn pompadour fashion, and a short bristling moustache. He, too, had laid his hat upon his lap, and his brown fingers, playing with its brim, were the only part of him which showed any trace of agitation.

"I was interested in watching him," Distant said. "He looks callous. But he turned his head away every time a horse was hurt."

"He's a very nice man, according to Father. I don't know him very well. He always has acted a little brusque, but Father says that's because he's really self-conscious, and has lived by himself so long. He's one of Dr. Torday's witnesses too."

"He is? The judge might as well hear the case here, mightn't he? I suppose they're here because they know Campos."

A roar drew their attention back to the west side of the stands.

"Campos has finished his speech," Distant examined. "He's going to pose for a picture."

The *matador* had moved back a few steps and taken up a theatrical stance, his left hand pointing a long bright sword at the sky.

The photographer, a young Mexican or American—they couldn't be sure which—stood in the runway and balanced his camera on top of the fence. He finished, and waved a hand to Campos.

The latter unfastened his cloak, flung it across the *barrera*, and took from an attendant a spiked stick over which was folded a scarlet cloth.

"The *muleta*," Distant said.

He squared his shoulders, raised and lowered his arms again, and strode towards the bull. He got to within three yards this time before he stopped. He extended the *muleta* in his right hand and began to move very slowly in a circle. The animal's head followed him as if the two of them were strung on a single invisible wire.

"Testing him. Deciding which pass to make. By George, he's going to try a *natural*."

"A *natural?*"

"Yes, watch."

Campos advanced and flicked the cloth toward the bull's nose. As the beast charged, he swayed, without moving his feet, and swept the *muleta* backward until the two of them had completed a quarter-circle. Then he flapped the lower part of the cloth again, stopped, and—magically—the bull stopped.

Distant nodded judicially. "The fellow's not bad. And left-handed, too! See what happens? The bull charges the rag, not the man. There they go again."

It was the same pass, even more skillfully executed. One had the illusion that the man's arm was swinging not only the bit of cloth but a black inert mass five times larger than he.

Campos went through four of these exhibitions, always coming to a standstill with his back to the sun. Then he went in for the kill. The Moment of Truth, Spaniards call it.

He raised his left hand and pointed the sword straight at the tiny vital spot between the bull's shoulder-blades. He moved forward, extending the *muleta* beyond his left side.

Again the bull charged.

But, as if a taut wire had snapped in a puppet-play, something went wrong. What looked like a spasm of pain contorted the man's face and he jerked his head to one side. His sword spun away from his hand, and the next moment he was writhing grotesquely through the air.

2
MURDER OF A MATADOR

I

BY THE TIME Campos struck the ground Rennert was on his feet, welded by the communicativeness of shock into the tiptoe-craning mob that always is startled by the very tragedy it has paid to witness. Like ten thousand others, he watched the matador make an effort to rise, then fall back, holding his left hand to his abdomen as with his right, in agony, he scooped up sand. For a long electrical moment, while the bull, uncertain of his victory, warily eyed the prostrate man, a hush of expectant horror gripped the stands. Then nimble little servants ran out from the *barreras*, shouting and waving cloaks.

The spell was broken.

"That's three."

"What?" Rennert turned to Dr. Lincoln.

The latter's thin sensitive lips were compressed into a straight line and there was a decided greyness at the corners of his mouth. He took out a handkerchief and passed it across his forehead. He disregarded Rennert's question and spoke in a voice so low that it was almost lost in the pandemonium: "I expect I'd better go down to the Infirmary. Though from the look of things there's not much anybody can do for Campos now."

"I'll go outside with you." Rennert glanced down into the arena, where the bull was wheeling in one direction and then another, confused by the simultaneous gadfly attack. The body was being placed on a stretcher. The crowd followed the operations closely, chattering, shouting directions, demanding to know if Campos were dead or alive. Rennert was disgusted, as always, by this aftermath of combat, the gush of blood-lust in timid people who never left the safety of the stands. It was worse than the attraction of throngs to the scene of an accident in the United States. . . .

The two men put on their hats and stepped into the aisle.

"Rennert, were you watching Campos's face when he went in for the kill?"

"Not his face so much as his sword arm. I wanted to see how he used his left hand. Odd. He seemed suddenly to lose control of himself. Could you tell what was wrong?"

"I may be mistaken—" Dr. Lincoln stopped abruptly, his eyes fixed on the ramp at the head of the aisle.

A group of police had appeared there. They were talking together excitedly, gesticulating and glancing down over the heads of the spectators in that section of the *tendidos*. They were youthful-looking fellows, in faded, drab uniforms, and a stranger from across the river might have taken them for Boy Scouts making a lot of fuss about some unimportant duty which had been assigned to them. Until he noticed the huge revolvers in unbuckled holsters at their sides.

One of them came hastily down the steps, his gaze on the runway at the foot. "*Siéntense. Siéntense*," he ordered curtly, as he brushed past Rennert and Lincoln.

"*Qué hay?*" the doctor called after him. When he got no response he turned to Rennert and smiled weakly. "We'd better obey and sit down."

"By all means."

Another policeman descended more slowly, scrutinizing each row in turn.

"*Qué hay, señor?*" Rennert tried a question as he came abreast of them.

The Mexican's keen black eyes rested on Rennert's face, and he answered in English: "Stay in your seats. There is a search."

"A search?" Dr. Lincoln put in.

"Yes." The officer studied him with ill-concealed suspicion. "Campos has said that a light was flashed from these seats"—he indicated the *tendidos* in section F—"into his eyes. There is a search for the mirror." He went on.

Rennert's and Lincoln's eyes met. The grey ones were troubled.

"I thought that's what it was. A mirror."

"Could you tell what part of the stand it was in?"

Lincoln shook his head. "Devilish," he said. "Devilish."

"I saw it done once at a baseball game in St. Louis. Someone reflected the sun into the pitcher's eyes. But this—"

Sharp staccato commands from behind made them turn. Reinforcements of police had come. An officer stood upon the second step of the concrete and was ordering the spectators in the last row to leave their seats one at a time. A youngster of fourteen or so was first. He smiled unconcernedly as hands went quickly and deftly over his clothing, then pushed him toward the exit.

A ponderous elderly Mexican in holiday attire was next. He stood undecided, filling the space between the seats with his bulk, and regarded the police stonily. His wife, fatter than he, immersed in pink flowered chiffon, retained her place, talking to him in a rapid, agitated undertone.

By this time that entire section of *tendidos* as well as the gallery were aware of what was going on. People were rising. An ominous quiet settled down—a quiet through which rustled the whisper of riot.

Rennert and Lincoln got to their feet, as if drawn upright by some compulsion. The latter's left hand went suddenly to his coat pocket, where it closed about something.

Rennert was speculating uneasily as to what would be the outcome if the police persisted in their search. Mexican crowds are different from those to be found at a popular spectacle in the United States. Zealous individualism delays concerted action. But there is probably more bitter resentment at real or fancied infringement of rights. Authority is vested with no special sanctity save that dependent on force, and a trivial insult becomes the symbol of threatening tyranny. And Rennert had noticed that upon this occasion, due to the influx of Texans, the customary examination for weapons had not been insisted upon at the entrance gates. He saw the sun glinting wickedly on beer bottles.

His attention was brought back to his companion by a low, "Rennert, I'm in a predicament."

"What's the matter?"

Lincoln glanced up at the box to which his daughter and young Distant had gone. Neither was visible. "Janell gave me her purse to keep. There's a mirror in it. I wouldn't like to have them find it on me."

"Don't worry. There'll be dozens of mirrors in this section. Over three hundred people."

"Women will have them, yes. But they might get suspicious if they found one on a man. I don't know what to do. If I drop it, I'll only call attention to it."

But he was not called on to make a decision. Somebody shouted. Heads jerked about. Fingers pointed. A small round mirror was sailing over the crowd, in the direction of the arena. Down it went, in a glittering arc, and shattered against the top of the wooden fence.

Mirrors of every description followed. Bottles. Fruit. A yell of triumph at the foiled representatives of the law. Men and women milled about in the aisles, some moving toward the exits, the majority scrambling down to the lower seats, regardless of the protests of those already in possession. The police, wisely realizing the impossibility of exerting any further control and doubtless secretly relieved at this termination of the affair, disappeared.

The band struck up a popular march, and everyone turned to the arena in high good humour. The bull had been drawn into a passageway, to be slaughtered unceremoniously, and men were smoothing out the sand where Campos had fallen. This was a gala occasion indeed, with three more bulls to come.

"For the love of heaven, Rennert," Dr. Lincoln said, "let's get out of here."

II

Rennert nodded and preceded him up the aisle, shouldering a passage through the throng. There is little shoving among Mexican crowds, so that these tactics, being unexpected, proved effective.

In a few minutes they had gained the exit and were descending the long ramp which sloped to the street level.

"I told Janell and Kent that I'd meet them at the foot here," Dr. Lincoln said. "I don't suppose they'll stay much longer. Kent came over in your car?"

"Yes. I'll wait for him."

"Will you and he take care of Janell until I get back. I—"

At the end of the incline Dr. Lincoln stepped back hastily to avoid collision with a young man who came dashing round the corner from one of the lower exits. At his side hung a camera, attached to a strap which went over his shoulder, and in his right hand he carried a long black case.

"Pardon me, Doctor. I'm sorry." He was, Rennert judged, of mixed Mexican and Texan parentage. An alert-looking fellow, stockily built, with a light olive face which would have been handsome had it not been for the preponderance of forehead and jaw.

Lincoln's loss of composure was but momentary. "Quite all right, Canard. My fault as much as yours."

The other hitched the strap farther up on his shoulder. "I got some good pictures of that fight. I was hurrying to get them over to the office in time for the late evening edition. Campos is dying, they say. The horn got him in the abdomen." He made no motion to go, but stood and glanced from Dr. Lincoln's face to Rennert's. His black eyes were bright and inquisitive.

"This is Mr. Rennert, Canard," the physician said in an offhand manner. "Juan Canard, of the *Brownsville Sun*."

The newspaper-man took Rennert's hand, and his smile was charmingly Mexican. "I knew you by sight, Mr. Rennert. It is a pleasure to meet you." He glanced speculatively up at the exit which they had used. "You were sitting on the east side?"

"Yes," Lincoln affirmed, with a very slight frown of annoyance.

"Can you tell me then about the mirror? Who used it?"

"We were next to the right aisle, about half-way back on the *tendidos*. We didn't know about the mirror until the police told us."

There was a quizzical glint in Canard's eyes as he looked at Rennert. "Even you didn't know, Mr. Rennert?"

"I doubt whether anyone did except the person who used it."

"Why do you say that?"

"Assuming that it was a man, he doubtless held his hat in his lap or between his knees. It would be easy enough to keep the mirror hidden from the view of those behind and beside him by the crown and brim of the hat. Only a person sitting directly in front of him could have seen. And there wasn't much danger of anyone turning round at that crucial moment."

"Very true." Canard glanced at Dr. Lincoln. "I believe Campos was to have been one of Dr. Torday's witnesses against the Mexican National Railways."

"Yes." The answer was stiff and cautious.

"I wonder how his death will affect the case?"

"I'm sure I couldn't say. If you'll excuse me, Canard, I must be going. If you want any statement you'll have to see Dr. Torday."

"About like interviewing the Lama of Tibet," was the dry comment.

"Talk to Jarl Angerman, then. There he is across the street. I'll be back as soon as I can, Rennert." Dr. Lincoln walked toward the rear of the amphitheatre.

Rennert's eyes followed Canard's through the white glare to the man who stood like a sentry by the gate of the improvised parking place opposite. He was well over six feet in height, and his body was given colossal proportions by the heat waves which went up from the asphalt. The sun beat with dazzling effect upon his clothing; a hat of hard white straw, a starched white shirt, an immaculate, perfectly creased suit of white linen, thick-soled white canvas shoes. It would have been difficult to determine his age; his Nordic features, bronzed by the sun, had such an impassive sculptured appearance. His eyes were on the vast vaulted spaces between the concrete pillars which supported the stands, searching methodically through the groups of men who were standing or moving about there.

"If Dr. Torday is as accessible as a Lama," Canard said, "Angerman there is as communicative as the Colossus of Rhodes."

"So that's Jarl Angerman!" Rennert spoke to himself as much as to his companion.

"Yes. Don't you know him?" Canard seemed for some reason surprised. "He's Torday's lieutenant, strong-arm man, or whatever you want to call him. Runs the sanatorium south of here. Acts as if one of his patients had escaped."

Rennert was a bit puzzled by the reporter's manner. Of Dr. Torday and his organization he knew very little. The air was full, of course, of emanations from his radio station, situated just outside the jurisdiction of the Federal Radio Commission of the United States. Interspersed among its bilingual programmes were short lectures by the crippled physician himself, subtle combinations of trite sermonizing and advertisement of the fountain of youth which he had fenced in on the shores of Tamaulipas.

"Have a beer with me, Mr. Rennert," Canard invited suddenly.

Rennert accepted, and they walked to a near-by *puesto*. Canard propped an elbow on the counter and watched the people who were leaving the amphitheatre. The majority of these were Americans, trying to appear unshaken by their visit to a shambles, and Mexican women with restive small children.

"I understand you're building a house outside Brownsville, near Rolf Jester's place."

Rennert told him that he was.

"Doing any more detective work?"

Rennert laughed heartily. "Good lord, no! That all went into limbo with my Customs job. I'm a farmer now. Or will be when my citrus trees begin to produce."

Canard regarded him with disconcerting directness, stroking his long jaw, where hairs showed blue-black beneath the closely shaven skin. "Honest?"

"Honest to God. Do you mind telling me why you asked that?"

"Sure not." Canard drank luke-warm beer as if he liked it. "You know about Torday's accident, I suppose?"

"I know he was injured in a train wreck down in Mexico. His neck broken. That's about all."

"It happened about three and a half years ago. On the *hacienda* that belonged to the father of this Carlos Campos. Rolf Jester had a party of prospective land buyers down there on an excursion. Their Pullman was put on a side-track. A train ran into it. Somebody had changed the switch. Dr. Lincoln's wife and a couple of other people were killed. Torday's neck was broken and they thought he'd die. So the Mexican National Railways offered him a thousand dollars a week indemnity. But he didn't die. He held them to their bargain. They have applied to the courts for relief. The case comes up next week." Canard drained his bottle. "One of the witnesses who was to have testified on Torday's behalf was murdered a few minutes ago. Quite convenient for one side, wasn't it?"

Another bull must have been sent into the arena, for a roar went up from the crowd within and over their heads—a roar that seemed to send pulsations through the solid concrete structure.

As he waited for it to subside Rennert saw Janell Lincoln and Kent Distant making their way down the incline. Both of them were smiling, but showed plainly the stress of emotion. The girl's face was chalk-white, her eyes were bright and the lids suspiciously red, her fingers played nervously with Distant's sleeve. A tightness about the young man's lips vanished as he caught sight of Rennert.

"We decided that we'd had enough for one afternoon," he said with unconvincing lightness. "We left as soon as the crowd thinned out at the exit."

Janell looked about anxiously. "Where's Father?"

Rennert explained Dr. Lincoln's absence, and, since Canard seemed attached to him, performed the introductions.

Canard's head went forward at the name Distant. "Any relation to the man who is going to testify in Dr. Torday's lawsuit?" he asked quickly.

"Yes, that's David Distant, my father."

"Is he here—or in Brownsville?"

"Not yet, but I'm expecting him any time."

"Where will he be staying?"

"At the Jester Hotel."

Over at their left an urchin tossed a fire-cracker in their direction, then scurried behind a pillar. At the sharp explosion Janell started and passed a hand across her forehead. "I'd like to sit down, Kent. This sun has given me a headache. I don't suppose Father thought to leave the keys to our car with you, Mr. Rennert?"

"He didn't. Take Miss Lincoln to mine, Kent. I'll wait here until her father returns."

"What was the excitement down in your section?" Distant asked as he took the keys from Rennert. "We drew our chairs back after Campos was horned, but I heard the yelling."

His eyes flashed as he listened to Rennert's account. "What a foul trick! And they didn't catch the person who did it?"

"No. It was the easiest and safest method of murder I ever saw. But I think you'd better not keep Miss Lincoln standing here any longer, Kent."

"That's all right." She laughed weakly. "Father didn't give you my purse either, Mr. Rennert?"

"No."

"Maybe it's just as well. I'd probably feel worse if I saw myself in a mirror. Glad to have met you, Mr. Canard."

They walked away and Rennert turned to the reporter. The latter's lids had drooped slightly, but there was a sharply speculative look in his eyes as they rested on the girl's back.

"You still haven't told me," Rennert reminded him, "why you thought I was engaged in detective work."

"Oh." The other jerked himself back to attention and smiled. "Why, I thought Dr. Torday might have hired you to keep an eye on his witnesses. To prevent exactly what happened to Campos."

"I have never even seen Torday. I have had no dealings with him at all." Rennert studied Canard, wondering whether he was being entirely frank. There was a seriousness behind his sang-froid. . . .

"Who are these witnesses?" he asked.

"I've got their names here." The reporter reached into his pocket and brought out a memorandum book. "I'm supposed to write a story on the case before it goes to court." He thumbed through the leaves, then folded back the cover.

"Dr. Paul Torday," he read. "His wife, Irene Torday. Her brother, Darwin Wyllys. Jarl Angerman, the big gladiator standing across the street. Dr. Lincoln. Professor Xavier Radisson. Roll Jester. Matt Bettis. David Distant, of Oklahoma. Know many of them?"

"Jester and Bettis. Radisson slightly. Dr. Lincoln, of course." Rennert frowned. "See here, Canard, if you have any information—"

Canard slipped the book back into his pocket and adjusted his shoulder-strap again. "I have no information," he said airily. "I'm looking for some. Can I give you a lift into Brownsville, Mr. Rennert?"

"No, thanks. And thanks for the beer."

"Don't mention it." The young fellow looked at him squarely. "To tell you the truth, I hoped it would loosen up your tongue a little. But it didn't. I'm afraid you're too good a poker player, Mr. Rennert."

"I'm a rotten poker player. I assure you, Canard, that my sleuthing is going to be confined to my fruit trees. Insect pests."

"Oh, yes?"

III

The ambiguous parting irritated Rennert, and he sought solace in another bottle of beer. He felt exactly as if he had been listening to talk in a foreign language of which he understood no word save his own name, used with what significance he did not know. He began to draw on his dignity.

And so paid scant attention at first to the actions of one man among the dozens under the stands.

This was an American, wearing an unpressed Palm Beach suit of good cut and obviously expensive material. He was of slightly above medium height, but slender to the point of emaciation. He was moving, with quick steps, in Rennert's direction, keeping inside the rows of pillars and taking care to place each group of idlers between himself and the street. Now and then he stopped—and watched.

Rennert forgot his beer. The man was watching Jarl Angerman.

The latter had not moved from his position. His hard blue eyes, narrowed against the sun, continued tirelessly to scan the scattering crowd. More than once the smaller man barely eluded their gaze by darting behind some shelter.

There was an open space between the booth where Rennert stood and the foot of the ramp. The stragglers who left the amphitheatre either turned to the left, towards the front of the structure, or continued straight ahead to the parking place. The fugitive (that's how Rennert thought of him) remained for a long time behind a pillar at the edge of this expanse, looking across in an attitude of indecision.

Rennert had an unobstructed view of his face. It was a delicately featured face, handsome and at the same time weak. The skin had an unhealthy indoor pallor, so that the eyes—black, deep-set, intensely bright—dominated the other features. There was a shifting, hunted look in them which gave Rennert a start.

A plump Mexican couple, in the midst of loud altercation, stepped off the incline and started for the street. The man darted behind them and adjusted his steps to theirs, keeping his head bowed and turned away from Angerman. But at the edge of the shade the pair changed their minds and, instead of proceeding towards the parking place, turned to the left.

The pale-faced man stood as if paralysed, and his eyes met Angerman's across the quivering heat waves which rose from the strip of asphalt.

Angerman did not speak or make any gesture at all, but kept his eyes fixed, rather sadly, on the other's face. The latter went deathly pale, his lips trembled spasmodically and, as if under the compulsion of some unspoken command, he moved toward the huge white-clad figure. In a seeming daze he walked into the sunlight and across the street, heedless of traffic.

He stopped directly in front of Angerman and the two faced each other without speaking. Then Angerman lifted an arm, ponderously, and laid it about the frail unsteady shoulders. He kept them in his embrace as he drew the man gently towards the automobiles.

From the arena came the muffled thunder of applause and the shrill call of a trumpet, almost drowning the grave voice of Dr. Lincoln at Rennert's elbow.

"Carlos Campos is dead. He passed away soon after they got him to the infirmary. Suffered horribly. There was no possible chance of saving him. These abdominal injuries—"

Rennert turned. "Did he make any further statement about the mirror before he died?"

Dr. Lincoln shook his head. His face looked grey and aged, and his kindly eyes were limpid. "There was no time. He died cursing the name of his saint." He cleared his throat. "Where's Janell?"

"In my car, with Kent Distant. Shall we join them?"

"Yes, Rennert. Let's get away from butchery."

They walked in silence to the street and paused on the kerb to allow a long steel-grey roadster to glide out of the parking place and speed past them towards Matamoros. Jarl Angerman was at the wheel, looking neither to the right nor to the left. His bulk almost hid the huddled figure on the seat beside him.

"Who," Rennert asked, "is Angerman's companion?"

Dr. Lincoln coughed in the powdery alkaline dust which the car had whipped up. "Darwin Wyllys," he said. "Dr. Torday's brother-in-law."

"One of Dr. Torday's witnesses?"

"Yes," Dr. Lincoln said absently. "Yes."

3
MAGIC VALLEY

I

CHRISTINE JESTER paused in the doorway of the bedroom and gazed at her husband's back. He was standing by the south window, in the full spate of sunlight which still poured between the green chintz curtains at the west. The warm cuprous rays burnished his fine auburn hair to redness and accentuated the healthy glow of the thick flesh at the nape of his neck. He was in his shirt sleeves. One hand was jammed into a pocket of his trousers, the other was plucking at his stubby moustache.

Although Christine couldn't see his face she knew that he was deep in thought or idle reverie. His legs were expressive enough. Rolf had never been able to correct entirely an outward set which a saddle had given to his knees in boyhood. He was sensitive on the subject and, except in rare moments of inattentiveness, took pains to maintain as straight-limbed a posture as possible. Now (Christine smiled fondly) those legs resembled nothing so much as a pair of sturdy parentheses.

"Day-dreaming?"

He turned, automatically forcing his knees together, and grinned so that little crow's-feet creased the corners of his candid grey-blue eyes. Except for the tan which darkened a ruddy complexion mottled by freckles, nearly fifty years of strenuous living had left slight mark on his lusty face.

"No." He slipped an arm about her. "I'm being practical. Counting pennies. Making plans."

"Plans?"

"Yes. Listen, honey." His soft voice lost some of its drawl as eagerness infused it. "Why don't we have the nursery built on now? Out over that terrace, like we talked about. So that it'll be all ready—for this spring."

She laughed and kneaded with her fingers the back of one of his broad hands: the left one, which still bore the brand of last fall's hurricane in the form of an ugly scar.

"Impatient, aren't you, dear? Don't be. There's plenty of time. We decided, you know, that we'd be better able to afford the extra room later."

"I know. But I hadn't counted on the money I made on that deal this morning in Matamoros."

"The sale of that Mexican bullfighter's ranch?"

"Yes. Darwin Wyllys is giving me a bigger commission than I expected."

Christine gazed thoughtfully down the long rows of grapefruit trees which stretched to the winding road a mile south of them, to be succeeded on the other side by Hugh Rennert's orange trees, not yet in fruit.

"Rolf," she said suddenly, "I wish you hadn't got mixed up in that business."

"But why, honey?" His voice was solicitous.

"I can't explain. But there's something underhand about it all. All the secrecy. I wish you wouldn't have anything to do with Dr. Torday's organization. I don't trust them."

He laughed reassuringly and pressed her close against his side. "You've been reading too many mystery stories, sweetheart. Torday's not any wicked old spider. And this deal only concerns Wyllys and Jarl Angerman. Let's forget about it and talk about the nursery. Do you still have those samples of wallpaper? The ones with the little monkeys chasing their tails about?"

Impulsively, Christine kissed him. "All right, dear. We'll go ahead with the nursery. Have it ready for a little red-headed roomer. But there's not time now. Hugh Rennert's coming for dinner, remember. And you have to fix the cocktails. Hurry now and get dressed."

"All right." He held her a moment longer. "Enjoyed our first Christmas together, honey?"

"The first one I ever did really enjoy. I didn't have you for the others."

"And this time next year there'll be three of us."

"And you'll be barking your shins on toys and wishing you were a bachelor again. There's Hugh's car now. I'll go down and meet him."

In a mood of complete and complacent happiness she left the room and went down the stairs.

She was reliving that gloomy New York morning when Rolf had come hesitatingly into the interior decoration department over which she presided. She remembered how disconcerted she had been by his eyes and his smile and his boyish exuberance as they discussed the houses which he was building in a country that was remote to her as the moon. During their frequent conferences she had found it increasingly difficult to maintain the mask of impersonal friendliness which she wore for buyers. They lunched together. Then in one short breathless week she had discarded all her carefully-formulated plans for a professional career and was journeying with him towards the sun and the valley which had fulfilled its promise of being a magic one.

She met Rennert at the front door. He was bareheaded and looked cool and unwilted in blue flannels. She wondered, as she did every time she observed the vitality of his mature yet unlined face, why he had never married, and learned what it was to be happy.

II

When the Brownsville–Harlingen Highway was paved and shortened by the elimination of unnecessary windings, a ten-mile loop of the old roadbed had been left stranded, as it were, in the midst of property owned by Rolf Jester. At its northern intersection with the main artery of travel stood the Jester Hotel; at its southern, the old-fashioned residence which Dr. Bruce Lincoln had purchased three years before. Neighbours on the distended arc which stretched eastward of these two structures were Jester's home, a square, severely simple example of modern architecture, and Rennert's bungalow, with its modest acreage of citrus trees behind it. There was formed, thus, a closely knit little community, with what amounted to a private drive connecting its members.

Rennert was thinking, as he accompanied Christine across the smooth grass towards a group of orange-red chairs, of how quickly he had become assimilated here during the past two months, so that even before his house was completed he felt like an old resident.

"You look happy," he commented. "A nice Christmas?"

She laughed. "A Christmas in a new dimension, Hugh. It isn't possible that there was a tree in Washington Square last night. Snow on the ground. Carols in the air."

"And frozen fingers and colds and coughs," he reminded, as he held a chair for her.

"Yes, those too." She leaned back and looked at the globules of fruit which hung like crystal pendants in the mauve haze that was gathering about the dusty leaves. The sun was touching the flat horizon at a point which would advance steadily northward to Cancer, now that the winter solstice was past. Already the air was perceptibly cooler, with a tiny breeze exploring their faces. From inside the house came Rolf's voice, uplifted in spirited song.

"How have you spent the day, Hugh? Sleeping, I'll bet."

"You lose. I went to the bullfight over in Matamoros this afternoon."

She turned her head in surprise. "Why, Hugh Rennert, whatever possessed you to do that?"

"Kent Distant over at the hotel had a couple of tickets. He found out I was going across anyway, so he talked me into going with him. I regretted it. A young *matador* was killed."

"Not Carlos Campos?"

"Yes."

She listened, frowning, to his account and repressed a shudder of repugnance. "How terrible! Rolf will be distressed to hear it. He knew Campos. Had some business dealings with him recently. How can you bear to sit through a bullfight, Hugh? I should think it would be sickening."

"It is—if one has a seat close enough really to see what happens. That's its primary attraction for people. They go the first time out of curiosity or to show that they have no prejudices. They go again for the perverse pleasure of having their feelings harrowed. After that, they either lose interest or become addicts. In the latter case, there's something responsive in their natures. I suspect it's the same thing that takes a lot of men and women to prize fights. Or hunting, so they can kill and mangle birds and animals and call it sport."

"You think that accounts for the flood of books on bullfighting in the United States?"

"In great part. Of course, it's a fad and won't last long. I can't decide whether these books smack more of the decadent, like Mirbeau's *Torture Garden*, or of the small boy's attempts to be shocking."

"I've never read any of them. Only an article that came out in some magazine a few years ago. An *exposé* of the cruel features of bullfighting. The illustrations gave me the nightmare. I remember the title, *The Last Trumpet*. Did you read it?"

Rennert nodded. "Yes. It caused quite a sensation in this country, or in Texas at least."

"Just lurid journalism, wasn't it?"

"No, it wasn't, Christine. The author knew what he was talking about. He took bullfighting merely as an example of the streak of cruelty which runs through Mexican life. A sort of childish cruelty, refined by a subtlety that goes back to the Aztecs with their blood rites. You can find it in all their literature. The stories of Mariano Azuela and the other Revolutionary writers. Bullfighting, the writer claimed, was far more dangerous and fatal in Mexico than in Spain. He listed internationally famous matadors who had met their deaths in the Mexico City ring. Antonio Montes, for one. He showed how deep-rooted the *afición* is, and quoted Lamartine: 'Brutality to an animal is cruelty to mankind—it is only the difference in the victim.' You can tell what an impression the article made on me."

"The Mexican Government got indignant about it, didn't they?"

"So much so that they barred the author from the country, as they did a well-known American novelist not many years ago. After a trip to Mexico she wrote a short story which they felt reflected discredit on their people. On the same principle they don't permit travelers to take photographs of the beggars who infest the railway stations. A sort of pugnacious national pride, which of course has some justification. I've been trying to think of the name of the man who wrote *The Last Trumpet*. It appeared in a little magazine called N.E.W.S, as I recall. I never read anything more by him. One would have expected him to take advantage of his publicity."

Christine looked around as the front door slammed loudly. "Here comes Rolf. He'll remember. We were talking about that article once."

Jester was carrying a tray with silver shaker and glasses. "Howdy, Hugh!" he greeted. "Ready for a Daiquiri?"

"I should say. I was afraid I was going to have to make it myself."

"The old man's a little slow to-night."

As Jester busied himself at the table, Rennert compared him with the fellow in corduroys and boots whom he had met for the first time less than a year before: a fill-blooded beefy man, given to backslapping, gusty laughter and ribald jokes. The diamond was out of the rough now, polished and faceted by a few months of married life. It would have been difficult to find, Rennert thought, a more suitable agent for this transformation than Christine. A little younger than he, attractive in a blonde Junoesque way, edged by city life, she formed his necessary complement.

She took a glass from him, and asked: "Rolf, what was the name of that man who wrote the magazine article on Mexico we were discussing once—*The Last Trumpet?*"

"Oh, that. Simon Secondyne wrote it. Why?"

"Talking about bullfights made us think of it. Hugh was over in Matamoros to-day. That young Mexican Carlos Campos was killed."

"Killed!" Jester echoed as he handed Rennert his drink. "How did it happen?" He lowered his big body on to the edge of a chair and listened, serious-faced, to Rennert's story. "Too bad." He shook his head. "Carlos was a nice young fellow. I knew him fairly well. Saw him only this morning, in fact."

"It was on his father's *hacienda* that the wreck occurred in which Dr. Torday was injured, wasn't it?"

"Yes. Manuel Campos was his father."

"Rolf, I'd like to hear the details of that accident. Do you mind? Or you, Christine?"

"I don't mind," she said. "I supposed Rolf had told you all about it long ago."

"I don't know why I never did." Jester settled back in his chair and stared into his glass. "It happened—let's see—four years ago next June. I was entertaining a bunch of people and trying to sell 'em land here in the Valley. I thought it would be a smart idea to let 'em see how nice it'd be to live in the United States, yet be able to be in a foreign country within an hour. So I arranged to take 'em over to Monterrey for one day, then down to the Campos *hacienda* for another. I knew old Manuel Campos pretty well and he'd invited me down on hunting trips. He had a big estate, I forget how many hundreds of acres, about a hundred and twenty miles southeast of Monterrey. The Tampico branch of the Mexican National Railroad runs through it. There's a signal stop about a half-mile from the house. So I chartered a Pullman and off we went. There were eleven of us. Dr. and Mrs. Lincoln, Dr. Torday and his wife and her brother, David Distant from Oklahoma, a couple named Perkins from New Orleans, Matt Bettis and his brother Charles."

Jester got up to replenish the glasses and Rennert said: "I didn't know Matt Bettis had a brother."

"Well, he hasn't—now. Charles was killed two years ago. He was out in the country near here and some hunter shot him accidentally."

Rennert was not surprised that no mention had ever been made of this fatality, nor that Rolf was obviously reluctant to dwell on it now. Such evasion was in accord with the doctrine which Chambers of Commerce have ingrained in residents of the Magic Valley:

death has no place within its boundaries. Newspapers publish birth but not mortality statistics. No stones or tombs betray the true nature of occasional pleasant meadows. The visitor's query as to the location of cemeteries is met by the bland assertion that the Valley is a healthy region where no one ever dies.

"It was Saturday noon," Jester hurried on, "when we got there. The Pullman was sidetracked to be picked up by the north-bound train the next day. Campos entertained us royally, and the visit was a success—up until the end. Dr. and Mrs. Lincoln, Dr. Torday, Mr. and Mrs. Perkins and the porter were in the car Sunday afternoon when the train came in. It was going to pass the Pullman, then back up and attach it to the rear. But the switch had been turned and, instead of doing that, the engine crashed right into the sleeper. The Perkinses, Mrs. Lincoln and the porter were killed instantly. Dr. Torday's neck was broken and we thought he was dying." Jester finished his drink and sat for a moment, staring into space and worrying the end of his moustache.

"Dr. Lincoln wasn't injured, then?" Rennert asked.

"No. He barely escaped, though. He stepped off the Pullman about one minute before it was hit."

"I understood that Professor Radisson and Jarl. Angerman were there. They weren't in your party?"

"No. Both of them were staying at the *hacienda*. Angerman was foreman. Radisson was a guest there while he made records of some of the native languages in that region. Well, we got Torday to a hospital in Monterrey as soon as possible. The doctors all said there wasn't any hope for him. They gave him only a few days to live. But he fooled 'em and got better. Manuel Campos sent his family lawyer to arrange for a damage suit against the railway. He had the old Spanish ideas about hospitality, and felt it was up to him to see that his guests got justice. The railroad people knew how much influence he had, and that if the case got into court it'd go against them. Then, too, they were making a big play for tourist travel from the United States and didn't want any more publicity than possible about the accident. So they settled out of court. They gave Dr. Lincoln and the Perkins's relatives large indemnities. They made Torday a proposition: to pay him a lump sum in cash or a thousand dollars a week as long as he lived. They hoped he'd take the last offer, of course, then die. He took it—but didn't die. For the last three and a half years he's been drawing his money every week. With it he has built his radio station and sanatorium. He capitalized on his injury to draw business. I don't have any idea how much he's worth to-day."

Jester turned his head at the faint peal of the telephone bell inside the house.

"About a year ago," he continued, "the Mexican Railways asked the courts for relief from further payment. They claimed the thousand-dollar-a-week offer had been made with the understanding that Torday's life was to be a short one. But from all indications he was going to live to a ripe old age. Torday fought their petition, of course. He got Manuel Campos to take his side again. Their combined influence was too much for the railroad, and the court said the contract was still binding."

The little Mexican maid came to the door and in a soft voice called Rolf to the telephone.

He got up and added: "Now that Manuel Campos is dead, the Mexican National is trying again. The hearing is some time after New Year, over in Matamoros. Odd case, isn't it? Christine says there was another like it somewhere in the East a few years back.— Pardon me a moment, will you?"

Rennert turned to Christine: "I recall that case. A woman had her neck broken. Twenty-three years later she was still living and drawing indemnity from the railroad."

"Yes. Rolf didn't say anything about it, Hugh, but he felt just as responsible as Campos. I know he had specialists examine Torday at his own expense. Just like Rolf—" She was silent for a moment then looked steadily at Rennert. "It was like Rolf, too, to pass over the significant thing about that wreck."

"The changing of the switch?"

She nodded. "He'd like to think it was an accident, but he knows it wasn't. Someone broke the lock to do it. I've never seen that country down there, but from what Rolf says it's desolate. Not a town within miles. Just a few little huts scattered through the mountains. It's not likely there was a tramp wandering along the tracks. Besides the railroad sent out patrols in both directions to pick up any suspicious-looking characters. They didn't find any. No, it was done by someone who was on the *hacienda* at the time. Someone"— her voice hardened—"who wanted to kill every soul in that party. I consider it a case of murder. And the guilt lies on Jarl Angerman."

"Angerman?" Rennert glanced at her in surprise.

Christine was silent for a moment, her tranquil face gradually assuming a purposive set.

"Hugh," she spoke firmly, "Rolf wouldn't like me to talk about this to anyone but you. It wasn't he who told me, in fact, but Bruce Lincoln. A few hours before that collision he and Torday were inspecting some of the buildings. They came across Angerman flogging a peon. They made him stop, of course. It could never be proven, but everyone was sure that the peon changed the switch out of revenge. That's why I say Angerman was to blame."

"He was to have left with the others on the Pullman?"

"No, but Bruce says that the peon may have thought he was. Or he may have held a grudge against all Americans for what Angerman had done."

Jester let the door slam again and came hastily across the grass. His face wore a quizzical smile. "You're still a notary public, aren't you, Hugh?"

"Yes."

"Well, that's Jarl Angerman on the 'phone. He wants you to attest some affidavits for him to-morrow. From the witnesses in Torday's lawsuit. Want to do it?"

Rennert hesitated. "How in the world did he come to call on me?"

"Don't know. Bruce Lincoln may have suggested you. He was the one who told Angerman where to find you. He's waiting for an answer."

"Why, yes, I'll do it. Shall I talk to him?"

"I can tell him. Nine o'clock suit you?"

"Yes."

"Talk about the devil!" Rennert turned to Christine.

She nodded in preoccupied fashion and her eyes rested on her husband's back as he made his way to the house.

"Hugh," she said suddenly, "I'm going to tell you the same thing I told Rolf a few minutes ago. It's a mistake to have any dealings with Torday or anyone connected with him. Especially this Angerman. Rolf thinks it's his duty to testify in this case because Torday was on an excursion of his when he was injured. I don't see it that way. There's certainly no need for you to be drawn into it."

Rennert drew slowly on his cigarette. "I won't be drawn in very deep merely by attesting affidavits. And I've got to admit I'm rather anxious to meet Torday, see what kind of a man he is."

"Oh, Hugh, you're impossible! He's just a charlatan. And you know it."

"He doubtless is. But he has a tremendous influence. I've listened to his radio talks. They're rather clever—advertisement of his health resort coated with the sugar of philosophy. I don't know anything about his treatments, but I've always felt that there must be some worth to them. Otherwise a reputable physician like Bruce Lincoln wouldn't be associated with Torday."

"Yes," Christine said unwillingly. "Rolf uses the same argument. Of course, Bruce really has very little to do with the sanatorium. He has his own private practice and is only called in once in a long while as a consultant. But there," she laughed, "I'm afraid I'm too suspicious about everybody. I have to be, though, to offset Rolf. He trusts the whole world."

Jester returned with word that dinner was ready.

"Angerman will call for you at the hotel at nine," he told Rennert. "I'll stop by there on my way to the office."

"What's the purpose of these affidavits?" Rennert asked, as they walked toward the house.

"Merely to prove that we're the persons who witnessed the wreck. We're American citizens, you see, testifying in a Mexican court. Torday's lawyers think it would be a good idea to be prepared in case there's any question about our identities."

At the door Christine stopped and laid a hand on the arm of each of them. "We're not going to have dinner spoiled by talk of Dr. Torday," she said firmly. "So Cassandra is going to make her last utterance now."

"Cassandra?" Rolf repeated blankly.

"Dear, Cassandra was a woman who made herself very unpopular by predicting evil. No one believed her until it was too late. You two men are going to regret the day you get involved in Torday's affairs. And, Hugh"—Rennert was surprised at her fervour—"you must take care of this husband of mine. Don't let anything happen to him. Because the world and I couldn't get along without him."

Rolf was concerned. "Why, what's the matter, sweetheart? Nothing's going to happen. What makes you think there is?"

"I don't think it, dear. I know it."

"But how?"

Her look was maternal. "How," she asked, "do you always know when a hurricane is coming?"

4
A RING ROUND THE MOON

I

ANY PERTURBING THOUGHTS which Rennert may have had previous to dinner had been dispelled by the time he left the Jesters. As he loosened his belt, settled comfortably behind the wheel and drove slowly down the road, everything contributed to his feeling of pervasive well-being: the secure knowledge that his pleasure in Rolf's and Christine's company was reciprocated; his new-found freedom from harness; and, of course, roast turkey, rum-essenced plum pudding, and the night.

The night was tropic in its softness. The moon, twenty-four hours from its full, in a cloudless sky brightly faceted with stars, silvered the leaves of Jester's trees and made distended balloons of the light-coloured fruit. A faint rim round the dead planet was, at this calm season, no portent of disturbed elements. The Gulf breeze had long ago relieved the earth of its effluvium of heat. It must have been to such a land of the lotus, Rennert thought, that Ulysses came, like himself, late in life.

The route which he was following was not the direct one to the hotel. It took him southward to the intersection with the highway by Dr. Lincoln's house. Had anyone asked Rennert why he was going in this roundabout way he would have replied that he was merely idling. But that wasn't the real reason. He wanted to look at his own home. He wanted to gloat over it in secret and simple fashion.

Critically, he watched it loom against the trees on his left. Low, one-storied, rambling, it formed an integral part of the landscape, he felt, tied there by its whitewashed bricks of uneven texture and the dull red tiles of its roof. A lot of planning had gone into it.

His own home! He repeated the words to himself and found them good, as only a man can who discovers belatedly the joy of being anchored by possessions. He reviewed the long years which he had spent in temporary quarters up and down the border, never knowing but that the next month he might be stationed a hundred miles away. There had been Del Rio, then Eagle Pass; Del Rio again, El Paso, Brownsville; Laredo, perhaps the best of the lot; one summer in the inferno of Presidio.

The night was very still, plated with moonlight, and the back-fire of a car on the highway ahead was a steel knife that cracked against glass.

Back-fire?

Rennert shut off his motor and listened.

The stillness had returned, intensified if that were possible, so that he heard very distinctly the gentle rustling of the leaves on either hand, the dispassionate ticking of his watch. Nothing else at all.

Damn it, his heart was pounding, and he felt the touch of indigestion.

Angry at himself, he started the car and sped forward. Utterly silly, this business of cruising about in the moonlight when he ought to be in bed. That explosion had been made by a firecracker, of course. Throughout the South, firecrackers are concomitants of Christmas, not the fourth of July. For the last week they had been popping continually.

But his eyes were keener now, scanning the dusty road.

The brick chimney of Dr. Lincoln's two-storied residence came into view. It was a landmark, that chimney, a conspicuous anomaly in a land where no fires are ever built for warmth. It dated the dwelling, back to the first influx of homebuilders into the Valley twenty years before. The house itself was attractive, with its walls of dipped shingles weathered to a rich buff, its shutters of yellowish green, its sloping roof that blended its colour with the foliage of tall palms. A driveway circled it, from the side road to the highway, and gave access to the former carriage house which Professor Radisson had converted into living quarters.

If the hour had been earlier Rennert would have been tempted to turn in there and call upon Radisson. Dr. Lincoln had gone to some pains to introduce them to each other as men with intimate knowledge of Mexico who should have much in common. Rennert, who knew of the monumental work on Mexican linguistics which Radisson was preparing, had been more expansive and cordial than was his wont. Consequently he had been inclined to take as a rebuff the reserve which the other had manifested. He was fully aware of his deficiencies in the matter of scholarship, and had thought that it was on this account that Radisson had not responded to what amounted to an offer of friendship on his part. But Dr. Lincoln had assured him later that the man was merely self-conscious and would welcome—

Startled, Rennert jammed on the brake and peered through the windshield. He backed a few inches, then jumped out of the car, walked to the front, and sat down on his heels.

The glare of the headlights yellowed the dust and reddened the dark little pool which fouled it. A wet and glistening pool that was soaking rapidly into sand.

Rennert got to his feet. Blood again, he thought, and sand.

He glanced at Dr. Lincoln's residence, where there were lights, and at Radisson's, which was dark. He stood for a moment, scrutinizing the road-bed.

It was seamed by tyre-marks and stamped by the imprint of a pair of shoes which had turned in the direction of the drive, accompanied by little pellets like thick black raindrops. No other object was to be seen.

Rennert locked his car, but left it standing where it was. He walked swiftly up the drive and cut across the lawn to the front of Lincoln's house. Although the living-room beyond the wide screened verandah was lighted there was no one in sight. He knocked.

There was movement inside, but it was several moments before Kent Distant appeared. "Who's there?" his voice was sharp.

"Oh, Mr. Rennert! It's you." He came to open the screen door and, in an access of relief, laid a hand familiarly on Rennert's shoulder. "Come in. There's been an accident. Professor Radisson's been shot."

"Seriously injured?" Rennert asked as he passed into the long, high-ceilinged room. Janell was there, sitting on the edge of a chair and tugging at the corners of a handkerchief. She looked very, very young—and frightened.

"I don't think so," Kent told him. "It's his hand. He's in the study with Dr. Lincoln."

"Go on in if you want to, Mr. Rennert," the girl spoke up. "I'm sure it'll be all right."

"Thank you. I know the way."

Rennert crossed in front of her and went down a wide hall towards an open door from which streamed hard white light. It was an orderly book-lined room on whose threshold he paused. Within, Radisson was leaning back in a chair with his eyes closed. His left hand rested in an enamel basin which was brimful of ruby-red water.

Dr. Lincoln stood beside him, deftly unrolling strips of gauze. He turned his head quickly, swallowed, and said in a low voice: "Come in, Rennert. Close the door, will you?"

Radisson opened his eyes and looked around. His dry chapped lips parted in a wry smile. "Hello, Mr. Rennert." The glitter in his brown eyes showed that he was in pain, but his voice was careful and precise as always. So careful and so precise that it alone put conversation with him upon an impersonal plane. (A characteristic, Rennert had decided, of professional linguists, who invest words with so much purely scientific significance that they lose spontaneity of speech.)

"I was driving in from my house. I heard what I know now was a shot. I saw the blood in the road. May I ask what happened?"

"You may ask, but I can't tell you more than that there was a shot." Radisson's body was tense, and Rennert thought at once of tightly coiled springs. He watched Lincoln as the latter prepared a tourniquet. "I was walking in the moonlight, a short distance in the direction of your house, Mr. Rennert. Then back. I stopped at the entrance of the drive and decided to smoke another cigarette before I retired. I lighted it. Then"—he shrugged—"I don't know what I was aware of next. Whether it was the shot or the red-hot pain that went through my hand. It rather stunned me for an instant. I caught my wrist to stop some of the flow of blood and ran in here. That's all."

"You don't know where the shot came from?"

"The highway. Cars were passing, but I paid no attention. There was one parked on the other side, without lights. When I looked again it was gone."

"Did you notice what kind of a car?"

"A small one. A roadster or coupe. Black or grey or some dark colour. But I couldn't say that the shot came from it. Another car— I don't know what kind—had just gone by."

"Your hand was by your side?"

"No, Mr. Rennert, my hand was close to my face. I had just started to put the cigarette between my lips. I had just tossed away the match with my right. I felt"—the facial muscles twitched slightly—"the taste of blood in my mouth."

Dr. Lincoln straightened and surveyed the tourniquet which he had affixed above the wrist. His forehead and temples, at the edge of his greying hair, were damp with perspiration. "Keep your hand in the water until I fix you an opiate. I'm afraid this is going to hurt a little. I've got to get the bullet."

Rennert was intensely curious. He wanted to stay, to learn what kind of a gun the bullet had come from, to ply both men with questions. But he felt that to do so would be to seem unduly officious. He resolved to give them an opening.

"Is there anything I can do?"

"Nothing at all, Rennert," was Lincoln's reply. "The bullet is lodged, probably, in one of the bones. But I don't think much damage has been done." He turned his back and began to explore the contents of a black leather case.

"I was wondering, Professor Radisson, if you wanted me to notify the police for you? Or the sheriff, rather, since we're outside the city limits."

Radisson's eyes met his in a steady neutral gaze. "The sheriff," he repeated. "What could he do?"

"Identify the car and the gun that were used, perhaps."

The other smiled without humour. "The car and the gun, Mr. Rennert, are crossing the bridge into Mexico by this time, I'm sure."

"Well, I advise you to get in touch with him anyway. I'll say good-night now. I trust the wound won't be serious."

"I trust not. Good night, Mr. Rennert."

Rennert opened the door, then paused. There was one question which he wanted very much to ask.

But Dr. Lincoln's back was still turned and Radisson had closed his eyes again. Rennert went down the hall in somewhat of a huff. Of course the newspapers had exaggerated grossly the results of his amateurish efforts at crime detection. But nevertheless he had learned a few things. And Dr. Lincoln had not even asked him to sit down.

II

The lights of Rennert's car were yellow cones alive with little insects that darted in and out and dashed to destruction against the glass. The stain on the dusty road-bed was innocent-looking now and no longer glistened.

Rennert stood on one side of it with Kent Distant, who had accepted his offer of a ride to the hotel. "You heard the shot, of course?" he broke the silence which had held them since they left the house.

"Yes. Janell and I were sitting on the verandah. We thought it was a firecracker. People had been throwing them from cars all evening. Dr. Lincoln was upstairs reading. He came out and asked us if we had heard a shot. Just then we saw Radisson coming across the lawn."

"Did you notice the automobile that was parked on the other side of the road?"

"No, I didn't."

"Or the last one that passed before the shot?"

"I didn't, Mr. Rennert. There were so many." The young man spoke apologetically.

"Was any part of this side road visible from where you were sitting on the verandah?"

"No, we were in the swing on the other side."

"You didn't hear a car enter or leave it during the evening?"

"No. All I can say is that there was none on it about half an hour before the shot. That was when we went to call Professor Radisson to the 'phone."

"Tell me about that, Kent."

"Well, the 'phone rang. Janell didn't answer it because she knew her father was upstairs. He called her though, said he had his slippers on, and asked her if she and I would tell Mr. Radisson someone wanted to speak to him. We walked around the house to the professor's apartment and gave him the message. That was the only time I saw this road after dinner."

"Radisson came to the telephone?"

"Yes, he came in, talked a few minutes, then went out again."

Rennert cast a last glance over the bare surface of the road. Sand and dried blood—symbols to him now of an evil which had no place in the Magic Valley—and nothing else.

"Let's go," he said abruptly. "This isn't any affair of ours."

They got into the car, Rennert turned on to the highway and headed north. "Kent," he asked then, "have you had any word yet from your father?"

"No, I haven't, Mr. Rennert."

"You don't know whether or not he has left Oklahoma?"

"No. You see, Dad's never in a hurry. He always gets where he says he's going to—eventually. So I'm just waiting."

"You had no definite date to meet here?"

"As definite as he ever makes one. The last letter I had from him, he said we'd spend Christmas together. So I expected him yesterday or last night."

There was no apprehension at all in his manner, and Rennert found himself exceedingly reluctant to continue. He took a deep breath. "Kent, do you know of the legal bout which Dr. Torday is having with the National Railways of Mexico?"

"Something, yes. Dad is going to testify if he's called on."

"That newspaper reporter I introduced to you at the bullfight hinted that an attempt was being made to intimidate Dr. Torday's witnesses. I'm being perfectly frank, Kent, because I know you have too much sense to get wrought up unnecessarily. But the facts are that Campos was killed this afternoon and Radisson was shot to-night. Both were to have testified. Don't you think it would be wise to find out where your father is and when he's due to arrive?"

"Yes, Mr. Rennert," the young man answered gravely, "I do. I'll put in a long-distance call as soon as we get to the hotel. Thank you. But it's hard to believe that the Mexican Railways would stoop to anything like this for a thousand dollars a week."

"That's why I'm worried, Kent. Because it is so hard to believe."

They approached the Jester Hotel in silence.

"Mr. Rennert," Kent spoke up, "there's something I want to ask you. Janell and I were talking to-night about Mexican food and places in Matamoros. She wanted to try them some time. So I asked her to go across with me to-morrow night to dinner. Dr. Lincoln's going to some kind of a medical affair. I suggested this night club they advertise so much. The Triumph of the Emotions. I thought I'd better ask you, though, if it was all right. You know what I mean."

"Well, Kent, I hate to throw a damper on your plans but . . ."

Rennert felt uncomfortably old and paternal as he slowed down at the signpost of the Jester Hotel.

The sign, small, with unobtrusive lettering and diminutive cap and bells, was the only indication of commercialism about the hostelry. This was a huge and ungainly old farmhouse, white with green shutters, which had been remodeled into small apartments designed to meet the needs of elderly people who were wintering in the Magic Valley. At this hour most of its windows were dark.

Rennert let Distant out in front, then drove to the garage on the north side.

Instinctively, he walked on tiptoe when he went into the lobby. A living-room it was, rather, with Mission furniture, bookcases and flowers. Potted palms discreetly screened the desk. A single lamp was burning by a table on which lay current newspapers and magazines.

One of the papers caught Rennert's eyes as he passed. He picked it up, carried it over to a chair, and sat down. It was the late evening edition of the *Brownsville Sun*.

On the front page, under the signature of Juan Canard, was an account of the death of Carlos Campos in the bull-ring at Matamoros. Rennert read, turned to the inside and smiled grimly at the conclusion:

> The authorities who operate the Matamoros arena express profound regret that the dedication ceremonies should have been marred by such an unfortunate incident. They state that in the future precautions will be taken against the malicious use of mirrors by spectators.

Yes, the reporter had done a good enough job of translating into English the sonorous and hollow phrases with which some Mexican official had dismissed the tragedy. They had been accompanied, doubtless, by a shrug deprecatory and at the same time expressive of the futility of further investigation.

There were four photographs: Campos standing in front of the mayor's box; a striking exhibition of his capework; a glimpse of the intent faces of the spectators; a grisly view of the *matador* being lifted from his feet by the horns.

Rennert studied the third of these. The section of the amphitheatre was the one in which he had been sitting. Only the faces in the first few rows, including those of Radisson and Bettis, were very clear. He located himself and Dr. Lincoln without difficulty, but doubted whether an acquaintance would have recognized them. A careful inspection revealed no one else whom he knew. Approximately two-thirds of the crowd, he calculated, were Mexicans. Most of the men had their hats upon their laps.

The camera must have been snapped within two or three minutes of the fatality. Rennert recalled lighting a cigarette about that time. And there it was, in his mouth.

It was an intriguing problem. Here before him was the face of a murderer. . . .

It was bed-time.

Rennert yawned as he went up the stairs and along thickly carpeted halls to his rooms on the third floor. The hotel served its purpose as a haven of rest. Night lights were dim and the heaviness of sleep lay upon the silent corridors. Snoring was stertorous in more than one of the rooms which he passed.

He reached his destination and took out his key. The passage in which he stood was a narrow one, at the rear of the building. At its end a short flight of steps led up to a door which gave, he surmised, on the attic.

This door opened now and a man backed out, pulling the knob toward him with his right hand. The automatic lock clicked sharply. The man started to turn.

"Good evening, Bettis," Rennert said.

Matt Bettis whirled, almost losing his balance, and his hand slid swiftly under his unbuttoned coat.

It came out almost immediately; he cleared his throat and descended the steps. He was carrying an empty china plate and, caught by his thumb, a water pitcher of white enamel. "I didn't hear you, Rennert," his voice was unsteady. "You startled me."

"I'm sorry."

"That's all right." The light was reflected from the blank panes of the spectacles. "These maids are careless. They leave things lying about everywhere, don't they?"

"I hadn't noticed it."

"Well, they do. Good night."

"Good night."

As Bettis hurried by he held his left arm close to his side. But Rennert's eyes detected the bulge in his coat, a bulge which could have been made only by a pistol in a holster.

Rennert wasn't as surprised by that as by the look which had been on Bettis's face in the instant that preceded recognition—panic.

5
LOTUS-EATER

I

COMFORTABLY TORPID from sound sleep, breakfast, and communion with sunshine, Rennert sat on the wide verandah of the Jester Hotel and eyed aloofly the cars which were passing with such speed and purposiveness along the highway. How thoroughly, he reflected, this sun could conquer a man's scruples against indolence, deep-grained though they had been by tradition and by years of machine-like adherence to schedule.

At the beginning of the construction of his house, he had been on hand, dutifully, each morning when the workmen put in their appearance. It hadn't taken him long to realize that his presence was not only unnecessary but hindering. He had no knowledge of carpentry, and soon saw the futility of standing about with his hands in his pockets, dodging ladders and betraying his ignorance by foolish questions. Now he was content to sit in a basket-chair, repress yawns, and listen to interminable life-histories of retired business-men. Only when he took stock of his expanding waist-line. . . .

He sat up as a long steel-grey roadster slid smoothly to the kerb.

Jarl Angerman, immaculate again in white, got out and strode up the walk. He paused at the top of the steps and directed his bleak blue eyes upon Rennert.

The latter rose. "Mr. Angerman?"

"Yes."

"I'm Mr. Rennert."

Angerman moved forward and extended a hand. "I am glad to know you, Mr. Rennert." He spoke with little movement of the lips, so that his voice was almost without inflection and marked by gutturalness.

"Will you sit down, or are you ready to go to work?"

"I will sit down for three minutes. Then it will be nine and we will make the affidavits."

He lowered himself into a chair with a crinkling of stiffly starched cloth. He removed his straw hat, adjusted carefully the sharp-edged creases in his trousers, and rested the hat upon his knees. He looked at Rennert in calm and unhurried appraisal.

Rennert reciprocated. Angerman's head was of a harmonic Nordic type: long for its breadth, with narrow nose and slightly prognathous jaw. His close-cropped hair was tow-coloured and showed a faint wave. The sun had given his skin an even patina of bronze, which glowed as if it had just been subjected to diligent scrubbing. Rennert had carried away from the dusty sunlight of Matamoros a decidedly unfavourable impression of the man's face. He had thought of it as stolid, with a great deal of inherent brutishness. Now he found himself revising that opinion. A passive and stoical countenance, rather; one which, if animated, might become likeable. He speculated as to Angerman's age. Thirty. Thirty-five. He couldn't be sure.

"I have come"—Angerman spoke ponderously—"from Dr. Paul Torday. I am to get affidavits from six men. Mr. Jester, Mr. Bettis, Dr. Lincoln, Mr. Radisson, Mr. Wyllys, and Mr. Distant. You will attest them. I have them here." He drew from his pocket six folded sheets of legal-sized paper and passed them to Rennert.

Each bore a typewritten statement to the effect that at 2.13 P.M. on June 20, 193–, the man named had been present at a flag-stop on the Monterrey–Victoria section of the National Railways of Mexico and had witnessed there a collision between a Pullman and a passenger train belonging to that line. There was a space for a signature, and at the foot the familiar lines:

State of Texas, County of Cameron. I, Hugh
Rennert, a notary public for and within said county,
in the State aforesaid, do hereby certify . . .

Rennert looked up. "Dr. Torday has saved me all possible
trouble. I'm acquainted with all these men except Mr. Distant and
Mr. Wyllys. Wyllys is Dr. Torday's brother-in-law, I believe?"

"Yes. He is at Tonatiuh. I will take you there when we have finished with the others."

"Wyllys is a patient there?" Rennert asked casually, as he returned the documents.

"Yes, he is a patient." Angerman consulted his watch and rose.
"It is nine. We meet Mr. Bettis in his room. Mr. Jester will come
there. You have your seal?"

"Yes." Rennert picked up the pasteboard box which had reposed
beside him in the chair.

They went inside and down a corridor in the left wing. Matt
Bettis opened his door at Angerman's knock and ushered them into
a large, plainly furnished sitting-room with wide windows open
upon the north.

He didn't present a very prepossessing appearance. The puffi-
ness of sleep was still upon his face, and his watery blue-green
eyes blinked behind the thick lenses of his spectacles. He was in
his shirt sleeves and the white cloth clung damply to his torso. He
greeted Rennert with a faint air of surprise, and said to Angerman,
"You're sure prompt. It's barely nine o'clock."

"I said I would be here at nine. Mr. Rennert will witness your
affidavit."

"Sure. Sit down." Bettis removed a coat from the back of a chair
and put it on. It was tight for him, and fully half an inch of white
cuff showed at each wrist. He took the sheet of paper which
Angerman tendered him, read it through laboriously, then said:
"O.K. Got a pen?"

Angerman, who had remained standing with military stiffness,
held out an uncapped fountain-pen. Bettis grasped it in his short

pudgy fingers, laid the sheet upon a table, and scrawled his name upon the proper line.

Rennert affixed his signature and seal, folded the paper, and handed it to Angerman, who said simply: "Thank you."

"When does this case come up?" Bettis asked.

"The first Monday of the New Year."

"Getting things ready away ahead of time, aren't you?" Bettis commented, as he went to the door in response to a rap.

It was Rolf Jester, wearing what Rennert was wont to call his Chamber of Commerce manner. He bade the three of them brisk good mornings, his eyes twinkled in friendly fashion as they met Rennert's.

"Well, Hugh, glad to see you routed out of bed once before the middle of the morning. You'll know how we working men feel. Got that affidavit ready, Angerman?"

"Yes, it is ready."

Angerman gave him a sheet, and, as Jester studied it, inquired of Bettis: "Is Mr. Distant here?"

The manager of the hotel shook his head. "He hasn't showed up. His son's expecting him, though. He ought to be here to-day."

Jester finished his perusal, carried the paper to the table, and signed his name in large, firm letters.

"How's the death of Carlos Campos going to affect Torday's case?" he asked.

"I do not think," Angerman replied, "that it will make any difference."

"You mean his testimony wouldn't have been needed?"

"No."

"Doesn't that apply to all of us? As I understand it, the Mexican National has already admitted their liability in the wreck. They did that when they paid indemnity to Torday and Lincoln and the relatives of that New Orleans couple. All they're doing now is to seek relief from the court as to the amount of the indemnity. That right?"

"That is right."

"Then these affidavits are just a matter of form. The chances are that none of us will be called on to testify."

Angerman took the second document from Rennert, folded it with care, and consigned it to his pocket.

"I am sure," he said, "that not one of you will ever testify."

Rennert had been attentive to this interchange. It seemed to remove the foundation entirely from the menace which he had seen taking shape since he had listened to Juan Canard's hints.

Angerman picked up his hat. "Are you ready to go, Mr. Rennert? We must see Dr. Lincoln and Mr. Radisson at nine-twenty. Then we must go to Tonatiuh."

Jester looked at him quickly. "Oh, you're going to Tonatiuh, are you?"

"Yes, we are going to get the signature of Mr. Wyllys."

Jester followed them into the hall. "Will you excuse us a moment, Angerman? I want to talk to Rennert."

"I will wait on the porch."

Jester caught Rennert's arm and drew him towards the rear. "I want you to do something for me, Hugh. When you get down to Tonatiuh, call Wyllys aside and tell him I've got the papers he wants. He'll understand. Tell him I'll be in my office at eight o'clock to-night. He can get them then. It'll save me putting in a call across the border. And be sure not to say anything to Angerman about this."

Rennert regarded his friend in some surprise. This was the first intimation he had had that Jester was involved in any dealing with Wyllys. Christine must have had this in mind last night.

"Sure," he said. "I'll be glad to do it, Rolf. By the way, have you heard about the shooting last night?"

"The shooting?"

Rennert told him of his experience on the way home.

Jester's full plain face became serious as he listened. "Well, I'll be damned!" was his soft comment. "I'm sorry to hear that. I'll have to stop and see Radisson. There was no way of finding out who did it?"

"Evidently not. I wondered what your theory might be."

"My theory? Good Lord, Hugh! I haven't any theory. It was probably just an accident. Somebody lit up and celebrating Christmas."

Rennert saw that Jester shared none of his suspicions. "That explanation satisfies you?" he asked.

"Why, sure. Why not?"

"Perhaps you can tell me then why Matt Bettis carries a gun at night? Why he's panic-stricken when he sees me in a dark hall?"

"Hugh, what in heaven's name are you talking about?"

Rennert continued his story of the previous night. "Do you know what he keeps up in that attic, Rolf? Almost every morning I'm awakened by someone—I suppose it's Bettis—walking about up there."

Jester laughed and laid a firm hand on his arm. "See here, old man, I'm going to tell you the same thing I told Christine. You've been reading too many mystery stories. You don't want to pay any attention to what she said before dinner last night. In her condition she's apt to brood and worry, you know. Let's go in and ask Matt what he's got upstairs."

Rennert shook his head. "Don't say anything to him about it, Rolf. I'd prefer you didn't. He and I aren't any too friendly, anyway, and I want my remaining days here in the hotel to be tranquil ones."

"You don't like him, do you?"

"Frankly, I don't, Rolf."

"I see. Therefore he's engaged in some devilment." Jester thrust a finger against Rennert's ribs. "Forget it."

This was the most forthright and guileless man, Rennert believed, that it had been his good fortune to meet. Intelligent and experienced, likewise, if a little too trustful.

Rennert left him with the feeling that there couldn't be anything wrong with their little world after all.

II

When he emerged upon the verandah Angerman was standing by the railing on one side of the steps, Kent Distant on the other.

The latter came forward, smiling. "Good mornin' Mr. Rennert. I thought you might eat breakfast with me."

"I ate long ago. Unusually energetic this morning." Rennert lowered his voice. "Did you call your father last night?"

The smile faded.

"I tried to. I called our home in Oklahoma but couldn't get an answer. I talked to one of Dad's friends. He said Dad left on the train last Wednesday. Three days ago. That should have put him in Brownsville Thursday night or yesterday morning. Of course," Kent added hastily, "he's all right. He stopped off somewhere to visit or he missed connections. He's always doing that. Do you think I ought to do anything more?"

Rennert almost regretted then that he had spoken as he had the night before. The morning was so bright and clean and peaceful. "It's easy to miss trains," he said. "He'll be here to-day, I feel sure."

"I'm sure he will, too."

Rennert joined Angerman, and the two of them went to the latter's car.

"Do you know," Rennert asked conversationally as they drove southward, "that Professor Radisson was shot last night?"

Angerman turned his head and for an instant his eyes rested on Rennert's—clear, cold-blue, searching. "Tell me."

He looked straight ahead as Rennert talked. His body was bent slightly forward to accommodate itself to the constricted space, so that any expression which his face may have had was hidden. But Rennert saw his hands tighten about the wheel. They were muscular hands, immensely strong, but well shaped and well cared for, even sensitive.

"That is bad. That is very bad."

Angerman made no further comment but turned into Dr. Lincoln's drive and stopped by the side of the house.

Both Lincoln and Radisson were sitting on the porch, evidently waiting for them.

The former got up to open the door. "Good morning," he said, to Rennert rather than to Angerman. "Come in."

Radisson, whose left hand was in a bandage, did not rise. Rennert judged that he was feverish, for a hectic flush was discernible beneath his tan, and his eyes were bright as oiled marbles.

Angerman gazed at him concernedly. "Mr. Rennert has told me what happened. I am sorry. I am very sorry."

The linguist's attitude towards Angerman was in marked contrast with that of Dr. Lincoln. "Thanks, Jarl. I'll be all right now."

Rennert inquired as to the nature of the wound.

"The bullet," Dr. Lincoln answered, "struck the trapezium, between the bases of the thumb and the second metacarpal. It did considerable damage to the bone. But not permanent, I hope, unless complications set in." He turned to Angerman and said almost curtly: "I haven't much time to spare. I must make my morning calls. Where's the affidavit Torday wants signed?"

Although he must have been aware of the hostility, there was no expression at all in Angerman's eyes or on his face as he returned the older man's gaze. He produced the documents and within a few minutes they had been signed and attested. With thoughtfulness and every evidence of deference, Angerman steadied the paper on the flat chair-arm while Radisson signed. When the latter got to his feet, with the remark that he was going to return to his apartment, Angerman held the door open for him.

"Rennert," Dr. Lincoln beckoned, and led the way into the living-room. Abstractedly he took his driving a table on which reposed his hat and instrument case. He spoke in an offhand manner: "I see by the morning paper that the death of Campos yesterday has caused quite a stir. I wondered if you had mentioned to anyone that I was there—and was carrying my daughter's mirror?"

"Why, no, Doctor, I never gave it another thought."

"Good. Would you mind not saying anything about it? I don't know what kind of investigation the Mexican police are making. But I cross over into Mexico almost every day, and it would be embarrassing to be detained and questioned."

Rennert frowned. "Of course I'll say nothing. But I fail to see any reason why you need worry."

"Oh, I'm not worrying. But—" Dr. Lincoln gently smoothed the gloves about his long fingers. "I might as well be frank with you, Rennert. I had in mind the man you're with this morning—Jarl Angerman. He knows that I have frequently urged Dr. Torday to dispense with his services. I consider him unscrupulous. He might welcome the opportunity to strike back at me. I hope you'll be on your guard while you're with him."

"Thank you," Rennert said evenly, "I shall be on my guard." He made up his mind quickly. "Doctor, since you have brought up the subject of that bull-fight, I wish you would explain the remark you made when Campos was gored."

Dr. Lincoln regarded him steadily. "Just what did I say?"

"You said, 'That's three!'"

"Oh. I meant that was the third accident"—he stressed the word—"which had happened to men who witnessed the railway wreck on the Campos *hacienda* three and a half years ago."

"Charles Bettis was one."

"Yes. Dr. Torday himself was the second. Exactly a year ago last night another car tried to force his into a ditch. In his condition the slightest jar would be fatal."

"I never heard that. So Professor Radisson was the fourth."

Dr. Lincoln put on his hat. "Radisson was the fourth. There aren't many more of us."

III

The steel-grey car sped smoothly past the long even rows of orange trees which paralleled the highway and abutted on the road which led past Rennert's house.

Jarl Angerman lifted a hand and stated: "A good grove."

"Yes." Rennert brought his thoughts back. "One of the best in the vicinity. It belongs to Dr. Torday, I understand."

"Yes. A whole section of land. Bounded on three sides by the highway, the road and by your house. You should own it, Mr. Rennert. It would even out your farm."

"I'd like to, of course. But I don't suppose it's for sale. And if it were the price would be beyond me. I'll have to be content with my modest acreage."

"It is not good," Angerman said sententiously, "to be content."

"Well, maybe not. But it's a lot more comfortable than being fired with ambition."

"But you are ambitious, Mr. Rennert. You do not think so now, but you will see. You will want more land. Every morning when you get up you will look at those orange trees. You will say, 'I wish they were mine.' You have never lived on a farm?"

"This is my first experience."

"But you are still living in a hotel. You do not know what it is to be a part of the land. To want to grow and not be able to because somebody has put up a fence. It is like clothes that are too tight. I know. I was born on a farm in Minnesota. A little farm. I could not stand it." He glanced sideways at Rennert and his eyes were friendly. "Do you understand what I mean? You were in the Customs Service. You quit. Maybe it was for the same reason that I quit the farm. You felt, the day you left, that you had got out of harness?"

"That describes my feelings very well." Rennert was thoroughly puzzled. Was all this merely a buildup for an attempt to sell him some land?

There was a dogged persistence about Angerman. "Then you will have the same feeling on a farm unless you make your land grow and grow and break down fences. You will see that I am right. Now you are loafing?"

"Yes. My house isn't finished. None of my trees will bear fruit for another season. Most of them not for two or three. I must say that I'm enjoying the chance to loaf."

Angerman shook his head almost severely. "You will get tired of that. You will want to be busy. You are not married?"

And so their talk went as Angerman drove expertly, at the exact maximum of speed permitted by law, through Brownsville's broad clean streets and towards the International Bridge over the

Rio Grande. Rennert found himself talking freely of his days in the Customs Service, of experiences which stood out in bold relief in his memory. Angerman attended gravely, prodding him gently with questions.

There was no delay at the bridge, for Customs officials of both nationalities recognized the car and waived examination.

They were in Mexico, passing between the low plaster walls of the shops and bars which Rennert knew, into squalid alleys where he had never penetrated, where dust and adobe emitted the peculiar noisesome exhalation of Mexico warmed by the sun.

Rennert thought he knew now why he had been brought along.

He was on his guard.

6
DUST OF MEXICO

I

DUST WAS A SHROUD that clung to the steel-grey car and billowed in its wake along the dusty road. Thin, stately columns of dust moved in the distance, disintegrating and forming again. Along the horizon mirages played, and in the hot blue sky vultures wheeled in lazy spirals. It was a land stillborn of heat and thirst, Rennert thought fancifully, and dust and mirage and vulture were the sinister emanations of its corpse.

"Beautiful!" Angerman spoke as if to himself. "It is beautiful. I see it every day and I always think it is beautiful." He was gazing ahead with a gleam that was almost ecstatic in his blue eyes.

"It's beautiful," Rennert agreed, "if one can escape from it, as we can. But look at it closely and you'll see the bleached bones that show how cruel it can be."

Angerman raised a hand from the wheel and tensed his fingers. "The desert is powerful and so it must be cruel. It has scared men off. The Indians. The Spaniards. The Mexicans. They have left it alone, as it was on the day of Creation. But some day men will come to it and conquer it. Some day coal and oil will be gone and they will have to come. Our children and our grandchildren, Mr. Rennert, will drive along here and see factories and foundries and mills. They will hear motors humming."

It was his belief, he explained, that solar heat would eventually be converted into cheap energy and take the place of mineral fuel. That industrial centres such as Pennsylvania and Lancashire, the Ruhr and the Saar would be abandoned for the Tropics. That Northern Mexico would become one great city.

It was curious, Rennert reflected, how frequently the visionary crops up in men of cold or gross exteriors. Yet there was nothing really chimerical about Angerman's simply expressed predictions. Shortly before there had been a demonstration in Washington of an engine run entirely by sun-power.

Long before he expected it, Rennert saw the twinkling blue waters of the Gulf appear among the undulating sand-dunes and, starkly outlined against them, a fence of heavy wire, higher than a man's head. Where it crossed the road in front of them was a gate and a small square box of a house. Over the gate was a huge sign, bright yellow letters splashed on white. Tonatiuh. And the flaming Aztec emblem of the sun.

A man ran from the shack to swing open the gate. He stood aside and as the car passed raised his right hand in salute. An American of the hard-bitten border breed, he had at his side a holster from which protruded the butt of a revolver.

The car leaped forward, down a gravel road which swerved in a regular arc towards the shore. Rennert watched the green roofs of buildings and the tops of small palms loom against the water.

"You keep the place guarded, I see," he remarked.

"Yes. We have to. Damn fools come here to gawk. They think we have patients that are mad. They think we are nudists. People will believe any story they hear about a place like this."

"I know. I've got to admit my own ignorance. What kind of patients do come here?"

"Ones who suffer from lung trouble: sinus, asthma. We give them lots of good food and sleep. They swim and lie in the sun. They get well quick. There are not many here now. It is Christmas and they have gone away." He turned to Rennert. "You like to swim?"

"Why, yes."

"Then we will swim."

Rennert was a bit taken aback. "I hadn't expected to. And I haven't done any swimming for years. There hasn't been enough water in places where I've lived. So I'm not specially keen about it if you have other business to attend to."

"My business, Mr. Rennert, is with you. I can attend to it while we swim."

The buildings, Rennert could see now, were ranged at regular intervals about a crescent-shaped beach, which was protected from the Gulf by a string of sandbars. There must have been twenty of them, each set in its plot of lush green grass and shaded by trees. The road forked, one branch going ahead towards what was evidently a second group of houses, beyond the southern tip of the crescent; the other, which Angerman followed, ending at the rear of a two-storey plaster building.

"The offices," Angerman said as he parked here, "and the Infirmary."

They got out, and he directed Rennert along a path of crushed sea-shells toward the front.

"May I ask"—Rennert watched his companion—"about Mr. Wyllys? It might make our meeting less awkward if I knew beforehand what his affliction is."

It was evident that the question was not a welcome one. A slight frown cut into Angerman's smooth forehead, and he answered briefly: "Nerves."

They turned to the right along another broader path which connected the cottages. These were all of a standard design, attractive enough with green paint and curtains at the windows, but with no sign of life about them.

Rennert was impressed by the stillness which lay upon the place, undisturbed except for the gentle rustling of the waves. His gaze roved over the beach that shelved smoothly down to the water. It was probably the sand which gave him a vague and altogether unreasonable feeling of uneasiness. It was yellow and hard-packed, and the Spanish word for sand is *arena*.

Angerman nodded in the direction of the first house. "That is mine. The second here is Mr. Wyllys's."

They went up the steps, and Angerman pressed a bell. The front door was open, but inside a frame of latticed fibre was closed against the sun.

This was opened, and a man spoke in what seemed to Rennert an artificial voice: "Good morning, Jan."

"Good morning, Darwin."

"Come in." Wyllys stood aside.

He was the man whom Rennert had seen outside the bull-ring the day before. He presented a disheveled appearance, in a maroon-coloured dressing-gown and pyjamas. His wiry black hair was tousled, and a lock of it straggled forward over his forehead. Rennert was struck again by the sallowness which underlay his complexion, noticeable even on his unshaven cheeks. His eyes had an oddly lucent quality, as if the pupils were slightly dilated.

Angerman introduced them. Wyllys did not offer to shake hands. His gaze rested for only a fraction of a second on Rennert's face, then darted back to Angerman's. "Sit down," he said nervously.

Rennert did so, depositing his seal on a table. The room was small but comfortably furnished. The walls were of light cream plaster, a dark brown rug covered the hardwood floor. Untidiness was everywhere, in the overflowing ash-trays, in scattered articles of clothing, in newspapers which littered the floor.

"Mr. Rennert is a notary public," Angerman explained. "He will witness your signature on the affidavit which Dr. Torday told you about."

Wyllys stood in the centre of the room, rubbing the palms of his hands together and intertwining his long, flexible fingers. "No, he won't," he said flatly. "Because I'm not going to sign."

It was exactly as if a taut wire had been struck and was filling the air with the violence if not the sound of its vibrations. Angerman stood motionless and looked at Wyllys, as he had looked at him across the Matamoros street. His face was set austerely and coldly, the blueness of his eyes was clouded by (Rennert knew he wasn't mistaken) sadness.

Wyllys's gaze fell, beaten down by that relentless scrutiny. He opened his mouth, ran his tongue over his lips, and repeated, "I'm not going to sign it," this time with a wheedling softness.

Angerman said gravely: "You must sign it, Darwin."

"I'm not going to."

Angerman sighed deeply. There was something incongruous in the heavy rise and fall of his chest and in the rasping exhalation of his breath. "I am sorry. I do not want to have to do this." He did not turn his head. "Please go outside, Mr. Rennert."

Rennert got up, hesitated. "Perhaps I'd better stay."

"Go outside."

Rennert glanced at Wyllys. "What do you say, Mr. Wyllys?"

The latter did not look at him but at Angerman. There was a twitching of the muscles about his eyes. "Yes, yes," he said with a trace of sibilance. "Go on. You must do as he says."

Rennert walked out upon the porch. He heard the outer then the inner door being closed, the window lowered and the shade drawn. No sound came from within.

He went to the steps, sat down and lighted a cigarette. Nothing in the prospect had changed. The sun still spread its dazzling sheen over water and sand and grass, giving colours of the paining lemon-yellow intensity of a Van Gogh canvas. The lulling quietness persisted. There was a thin film of perspiration on Rennert's forehead. The board upon which he rested was uncomfortably warm. Yet he had to repress a shiver. It was the recoil of his whole healthy being from what he knew was going on inside. Or what he thought was going on.

Four or five minutes passed.

The door opened and closed and the flooring echoed hollowly under a heavy measured tread. Rennert felt the wood sag under him as first one shoe and then another came down. The shoes were of white ventilated canvas, huge, square-toed, and soled with thick slabs of rubber.

"Now," Jarl Angerman said with satisfaction, "we can go for a swim."

Rennert rose and faced him. Angerman was gazing out over the sea, a far-away brooding look in his eyes. His features were smooth and symmetrical, but were losing their austerity.

"My hat and seal," Rennert said, "are inside the house."

"Leave them. We will come back."

"Is there any reason to come back?"

"Yes, Mr. Wyllys will sign that paper."

"He changed his mind?"

"Yes, he changed his mind."

"Then why not get it over with now?"

"We must let him rest. He does not feel well now." Their eyes met.

Rennert flicked away his cigarette. "I understand," he said thoughtfully.

"I knew"—Angerman's voice was level—"that you would understand."

He did not speak again until he held open the door of the first cottage. "This is your house, Mr. Rennert, as they say here in Mexico. The door is not locked, you see. We do not have to lock doors here in Tonatiuh. I will go now to the office and get you a bathing-suit. We keep them for visitors." He eyed Rennert's body and gave his size accurately. "I will bring one to fit you."

Rennert was left to look at wood carvings. They were everywhere in a room which was similar to Wyllys's in design and furnishing, but clean and orderly. There were statuettes of men and women, many Mexican, done with scrupulous attention to detail. Masks lined the walls. There were book-ends, picture-frames, ashtrays, paper-weights, knives. On a pedestal in a corner stood the uncompleted torso of a man, mutilated of head and limbs. Chisel, hammer and knife were beside it.

A hobby, evidently, which Angerman pursued without stint. And a man's hobbies are always revelatory.

"Thanks," Rennert said, when Angerman came in smiling and handed him a black suit. "I've been admiring your work. It's excellent."

The other showed his delight. "They are not much. The Mexicans do much better. I learned from them."

They went into the adjoining bedroom, almost monastic in its simplicity.

"You've spent a great deal of time in Mexico, I judge," Rennert said as he started to undress.

"Four years. Here and in other places. I was *capataz*, foreman, of an *hacienda* once. At first I did not like the country. I got impatient with it. Now I could not leave it."

Rennert brushed dust from the collar of his coat. "You know the Mexican saying: 'When the dust of Mexico settles on a human heart, that heart can find rest in no other land.'"

"That is true. I would be happy to live on that *hacienda* where I worked. And die there."

As Rennert moved to a chair his eyes rested on the small framed photograph which was the sole occupant of the top of a chest of drawers.

It was a woman's face, as finely chiseled as some of those wooden ones in the other room, beautiful in a full-blown way. If there was no indication of great intellectual force, the lack was compensated for by the strength and resolution inherent in the chin and mouth. And by the eyes . . .

Rennert sat down and began to unlace his shoes. "That was the Campos *hacienda?*"

"Yes." Angerman folded his trousers over the footboard of the bed so as to leave the crease undisturbed. He seemed to be ambidexterous.

"I know the region."

"You are to be one of the witnesses in Dr. Torbays case then?"

"No, I am not one of the witnesses. I did not see the wreck. I was near. I heard it. But I did not see it."

Rennert stood up and cast another glance at the picture. The eyes were the woman's most attractive feature. They were large, deep-set and luminous, and gave her a faintly exotic appearance. There was a similarity between them and those of Darwin Wyllys. Put this calmness in place of the febrile intensity of the man's, draw that terrible dilation of his pupils . . .

"Perhaps," Rennert said, "that is fortunate for you. It looks as if those who saw the wreck are not finding the Valley a very healthy place to live."

Angerman was fastening the buckle of a pair of snugly-fitting black trunks. "That is what you and I are going to talk about, Mr. Rennert. Shall we go?"

Rennert looked once more, surreptitiously, at the photograph. He was sure it was that of Mrs. Torday.

II

The sun stared obliquely from a sky of profound blue. The air was heady with the smell of blistered pine boards, of vapours rising from the waves that lapped gently against the float, of salt water drying on Rennert's bare shoulders and arms. Slightly winded from the swim, he sat tailor-fashion and felt a pleasing lassitude creep over his limbs.

Angerman lay outstretched, his hands clasped behind his head, his eyes fixed on the sky.

"Let us go back," he said. "Last night Professor Radisson was shot. Yesterday afternoon Carlos Campos was killed. Did you know that a year ago somebody tried to kill Dr. Torday?"

"I knew it." Rennert thought it wise not to divulge the source of his information. "But none of the particulars."

"Not many people know it. He has a car built for his wheelchair. One that will not jolt. Now *I* drive him back and forth from the radio station. But before a chauffeur did it. He broadcasts twice each night. At seven and at nine. He was going back to his house after the last broadcast. Someone tried to crowd him off the road at the edge of Brownsville. The chauffeur was too scared to see what kind of a car it was. It was a narrow escape." Angerman stopped as if he had rounded out a period.

"Two years ago," he went on, "Charles Bettis, the brother of Matt Bettis at the hotel, was shot and killed. That was before I came here, and I do not know much about it. But they found him out in the country. Shot through the head. A bullet from a long-range rifle, like deer hunters use. Everybody said it was an accident. But Dr. Torday does not think so."

"He believes, I suppose, that there is a plot on foot to do away with himself and his witnesses."

Angerman turned his head so that his eyes met Rennert's. "That is what he wants you to find out."

Rennert smiled. "So that's why I'm here."

Angerman's smile matched his. "That is why you are here. I am offering you a job."

Rennert was silent for a moment. "Be more specific," he said. "Just what is it Dr. Torday wants me to do?"

"To find out if there is a plot against him or his witnesses. To get evidence one way or the other."

"I see. Didn't I make it plain on the way over that I quit work of that sort when I left the Customs Service?"

"Yes, Mr. Rennert, you made it plain." There was a glint of humour in the blue eyes. "I think maybe you knew what was coming and tried to make yourself—not me—believe you did not want to do it." Angerman sat up. "But you can keep on believing what you said—and still take this job. It will help make you a farmer quicker than sitting on your—I beg your pardon, Mr. Rennert—than sitting in a chair at the hotel all day."

"How?"

"Dr. Torday will give you that section of land next to your house. The orange trees that we looked at. The trees that you will look at every morning and want—if you do not take this job."

Rennert laughed outright, partly in satisfaction. "Do you mind telling me what part you had in planning this campaign?"

Angerman's face beamed with pleasure that he made no attempt to conceal. "Last night," he said, more thickly than usual, "Dr. Torday called me to his office. 'Jarl,' he said, 'I have a job for you. Go out and engage Mr. Rennert's services. Have him here at noon to-morrow.' At noon you and I will go to his office and my job will be done."

"I don't like to be bluntly mercenary, Angerman, but is the offer of that orange grove made by you or by him?"

"By him. But I thought of it. I thought of it this morning. After I met you I told myself that you would be more likely to take that land than money. You told me you would like to have it. A few minutes ago, when I went to the office, I 'phoned Dr. Torday. I asked him if I could offer you the orange grove. He said, 'Yes.'"

"Was it your idea to have me attest these affidavits?"

"Yes. Dr. Torday had told me to get them fixed, but there was no hurry. I found out you were a notary. I thought it would give me a chance to know you, to feel you out."

"It's true then that the testimony of these men is of no importance to Dr. Torday?"

"No, it is of no importance. Now"—Angerman sprang to his feet, swaying the solid raft—"we will call it settled, won't we?"

"I'm going to withhold my answer until I've talked with Dr. Torday. But I see no reason why I shouldn't accept his offer." Rennert realized what a disadvantage it is to have to look up to meet a man's eyes. "I trust this means that you and I are going to be frank with each other?"

"Yes, of course."

"I want you to tell me, then, about Darwin Wyllys."

"That is a private matter, Mr. Rennert."

"I'm not going to get very far if you take that attitude. For instance, I was at the bullfight yesterday afternoon. I saw you and Wyllys meet outside."

"Neither of us was inside. That is enough." Angerman turned his back and stepped to the edge of the float, where he stood, a flaming bronze and black colossus straddling seashore and houses and palms. "I think it will be much better," he said firmly, "if you do not ask any more questions about Darwin Wyllys."

He dived.

III

A remarkable change had come over Darwin Wyllys when he ushered them into his living-room the second time. He was fully dressed in whites. He had shaved and combed his hair. His face was flushed with colour, as if from the effects of a cold shower. His pupils had lost most of their dilation.

"Enjoy your swim?" he inquired affably.

"I always enjoy a swim." Angerman preserved some of the defensive hauteur which he had manifested since he and Rennert left the float.

"I haven't been in lately. Sit down. Or do you want to get this affidavit fixed up right away?" Wyllys turned to Rennert and smiled. "I didn't understand about it at first, Mr. Rennert. Jarl here made things clear to me. I'm ready to sign it now."

"We cannot stay," Angerman said. "Here it is."

Wyllys took the sheet from him, moved to the table, and affixed his signature. Rennert completed the document and handed it to Angerman.

The air of strain about their departure was very slight.

On the walk outside Rennert stopped suddenly. "I forgot my seal," he said as he turned back. "Just a moment."

"I will get it for you," Angerman said quickly.

"I'll do it."

Rennert crossed the porch, rang, and stepped inside when Wyllys came to the door.

"I have a message for you," he said in a low voice as he secured his seal. "Mr. Jester has the papers you want. He will meet you in his office at eight o'clock to-night."

Wyllys's eyes brightened. "Good! Now I will be able to please Jarl."

"To please him?"

"Yes, by giving him what he wants more than anything in the world. The *hacienda*."

"The Campos *hacienda?*"

"Yes. Didn't you know?"

"No," Rennert said slowly, "I didn't know."

7
THE BROKEN MAN

I

"DR. TORDAY," Angerman broke the silence, "lives here."

"Yes," Rennert said, "I know."

The estate, on the northern fringe of Brownsville, had been pointed out to him more than once. Due to its isolation and the peculiar circumstances of its owner's life, popular gossip had been rife and inventive regarding what lay behind its stone boundary walls. Rennert had been told, in all seriousness, that the crippled physician maintained there an Oriental seraglio, replete with eunuchs, slant-eyed dancing girls smuggled across the Rio Grande, a retinue of dwarfs and deformed buffoons and other horrors which the clean-minded Anglo-Saxon knew of only from the *Arabian Nights*.

The walls *were* high. The man who swung open the iron gates at Angerman's signal was ostensibly a gardener, but wore a revolver and stood at military attention as they passed. Otherwise, Rennert thought as he was carried between smooth green lawns, clustered shrubs and flowers and rows of tall palms, it might have been the home of any successful *bourgeois* businessman.

Angerman parked in front of the house—a large rectangular mansion of cream-coloured brick and stucco—and got out. He glanced at his watch and unobtrusively straightened his tie as Rennert walked round the car to join him.

A Mexican maid let them in, and Rennert noted a softening of the black eyes that rested for a moment longer than necessary on the broad white-clad form of his companion.

The latter disregarded her. "Will you sit down, Mr. Rennert? I will see if Dr. Torday is ready."

Rennert sat in a living-room which occupied the east side of the residence. It was a beautiful room, done in a modified Regency style, with wallpapers of a deep but vital blue, white classical figures and light graceful furniture which increased the feeling of spaciousness.

His eyes did not detect a single discordant note in the *décor*. That, he decided, was the trouble. It was a singularly impersonal room, too formal, lacking the little disarrangements which are significant of human occupancy.

A woman came in from one of the two doors at the rear, paused for a fraction of a second before Rennert turned his head, then advanced toward him.

She wore a severely simple dress of white. Her arms and throat and face were white as alabaster. As Rennert rose he recognized the features of the photograph which adorned Jarl Angerman's bedchamber. She was older now, a little of the firmness had gone from her mouth, but her eyes were unchanged.

"I am Mrs. Torday. I believe you are Mr. Rennert. Dr. Torday told me that he was expecting you. Jarl—Mr. Angerman—is with him now?"

"Yes."

"He won't be long. Sit down, won't you?" Her voice was low and pleasant, with no trace of strain. Yet there was an absent quality to it, purely negative in its force, as if from habit she were giving but perfunctory attention to what she said.

"I hope you can relieve Dr. Torday's mind, Mr. Rennert. He didn't rest well last night. In his condition rest is essential. I've tried to convince him that he is letting his imagination run away with him, but without success. Don't you agree with me that it is fantastic to suspect the Mexican National Railways of any plot such as this?"

"It certainly strikes me as fantastic, Mrs. Torday. But I know very little about the matter as yet. Mr. Angerman told me of it only this morning. When he took me to Tonatiuh to attest the affidavit of your brother, Mr. Wyllys."

"Yes." The monosyllable was colourless.

"I hadn't met your brother before. I was sorry to hear from Mr. Angerman that he was suffering from nervous trouble. I trust that the sunshine and quiet of Tonatiuh will relieve him."

"Nervous trouble?" He thought, but couldn't be sure, that there was a faintly speculative look in her eyes. "Oh, you're mistaken, Mr. Rennert," she said calmly. "There is nothing wrong with Darwin. He's merely living down at Tonatiuh in order to be with Mr. Angerman. They have been friends most of their lives. Darwin worships him. He has never been very strong himself."

"Oh, I'm sorry I misunderstood. I was glad of the opportunity to visit Tonatiuh. Do you go there often?"

"Very seldom. Dr. Torday likes his patients to have as much privacy as possible. He discourages casual visiting. And I don't like to set an example to others."

Rennert never knew how long Jarl Angerman had been standing in the hall, exactly like a garbed piece of statuary. It was no movement on his part but rather the consciousness of his presence which made Rennert turn.

Angerman came in, setting thick rubber soles carefully on the deep nap of the rug, and said: "How do you do, Irene."

"How do you do, Jarl. Is Dr. Torday ready to see Mr. Rennert?"

"Yes."

Their eyes met briefly.

Mrs. Torday rose and held out a hand to Rennert. "I'm so glad to have met you, Mr. Rennert. I expect we shall see you here frequently now."

"I hope so, Mrs. Torday."

Rennert went with Angerman across the hall and into a room on the southwest. It was a large nondescript room which seemed to do duty as office and library. There were metal filing-cases, a desk with a typewriter, cases crammed with books and papers, a suite of living-room furniture.

Two high-backed Spanish chairs were ranged side by side, facing the French windows on the south. Facing, also, a wheel-chair. Deep in the latter, his back to the sun, a man sat.

"Dr. Torday," Angerman said, "this is Mr. Rennert."

II

Rennert was faintly amused at his own surprise. It told him how actively his fancy had been at work, without his full awareness, in conjuring up images of Torday. What sort of an individual he had expected to meet, he didn't know. A patriarch, perhaps. Or a grotesque, even sinister, invalid. But certainly not this crabbed insignificant little man who was busily appraising him with such shrewd black eyes.

Dr. Torday wore a grey sack suit. A black silk scarf was wound loosely about his neck, entirely covering the cast which must have been there. His head, with its little wisps of grizzled hair, rested upon large cushions. His voice was the mildly incisive one which Rennert had heard over the radio.

"So this is Hugh Rennert! Do you mind standing right where you are for a moment, Mr. Rennert? I can't turn my head, you know, and I'm curious to get a good look at you." He gave a little bark of laughter. "It's rude, I know. But I dare say you're just as curious about me. So we'll toss the conventions overboard."

For a full minute he studied Rennert's face.

"I'm agreeably surprised, Mr. Rennert. I'd expected a younger man. One of those fellows with bulldog jaw, tight lips, hard eyes. You have good features. A well-proportioned body. Getting just a little bit fat. Better go down to Tonatiuh sometime and have Jarl show you some exercises that will take care of that. Turn your head just a bit, will you? Yes, I thought so. Well-modeled ears. I'd be inclined to put confidence in you if I saw only your ears. People never look at ears. I think maybe they're the most expressive things about a man. He doesn't have any control over them, as he does over his eyes, for instance. Or his mouth. I've had to study physiognomy. I'll wager I know what your voice will be like. Soft, but none of this southern slurring. Say something, won't you? I'll keep still now and give you a chance." Another laugh. "You might say this: 'You're taking advantage of the fact that you're an invalid, Torday.' Go ahead. I'd much prefer you to be frank. And I know that's what you're thinking."

"I don't think you're taking advantage of the fact that you're an invalid, Dr. Torday."

Torday sighed. "I'm disappointed in you, Mr. Rennert. You don't need to toady to me."

"I think you're taking advantage of the fact that you have something I want. You would act exactly the same way regardless of your physical condition."

The invalid's laugh was loud and clear and happy. "*Touché*, Rennert! You're absolutely right. You and I will get along together. I'm going to apologize to you—sincerely—for having kept you standing. Sit down. Jarl, you must attend to the refreshments. What will you have, Rennert? Don't be hesitant in expressing your wishes. I'm not by nature a hedonist, but I keep myself supplied with such pleasures as I can have. In compensation for those I can't have. What will it be? Whisky-and-soda? Brandy? Anis?"

"Brandy, if you please."

"Fine. Jarl, there's a special bottle of Martell in the lower compartment of the bar. Open that for us. We must toast Rennert in the best."

His eyes followed Angerman as the latter moved toward a movable chromium and nickel plated bar by the window. "You and I will have to drink alone, Rennert. Jarl is an abstainer. He gets his enjoyment out of mortification of the flesh. Takes icy baths, I suspect. He'll look on at our dissipation with a severe Spartan aloofness. Nordic, rather."

He fell silent when Angerman passed out of his range of vision, then pitched his voice a little higher. "Remarkable, isn't it, how this analogy keeps cropping up in history? I know how those weak Byzantine emperors felt when they looked down on the blond blue-eyed Northmen who were guarding their thrones. What were those mercenaries called? Varangians. Poor bargainers then, poor bargainers now, the Vikings. It may be fortunate for me that Jarl doesn't read history. Some of his ancestors found out after a long time that those thrones were comfortable places to sit. But no"— he watched Angerman returning with decanter and glasses—"the discovery was always forgotten. Haven't been studying up on the Varangians, have you, Jarl?"

Angerman set the tray upon the table at his employer's left hand.

"No," he said, with no alteration of his face, as he proceeded to pour out the liquor.

"Do you know who they were?"

"No." Angerman kept his eyes averted as he served Rennert.

"Ah, there we are! History is discussed before Jarl, and he doesn't even listen!" Torday fumbled in the depths of a square box of carved wood, brought out two ivory cigarette-holders, also ornately carved, dropped one back and put the other between his thin, bloodless lips. "He'd rather spend his time carving things than reading. Wouldn't you, Jarl? This holder is a specimen of his work, Rennert. My wife had him make me some as a Christmas present. What do you think of it?"

"Very fine work."

Angerman passed a flat box full of various brands of cigarettes—American, Mexican, Turkish—and held a match to the one which Torday inserted into the long tube.

"Now, Jarl, you may sit on the right side of Mr. Rennert. No, move your chair a little closer to him." The cripple drew slowly and contentedly upon tobacco whose sweet odour scented the room. "Rather like the line-up, isn't it, Rennert?"

Angerman sat bolt upright and stared out of the window. The curtains were drawn back and the noon sunlight was beginning to creep towards them over the waxed floor.

Torday took his wide-mouthed glass in extremely white, delicate and flexible fingers. He was, Rennert had already noted, left-handed.

"A toast, Rennert, to your success!"

He set down the glass and said almost querulously: "Too much stage-setting, I'm afraid. What follows will be in the nature of an anticlimax." He stared at Rennert's tie, frowning and pursing his lips. "I scarcely know where to begin. It's so much like trying to spear something in the atmosphere. Or catch hold of a bit of cloud."

"Suppose you begin," Rennert suggested, "by telling me how you came to think of me in this connection."

Torday laughed. "I wish I could say that as soon as I suspected there was a plot on foot against me I thought of you as the one man in the world who could foil it. In fiction, I believe, that's the way the threatened man appeals to the detective. But, alas! it's not true. I knew of you, of course, and was aware that you had settled here. But this meeting wouldn't have taken place, I fear, had it not been for a newspaper reporter. Juan Canard, of the *Brownsville Sun*. A hasty but capable youth. You met him yesterday at the bull-ring, I understand."

"Yes." Rennert wondered if his face showed his surprise.

"He has been trying to get an interview with me about my case against the railroad. I don't care for that sort of publicity, so I kept putting him off. But he persisted, and I received him here yester-day afternoon, after he returned from Matamoros. Bluntly he out-lined a theory of his and asked me to verify it. He linked the mur-der of Campos with the shooting of Charles Bettis two years ago, and with the attempt to force my car off the highway. There seems to be no keeping of secrets from the news clan. It showed, he said, that some agency had been at work all that time, 'grimly deter-mined'—I believe those were his words—to destroy me or, failing that, my supporters against the Mexican National. He pointed out that less than a week remains until the case comes up for final settlement. Judging by the death of Campos, that week would hold danger for us."

Torday sipped brandy slowly. "Frankly, I was astounded at his words. I told him that the whole thing was a figment of his imagi-nation. He kept on, however. I got to thinking. And I began to see that it wasn't so preposterous. There it was! Two of the witnesses to my accident had met violent deaths. I had barely escaped one. I didn't commit myself, but brought the interview to a close. Just as he was leaving he asked me if I knew that Hugh Rennert was living near me. I could see that he wasn't sure whether to believe me or not when I told him that I had never met you. He came straight out with his question then. Had I employed you to look into this matter? I said, of course, that I hadn't. He explained that he had seen you at the bullfight with Dr. Lincoln and had wondered if you weren't there to safeguard my supporters. I think I convinced him that he was wrong. Why, then, he wanted to know, didn't I

establish contact with you? He pointed out that you were the logical man to undertake an investigation. I couldn't very well appeal
to the police, since Bettis was killed in the United States and Campos in Mexico. Someone was needed who was acquainted with both
sides of the Rio Grande. You spent a long time in the Customs and
knew the border. Furthermore, you were a neighbour of four of the
witnesses. You would be able to 'keep an eye' on them, he expressed
it. He urged me to think about it and left. Well, I thought about it.
And began to get uneasy. I called Bruce Lincoln and asked him
something about you. I didn't tell him why I was interested, as I
didn't want to alarm him. He gave you high praise. So"—Torday
spread a palm in Rennert's direction—"I commissioned Jarl to sound
you out and bring you here if possible. You're here. In the bright
light of day I was inclined to think the whole thing a mare's-nest.
Until I heard that Xavier Radisson had been shot last night. Now—
I don't know what to think. What's your honest opinion, Rennert?"

"I'm going to hold back my answer for a moment. Canard's
theory is based on the assumption that the evidence of these men—
Jester, Lincoln, Radisson, Bettis, Wyllys, Distant—is essential to
your case. Is that true?"

The other took a long time to plant another cigarette into the
holder. Angerman rose, like an automaton, and struck a match for it.

Torday emitted a ring of smoke, then said explosively:

"You've put your finger on the crux, Rennert. As far as I can
see, the testimony of these men doesn't amount to a tinker's damn.
The railroad is not raising any question as to its liability. It's merely
contending that the indemnity which I am getting was agreed to
under a misunderstanding. They thought I'd die but"—a wry smile
twisted his lips—"I didn't. I can see a very good motive on the part
of the railway for doing away with me. But none at all for attacking
anybody else."

"Another point, Dr. Torday. Do you really believe that an organization like the National Railways of Mexico would resort to such
tactics in order to avoid payment of an obligation?"

Torday's laugh was dry and humourless. "You know the history of railroads and other corporations in this country, Rennert."

"Certainly. I have no illusions about big business. But neither am I ready to believe it entirely unscrupulous, without proof. But it's futile to argue that point now. We seem to be agreed that even if the railroad people were deep-dyed villains they would have nothing to gain by this. Do you know of anyone else, any individual or group, who would like to see you lose this case? Or the stock question: Have you any enemies? Enemies who might believe the testimony of these men more important than it is."

The cripple smiled. "I'll be frank with you, Rennert. I have business enemies, I am well aware. Rival radio stations. Medical interests. Landowners, perhaps. But they would gain nothing except by killing me. And I'm sure they all know that."

"Another personal question. How important to your continued operation of the radio station, sanatorium and so forth is this indemnity you are receiving?"

"Would its loss leave me bankrupt, you mean?"

"Yes."

"It would mean very little. A few years ago it would have been different. But now I could continue very well without it. Not"—Torday hastened to add—"that I am as rich a man as people think. One thousand dollars a week to me means a great deal of comfort, of luxury even, that I should be loath to lose. Especially since I feel it is only my right to receive it. This brandy, for instance. And that reminds me, Jarl, you're neglecting Mr. Rennert. His glass is empty. Attend to it at once, please."

"Thank you," Rennert said. "No more just now."

Torday seemed disappointed. "You can fill mine, Jarl. I know Mr. Rennert will pardon me if I go ahead." There was deep amusement in his eyes as he watched the big hands tipping the decanter. "You don't seem to be taking much interest in this discussion, Jarl. Surely you would know if I had any enemies."

"I am sorry," Angerman said very seriously, "but I do not know of any." He went back to his chair and moved it a few inches farther away from Rennert's.

Torday's smile was quick and malicious. "Please, Jarl, put your chair back where it was. You know that it pains me to shift my eyes back and forth so far. And Mr. Rennert may think you dislike being in such close contact with him."

"It is not that. It is the light."

"Oh, the light. I see. But you shouldn't object to that. You take sunbaths. Sit down, please."

Deliberately Angerman returned the chair to its former position, and lowered himself into it. He rested his hands on his knees, taking care to cup them so that the palms would not disturb the crease in his trousers.

Rennert glanced sideways at his face. The sunlight had encroached into the room so that it struck the top of the bar by the window. There was a quantity of glassware there and the reflection was a broken halo that played upon the bridge of Angerman's nose. It must have taken stern self-control to sit as the man did, staring straight into it without a flicker of an eyelid.

Rennert piled orange trees, golden-fruited, against the disgust which was settling upon him. Before he could see which way the balance was inclining, he said: "There's one more question that I'd like to ask, Dr. Torday."

"Oh, yes. Certainly." The other took his gaze from Angerman.

"You spoke a few moments ago of spearing at something in the atmosphere. That may be what I'm doing now. But"—Rennert leaned forward—"did you ever consider the possibility that the attacks on you and Radisson, Bettis and Campos are not only interlinked, but linked with something that goes farther back into the past?"

"What?"

"The wreck in which you were injured. The wreck that was caused by the deliberate changing of a switch."

III

Torday made a pyramid of his fingers and scrutinized them amusingly, as a faint smile played about his lips. "What makes you ask that, Rennert?"

"I've heard this matter discussed by you, Dr. Torday, and by others. I've been struck by the fact that all of you pass blandly over the question of who turned that switch. And why. Unless it was a random bit of sabotage it was done for the purpose of killing one or more of the individuals on that Pullman. The likelihood of a general holocaust didn't deter the person who did it. I've heard one explanation. If it is true, I think it would be far-fetched to find any connection with the other tragedies. But I should like to hear your explanation."

"Mine," Torday repeated. His eyes moved slowly in their sockets and fastened on Angerman's face. There was a calculative narrowing of the lids. "I think at this point we must insist that Jarl break his silence. He can tell us who changed that switch. He can tell us why. Tell us, Jarl," he urged gently.

Angerman stared blankly into sunlight.

Torday waited. When he saw that no reply was forthcoming he went on, in a voice which was perceptibly edged: "Then I shall have to tell him, Jarl. I can understand your reluctance to talk about it. Rennert, I suppose you know that Jarl was acting as foreman of the Campos *hacienda* at the time of my unfortunate visit there with Mr. Jester's party to the moment of our departure our stay was marred by only one bit of unpleasantness. While strolling about enjoying the coolness of morning, Dr. Lincoln, another gentleman and I were attracted to one of the buildings by the sound of blows and by cries of pain. We came upon a most ugly scene. One that astonished and nauseated us. Jarl was flogging a peon."

Torday had been talking in a monotone, and his eyes had taken on the deep glow of concentration. He drained his glass hastily and dried his lips with the end of the black scarf.

"We put a stop to it, of course. Jarl marched away without a word. We consulted with Mr. Jester and informed the owner of the ranch. He expressed his regrets and said that he would speak to Jarl. No further reference was made to the matter. But we heard before we left that the peon had been dismissed. I have never had any doubt that it was he who tampered with the switch. A case of misdirected revenge. Either he thought that Jarl would be on the Pullman or he was filled with resentment towards Americans in general. Perhaps he blamed the Campos family and struck at them through their guests." His eyes came sharply to Rennert's face. "You spoke of an explanation which you had heard. Was that it?"

"Yes. Did the railroad accept it?"

"I believe so. They were never able to locate the man, however, so couldn't prove anything. Do you know that country, Rennert? Oh, of course you do. It was in that region that you investigated a murder case a few years ago, wasn't it? Also on the Tropic of Cancer. A coincidence."

Rennert nodded.

"Well," Torday went on, "you know then how isolated those *haciendas* are. It was extremely unlikely that it could have been the work of an outsider. I see no reason why the blame should not be laid on that peon. Do you?"

Rennert phrased his reply carefully: "I see no reason at all why the blame should not be laid on the peon."

Torday's eyes bored into his, puzzled. "But you aren't satisfied, I can see that. Why aren't you?"

"I assure you, Dr. Torday, that I cannot give a single specific reason why anyone should doubt that some nameless Mexican peon changed that switch."

Rennert started to get to his feet. He thought that an attack of some kind had come upon Torday and that the man's head was being forced forward. He was trembling violently and his eyes were dulled as if by shock. But he regained his composure suddenly, and began consuming his cigarette with quick, nervous inhalations. He looked at Angerman. His eyes glowed, then flared into bright pin-points which could be reflections of but one thing banked within him—hatred.

"Of course," he said fiercely, "I've always known who was really to blame."

Of course! Rennert was surprised that he hadn't grasped at once the explanation for the cripple's attitude toward Angerman, his studied taunts, his delight at seeing the broad, strong back bent to menial tasks before a spectator. It was a studied and subtle form of revenge against the man whom he held responsible for his broken body.

Rennert's gaze went swiftly to Angerman. The latter's eyes maintained their unblinking stare, but had a different blueness. They were glistening and were as dark as the vermiform vein that throbbed on his temple. How, Rennert demanded of himself; could anyone be so insensate as to fail to gauge the emotional forces so resolutely held in check there? Torday didn't fail to gauge them, of course. He was calculating them to a nicety, weighing them against some foil which he held.

The answer clicked in Rennert's mind, and he swore fervently to himself.

The foil was Mrs. Torday.

God, what a poisonous swamp he had stepped into!

Torday talked in a dry little patter: "What a lusty young stallion he was that morning! Standing stiff-legged and solid in flaring riding-breeches, brand-new boots and polished spurs. It was dank and cool in that adobe room. But his face gleamed with sweat. For he had been working hard and long. One whip had come to pieces during the preliminaries. He was giving himself a few capricious moments with the left hand as he got the feel of a new one. Exploring with the beaded tip and testing his knowledge of anatomy—"

Angerman got to his feet and shoved the chair aside. Twin depressions at his knees showed where his moist palms had flattened out the creases.

"I think," he said gravely, "that you are mad."

"No, Jarl," Torday's voice regained its level monotony, "I'm not mad. But I have been, I think. Not to understand sooner. I didn't give you credit for enough intelligence. I saw that you were doing a thorough job with that whip. But I thought it was all a part of your day's work. I see now. You wanted to leave your brand, didn't you?"

"I don't know what you mean."

"Oh, yes, you do. You wanted to be able to point to that man's back and say, '*He* changed that switch. *He* had a motive.' You wanted exactly what you got. A scapegoat. And we were fools enough, all of us, to let you get by with it."

Angerman's stony voice broke in: "You don't think that *I* changed that switch."

"Of course you did. You were willing to kill a dozen people to get me out of the way. You tried again a year ago, and failed. You came to me and I gave you a job. You've got another scapegoat now—the Mexican Railways. You thought you could turn my car into a ditch some night and say a mysterious stranger crowded us off the road. You don't dare let any suspicion rest on yourself. If you did you'd lose everything you're trying to get. I even wish I could make you turn my chair over this minute. With a witness to prove you did it. Then I'd die knowing that I had beaten you for ever."

But Angerman was gone. They heard his tread in the hall and in the living-room. Through the open windows came the throb of a starting motor and the crunch of gravel beneath fast-spinning wheels.

Torday's eyes closed. He caught his breath with a little sucking sound. "Will you ring, Rennert? This has been too much for me. I let myself be carried away. I must go to bed. I will need your help now far more than I expected."

Rennert rose. "You will need," he said, "far more help than I can or am going to give you."

8
SHERIFF

I

PETER BOUNTY was serving his second term as Sheriff of Cameron County. Of obscure genesis and no political affiliations, he had been elected to office as a dark horse. He had been kept there by the devotion of two mutually antagonistic elements. To the Mexicans he was Don Pedro, who sat at table with them and acted as god-father to their babies, who was as quick to take their side in mat-ters of racial discrimination as he was to punish their peccadillos. To the booted, Stetson-hatted gentry of the ranches, whose power was on the wane, he was Pete, a rare comrade untouched by affec-tation or effeteness.

The bustling young businessmen who have made the sands of the Rio Grande to blossom and pay dividends looked at him askance as a picturesque but slouchy remnant of a past which had gone the way of the Texas Rangers. The Magic Valley was urban now, and its law enforcement should be taken care of by a product of the schools of crime detection, who would join their civic clubs and whom their wives could ask to dinner and to bridge.

Bounty was an imperturbable, mildly sensuous man of slight but wiry build. There was something feline about the indolent movements of his body, which always seemed clad in the same blue serge, worn thin and shiny on the seat, the elbows and the shoul-der-blades. His virile, finely featured face and sleek flaxen hair, too oily, gave him an illusory appearance of youth. His eyes were a baffling blend of blue and hazel. They were slightly glazed this afternoon, as if by digestion, and betrayed nothing at all of what he was thinking as he perched on the end of his spine in a padded swivel-chair and gazed across a cluttered desk at Rennert.

Rennert had been talking for some time. He finished, settled down on the end of *his* spine in a chair which wasn't padded, and said: "There are the cards. It's your game, not mine."

He was immensely relieved to be rid of responsibility. Although heretofore he had exchanged less than a dozen words with Bounty, his liking for the sheriff had been instantaneous. On the occasion of their first meeting, at the Customs office, he had known that the man was (Rennert would have had to use a Spanish word for which the English has no equivalent) *simpático*.

Bounty ruminated on the end of a match. His voice was slow and rich: "Um-huh. Partly my game. I'm sheriff of Cameron County, not Mexico. If any citizen of this county comes to me and asks for protection I'll see that he gets it. All these men know that. Why don't they come?"

"Most of them don't realize that they are in any danger."

"Torday does."

"Yes, and my guess is that he will be appealing to you now that he knows I'm not going to work for him."

"Mind telling me just why you turned down his offer? That's a valuable orange grove. The hurricane last fall didn't hurt it much."

"I wasn't at all sure just what I'd be letting myself in for."

Bounty's lids drooped and rose.

"Is that hedging it or isn't it?" he demanded of himself.

"It isn't. It's an exact expression of my feeling."

"Maybe I was hedging then." Bounty looked at him. The glaze was leaving his eyes now. They were hard and clear, and the muscles about them were tight. "Do you believe Torday's accusation against Angerman?"

"I don't know."

The swivel-chair rocked a bit. "What sort of a woman is Mrs. Torday? I've never seen her."

"I saw her for perhaps three minutes."

"That's enough."

"Banked fires."

"That's bad. How well banked?"

"Deeply. By religion, for one thing. Her church doesn't sanction divorce."

"That's worse. I was wondering why she didn't divorce Torday. Thought maybe it was pity."

"That probably plays a part."

"Are she and Angerman lovers?"

"In the sense you mean, no. I saw them together for thirty seconds."

Bounty had an extremely pleasant smile. "If we keep on like this we'll be psychic, Rennert, and can set up a private inquiry agency of our own."

"I'll give you another reason why I refused Torday's offer. I don't like sadism. I don't like contact with it. I'm afraid it might be catching."

"Sadism." The sheriff considered this as he swayed the chair back and forth with a regularity which would become irritating in time. "Wouldn't you say that Angerman is the sadist rather than Torday?"

"No. It was Torday who told the story of that flogging and gloated over it. I'm not defending Angerman. He may be brutal, although I confess he doesn't seem so. His acts would be those of an animal, lamentable but not perverted. It's when man begins to refine on the animal that I get disgusted. And, I don't mind admitting, afraid. That's the reason, I think, why I came to you."

Bounty spat out a sliver of wood. "I judge you think I ought to do more than give protection to these men if they ask for it?"

"I do. I hope that doesn't sound as if I were trying to tell you how to run your office."

"Not at all. These murders and attempts at murder that you've been telling me about. How would you describe them in the terms you were using just now?"

"I can't decide. That's what worries me. I'd be inclined to say that it's cold and purposive work. The mind of the man who's doing it may be warped or it may be as clear and logical as yours and mine. He seems to adhere to a schedule that I can't see rhyme or reason to."

"A schedule?"

"Yes, he's active only at the Christmas season."

II

Bounty gave a low whistle. His chair gyrated slowly toward the sunlight which was pouring in the window behind him. He spread out his legs and stretched them, as if getting a voluptuous pleasure out of the warmth on his thighs and loins. A sleek and graceful leopard sunning himself upon a rock. . . .

"It can't be a coincidence," Rennert pursued, "that all these crimes have been committed then. Two years ago, you recall, Charles Bettis was killed on Christmas Eve. Last year Torday had his escape on Christmas night. Yesterday was Christmas again. Campos was killed. Radisson was shot."

"Odd." Rennert thought that the sheriff's tone was concessive. "I remember the evening we brought Charles Bettis's body into town. The radios playing *Silent Night*. The lights and firecrackers and bells. The tinsel and the stuffed Santa Clauses in front of the stores. The kids. I love kids, Rennert. A bunch of 'em saw us take him out of the car. They got scared and cried. And the poor fellow had been cutting down a mesquite bush to use as a Christmas tree when he died. His blood was on it." Bounty shook his head. "It got me. It got Jester too. We went and had a drink together afterwards. He put into words just what I'd been thinking. That it was against nature. A sort of judgment on Bettis to go out like that, at that time. I don't put much stock in religion myself, Rennert, but I'm not an out-and-out atheist like Bettis was. You didn't know him, did you?"

"No."

"You wouldn't have liked him." Bounty fell silent, frowning. He hitched his thumbs about his wide belt, and his finger-tips plunked at his abdomen as if it were a sound, ripe melon.

"I'd like to know more about Bettis's death," Rennert said after a moment. "I'm asking purely out of curiosity."

Bounty spoke slowly: "I was eating supper, I remember, when Rolf called me. Just after sundown. He and Matt had been out looking for Charles and found the body. Matt stayed with it while Rolf came in to town. I got hold of the county doctor; we picked up Rolf at the hotel and went out. Bettis had been shot through the head with a high-powered rifle. It was deer season, and the brush was full of hunters. A stray bullet had killed a Mexican about a month before that. The only thing that made me a little suspicious was this Matt Bettis. He was so darned positive that it was an accident. Kept wanting us to go and quit talking. Acted nervous. It was hard ground there, but it seemed plain that there weren't any footprints near except Bettis's. And Doc McHenry said the shot had come from a distance. I let it go at that, but got to inquiring around later. Matt Bettis didn't gain anything by his brother's death. No insurance. A lot of debts. And Matt had been at the hotel at five o'clock, there wasn't any doubt. When Charles fell, his wrist-watch was smashed on a rock and the hands stopped at about five. That corresponded with the doctor's finding as to the time of death. Charles had a revolver on him, but it hadn't been fired. And it couldn't have been suicide anyway, because the wound was on the wrong side of the head—the right. So the verdict was accidental death."

Rennert was puzzled. "I don't quite follow that. About the wrong side of the head being the right. Unless—oh, my God! Bounty, was Charles Bettis left-handed?"

"Yes, I should have mentioned that. If he had shot himself, of course, the wound would have been on the left side."

Rennert was staring at him. "Bounty," he inquired softly, "what percentage of people would you say were left-handed?"

"Search me."

"Three out of ten. A larger number than usual, I'd say." Rennert sat up. "It's time to go quietly crazy now. There were ten witnesses to that railway wreck, weren't there? Well, three of them were left-handed. Those three were Charles Bettis, Carlos Campos, Dr. Torday."

"Torday is left-handed?"

"Yes, I noticed that to-day. If you want something thrown in for good measure, Professor Radisson was wounded in the left hand." Rennert picked up his hat. "A railroad accident. The left hand. Christmas. Multiple murder. I'm going to a movie, Bounty. Sorry you have to stay here and figure it out."

But the sheriff waved him back into his seat. "Don't be in such a hurry. I want to think. That movie will wait. That's about all you're doing now, isn't it? Going to movies?"

"That's about all."

Bounty, too, was sitting up now, as if galvanized, and facing him. "First, Rennert, I want to make a confession to you and an apology. When you came in here I thought this was some monkey business of Torday's. He's slick as an eel, and I suspected that he was trying to make use of me and my office in some way. I soon saw that wasn't it, that you were here on your own account. Then I decided you were letting your imagination run away with you. I apologize. There is something rotten in Cameron County. Rotten as hell. I'm going to get to the bottom of it. Now I know my own limitations. I've never come up against anything like this before. I want you to help me, Rennert. I'm not giving you any spiel about your duty or anything of the sort. Though you might consider that. I'm asking it as a personal favour. You and I talk the same language. Going to stick by me?"

"Of course I'll do anything I can."

"Good."

The sheriff swung out of his chair, lounged to the window, and stood with his back to Rennert and his hands jammed into his pockets. He began to teeter on the balls of his feet and to whistle *The Eyes of Texas*, dirge-like:

"Do not think you can escape them
From night 'til early in the morn . . ."

Bounty wasn't at his best, Rennert had to admit, viewed from the rear. The sunlight against which he was silhouetted glossed the blue serge too brightly at the spots where his muscular body had constant contact with a chair.

He wheeled about suddenly and smiled at Rennert. "I ought to be booted for not thinking of it sooner!" His voice was happy. "Why don't I appoint you a special deputy? No salary, of course, but you'll have authority and a gun and, by God, I'll stand by you if you have to use them!"

Rennert started to laugh and settle back in his chair. Instead he set his feet squarely on the floor, his elbows on the desk, and said: "Well, why don't you?"

9
DEATH ON THE LEFT

I

THE DEPUTY SHERIFF'S BADGE was of nickel. It was large and heavy and, now that the novelty of its possession had passed, Rennert was inclined to think it ostentatious. Since the weather was too warm for a vest, he wore it pinned to the inside of his coat, where it made his lapel sag conspicuously. He had half a mind to take it off and consign it to a pocket. Instead, he buttoned his coat and straightened his shoulders. "Leave it on," Bounty had admonished him. "It will make you feel snug and confident."

Rennert got out of his car and walked toward Professor Radisson's door.

The latter's quarters, he judged, occupied the entire upper floor of the old carriage house and shared the lower with the garage. A glance had told him that the linguist's battered dust-grey coupé was in place but that Dr. Lincoln's familiar black saloon was not. Rennert wanted to see both men.

He pressed a bell, but had to wait several moments before he heard footsteps within. Radisson opened the door, smiled wanly and did his best to make his welcome a hearty one. The slight primness which usually characterized his exterior was altogether lacking. He was in his shirt sleeves and wore no tie. He looked a wretchedly sick man and Rennert was concerned at the deepened ravages of fever since their meeting that morning.

"I stopped to see how you were feeling," he said, "and to have a little talk with you. But perhaps I'd better not come in."

"No, no. Come on in, Mr. Rennert. I'll be glad of your company. Maybe you can brighten things up. I'm rather distraught this afternoon."

As Rennert passed him he caught the tang of whisky and decided that his host had been drinking rather heavily.

He found himself in a large, nondescript, thoroughly masculine room, with dark paneling and walls of dark green beaverboard. A staircase rose at the rear. There was a great deal of bulky old-fashioned furniture which might have seen service in Dr. Lincoln's home. Mexicana was everywhere: colourful Saltillo *sarapes*, pottery and basketry, some clay images which looked ancient and doubtless were.

Radisson indicated a comfortable leather chair. "Since you're a bachelor yourself, Rennert, I'm not going to apologize for the helter-skelter state of my house. It's more or less a *pied-à-terre*, anyway, where I store things I've picked up. I'm only here a few weeks out of the year, but I like to have roots somewhere."

"I appreciate your feeling. I'm looking forward to getting settled myself. I'll be satisfied when I get this much of an air of comfort and permanency."

"You're probably referring to the soft chairs and the cushions. Out in the mountains a burro is my usual means of transportation. I'm just recovering from a three weeks' ride." Radisson paused by a table on which were a siphon and a bottle. "Let me give you a whisky-and-soda, Rennert? I've had to have recourse to it several times to-day myself. I've needed bucking up."

"I'll have one, yes. But let me fix it."

"All right, if you will." Radisson sank into a chair. There was a brittleness about his manner which spoke of overwrought nerves as well as the excitation of liquor. It rather bothered Rennert because it was so at variance with his former taciturnity.

"You haven't told me about your hand. You don't mind my saying that you look feverish?"

"I seem to have a bit of fever." With set lips Radisson adjusted his bandaged hand upon his lap and pressed delicately upon the left forearm and elbow.

"The arm hurts?" Rennert inquired as he set a glass within the man's reach.

"It hurts abominably. Pains began shooting up it about noon."

"Has Dr. Lincoln looked at it since morning?"

"No, he dressed it then, but didn't seem to think that I'd have any trouble with it. He's not at home now. As soon as he returns I'll have him take a glance at it."

"You want to watch out for infection."

"Oh, I don't think it's that. Lincoln would have noticed it." He forced a laugh. "I'm not a tractable invalid, I'm afraid. I'm making much ado about nothing. What really worries me is the possibility of being laid up here. I've got to get back to my work. That's all that matters to me."

"Is it nearing completion?"

"Completion?" There was something of his old shortness in Radisson's manner. "Good God, no, it's not nearing completion! It will take another ten years at least. Ten years of solid application. There ought to be a dozen men doing it instead of one. Here's to you, Rennert." He drank long and deep.

Rennert followed suit, then said: "Mr. Radisson, I'd like to talk to you about last night's shooting. Officially or unofficially, as you choose." He was on the point of unbuttoning his coat and display-ing his shield, but refrained from that bit of melodrama. "Sheriff Bounty has appointed me a special deputy" sounded modest enough.

"A deputy?" The stare was blank and unreadable, but Rennert was afraid for a moment that Radisson was going to laugh. "I don't believe I understand. You can't mean this injury of mine was im-portant enough to warrant that?"

"Not in itself. But we"—Rennert stressed the word—"believe that your wound is not an isolated incident. You were one of the persons who witnessed the wreck in which Dr. Paul Torday was crippled. Are you aware that two of those individuals have been killed and that you are the second to meet violence?"

"You refer, I take it, to the brother of this Bettis at the hotel, Torday himself and Carlos Campos." A bit of acerbity crept into his speech. "A gambler, a quack doctor, a bullfighter. Fine company to find myself with!"

"You know, then, what has been happening?"

"Yes." Radisson continued to study Rennert's face for a moment then sank back and gazed at the wall. "Mr. Rennert"—although he gave care to his syllables they emerged thickly—"I've felt bewildered ever since Lincoln told me last night of his suspicions. Bettis was almost a total stranger to me, since our paths seldom crossed after his visit to the Campos *hacienda*. I knew of his death, but assumed that it was an accident, like everyone else. I saw Campos killed yesterday. It was a shock to me, since I knew the boy rather well. I dislike bullfights intensely, but I went to see him in his first public appearance. I took it for granted that the mirror had been used by some mischievous boy or by some follower of a rival *matador*. I must say I gave it little thought. When you saw me last night I was in no condition to concentrate on the question of who had shot me. Then, as I said, Dr. Lincoln told me that he was convinced that the National Railways of Mexico were trying to intimidate these witnesses. I—well, I'll be frank with you— I was inclined to laugh at his suspicions. But to-day, I dare say because I've felt so rotten, it all seems perfectly plausible. I've kept a grip on myself, but it would be easy to let myself get into a panic." He hesitated. "A stranger came to the door this afternoon. He rang and rang, but I didn't answer. Silly of me, I suppose. And I admit I looked from a window at you before I answered your ring."

"What did your other caller look like?"

"A young fellow. Mexican or part Mexican. A salesman, I imagine."

"Rather stocky build, good-looking face with too much forehead and jaw?"

"Yes, that describes him."

Rennert was thoughtful. "I think that was Juan Canard, a reporter for the *Brownsville Sun*. Do you know him?"

"Canard? No, I don't. Why should he come here?"

"For an interview. Perhaps it's just as well you didn't see him." Rennert didn't pursue this lead. "Professor, I understand you received a telephone call at Dr. Lincoln's house about half an hour

before you were shot last night. I don't like to pry into your affairs, but the close sequence of events made me wonder about that
call. Would you object to telling me who it was from?"

Radisson had recourse to his glass before replying. "I don't
know who it was," his voice had a convincing ring of sincerity. "I
only wish I did." He looked straight at Rennert as if inviting the
latter to read in his eyes the truth of his assertion.

Rennert believed him, but also speculated at the impression
which he received that Radisson was putting an importance on that
incident which he had not done.

"Just what was said?" he prompted.

"A man's voice, very low, asked if I were Professor Radisson.
Then he inquired how long I was going to be in Brownsville. I told
him my plans were indefinite, that I should probably leave the
middle of next week. That was all. He hung up. I called the opera-
tor and asked her to trace the call. It came from a telephone-box
in a drug-store, that was all I could learn."

"The voice was not familiar?"

"No."

"You do plan to leave the middle of the week?"

"As soon as some typing is completed. That should be before
New Year."

"You don't intend to stay for the hearing of Dr. Torday's case then?"

"I hadn't considered that in my plans. I signed the affidavit for
Jarl Angerman this morning. According to him, that was all that
was necessary. I shouldn't object to testifying on Torday's behalf
if it suited my convenience, but I certainly don't intend to
discommode myself for him."

Whatever it was which had vibrated within the speaker had
quieted now. He was a pain-wracked man, a worried one, perhaps
a frightened one, who was passively answering questions. There
was something here, possibly irrelevant to the case, which Rennert
felt was eluding him. He thought of that bare expanse of sandy
road-bed and the blood which had glistened in the moonlight.

"Then that telephone call did not cause you to take your stroll
last night?" he asked.

"No. Well, indirectly it did, I suppose. It served to interrupt my work. On my way to and from Dr. Lincoln's house I got a few breaths of fresh air and wanted more."

"You're certain that nothing at all was said which would lead the person at the other end of the wire to think you might walk along that particular stretch of road?"

"No, I'm certain there wasn't."

"Is it possible that someone might have designs on your life for some cause unconnected with Dr. Torday's case?"

Radisson shook his head. "I know very few people here. I come to the Valley two or three times a year to get my notes typed, my teeth taken care of, that sort of thing. But I have made very few acquaintances. Lincoln's friends, mostly, like yourself."

"You are usually here at Christmas-time?"

"Yes, it's the one season of the year when I get a nostalgia for the United States. A week or so and I'm ready to leave."

"You have been here the last two Christmases?"

"The last three or four, as I remember. I ran across Lincoln once and we renewed the acquaintance which we had begun at the time of his visit to the *hacienda*. This old carriage house wasn't in use, except one room as a garage. I had it fixed up as you see it now. I can come here and feel at home. While I'm away I know that my possessions, such as they are, will be looked after. A very satisfactory arrangement. Oh"—he became more aloof—"I see what you mean by your question. Yes, I was here when Bettis was killed and when Torday had his escape."

"Has it struck you as odd that all these crimes, including last night's affair, should have occurred at the Christmas season?"

Radisson gave a decided start and passed his tongue quickly over his lips. "Christmas! They have occurred then. I never thought of it. Of course, Torday's suit against the railroad comes up right after New Year. If there is any skull-duggery going on it would have to be done now."

"These crimes have another point in common. I'd like very much to know if you can throw any light on it. Bettis, Campos and Torday have all been left-handed. You were shot in the left hand. Does that mean anything to you?"

Radisson moved uneasily, took a handkerchief from his pocket and passed it over his face. "Mr. Rennert, you are an amazing man. I know something of your past experiences. Once you take charge of a case it leaves the realm of the commonplace and becomes bizarre." He regarded his bandaged member thoughtfully. "You know all the connotations of the left hand. Our word 'Sinister' comes from it. Inauspicious, ill-omened. From the Roman auguries. Although I don't believe all of them agreed. Some held that the left hand was a favourable one. But nowadays we always look on it as unfavourable. We speak of the bar sinister and the sinister aspect of the planets. I say, Mr. Rennert, isn't that reading too much into this?"

"Probably. The mention of the left hand means nothing to you in connection with anything that ever happened on the Campos *hacienda?*"

"On the *hacienda?*" Radisson's head moved slowly in a negative. "Carlos Campos, of course, was left-handed, as you have said. I believe he owed some of his success as a bullfighter to the fact. But I can think of nothing else."

"About that wreck. What was your theory as to who turned the switch?"

The other's gaze wandered from Rennert's face to the table. "Do you mind filling the glasses again, Mr. Rennert?" He requested a strong drink for himself. "I am adverse to talking about that wreck," he stated when Rennert was back in his chair. "To do so, especially in this connection, would be unfair to a certain individual. I feel that he has suffered quite enough for the indirect part he had in it."

II

"You refer to Jarl Angerman and his flogging of the peon?"

Radisson frowned quickly. "Yes. I suppose Bruce Lincoln told you of it?"

"Dr. Lincoln has never mentioned the matter to me."

"I suppose the account you heard originated with him, though," Radisson said rather querulously. "Bruce conceived a dislike for

Jarl on that occasion. It has coloured his actions and thoughts with regard to him ever since. I have never been able to convince Bruce that he is doing Jarl an injustice."

"You believe that he is?"

"I know it. Rennert, I know Jarl Angerman far better than most people. I was thrown into intimate contact with him during my stays at the Campos *hacienda*. I was there the day he drifted in, on his way to the Tampico oil-fields to look for a job. Old Manuel Campos took an immediate liking to him and offered him a place. Jarl was a good worker and popular with everyone. He is as fine a type of manhood as I ever expect to see. That surprises you, doesn't it?"

"I admit it does. I'd like to hear you amplify."

"Everyone judges Jarl by his exterior, thinks of him as a block of bone and muscle. Which isn't true at all. Jarl is a simple soul, a lovable one. He's extremely unfortunate in that he is intensely high-strung, proud and sensitive, but all his life has repressed outward show of emotion. As a result, it eats away on him, so to speak. It makes him miserable and he draws more into himself. On rare occasions it culminates in an outburst. Particularly if he drinks a little, something he very seldom does. He's so immensely strong that he is liable to do more damage than the ordinary man under such circumstances. Now, I know nothing of this flogging. It occurred just before the wreck and, naturally, we had all we could think of afterwards. I left the *hacienda* soon after and Jarl never had an opportunity to tell me about it. I believe he would have done so eventually because he had gradually come to confide in me. I never urged him, however. From that day to this no mention of the matter has been made between us. Either Jarl was in one of his rages that morning or he had a reason for what he did. A reason that to him made it right. If that were true, no power on earth could stop him from going ahead. I've always defended him and I'm going to continue to do so."

Radisson had been talking forcefully, almost fiercely, and he sank back now as if exhausted.

"Thank you," Rennert said, "that has been most illuminating. You say he was popular with everyone. You include the men who worked for him, the peons?"

"Certainly. They adored him." Radisson smiled weakly. "It was the old story of Quetzalcoatl, the White God. Jarl was big and blond where everyone else was small and dark. I could understand how the Toltecs came to worship the original Viking who was shipwrecked on their shores. I could understand why the legend is so curiously persistent in Mexico."

"Have you seen much of Angerman lately?"

"No, I haven't, I'm sorry to say. He visits me here occasionally, but Dr. Lincoln's attitude toward him makes it a little awkward. I spent a day and a night at his house down in Tonatiuh after I arrived the first of this week. I came away feeling invigorated. I spend a great deal of my time alone, as you know, Rennert. When I come suddenly into contact with the city again I'm disconcerted by its materialism, its suborthnation of everything to the scramble for money and power. It's a relief to associate with a man like Jarl, who has ideals and isn't ashamed of them. That sounds terribly old-fashioned and Sunday-schoolish, doesn't it? But it's the way I feel."

"I'm exceedingly glad the subject came up, Professor. I only met Angerman this morning. I wonder if you would do me, and perhaps Angerman as well, a favour when you have the opportunity? Advise him to make a clean breast to me about that flogging."

"Why, yes"—it was said hesitantly—"I will if you think it best. Although I admit I don't like to broach the subject, just why do you want to know about it?"

"I want to make certain that it was the peon who changed the switch."

Radisson set down his glass with a thud. "What do you mean to imply?"

"There's no real evidence that it was he, as far as I have learned. Do you know of any?"

"Why, no. Everyone took it for granted that he did it."

"Was he seen in the vicinity of the switch? That would be circumstantial evidence at least."

"Not that I know of." The wounded man spoke inattentively, as a car had come to a stop in the drive.

"Can you tell me where the members of Mr. Jester's party were from twelve o'clock noon on?"

"Noon." Radisson frowned. "That has been so long ago, Mr. Rennert. I don't think I know where any of them were. No, I know I don't. The day before I had received some completed recordings of native speech that I had made. I was listening to them in my room. Dr. Torday and Darwin Wyllys came in. I left them there and took my gramophone outside, found a shady place by a wall, and played my records. I must have been there for half an hour or longer."

"I judge that Torday and Wyllys wanted to be alone."

"Well, I thought it better to leave them alone." Radisson turned to the door, through which the tall and stalwart form of Dr. Lincoln could be seen approaching. "Wyllys had been riding and had suffered a slight touch of the sun. His brother-in-law thought he ought to rest before returning to the Pullman."

"He recovered?"

"Oh, yes. Hello, Bruce."

Lincoln paused on the threshold, glanced inside, then entered at once. "Good afternoon, Rennert." His eyes sharpened as they rested on Radisson. "You look as if you weren't feeling well, Xavier."

"I'm not. My arm is hurting."

"It is?" The doctor scrutinized the bandage, felt the pulse, and frowned deeply. "I'm going to put you to bed," he said crisply. "You shouldn't have stayed up talking like this."

"I'm sorry." Rennert rose. "It was my fault. May I wait and see you for a moment, Doctor, when you are through?"

"Why, yes. What is it?"

"I want to get the bullet which you took out of Professor Radisson's hand."

Lincoln tucked his black case under his arm. "Oh, that bullet. I'm sorry about that, Rennert. It's gone."

"Gone?"

"Yes, I left it in the basin after I extracted it. This morning the maid was cleaning up my study and emptied the water down the drain. The bullet went with it. I suppose you had identification in mind?"

"Yes."

"It's unfortunate, isn't it?"

The badge pressed, hard and reassuring, against Rennert's chest. "It's more than unfortunate, Doctor," he said. "It's criminal."

10
THE TRIUMPH OF THE EMOTIONS

I

IN THE GOOD old days of Don Porfirio, before the *Contrato Social* was read in Mexico and before thirsty *yanquis* began to pour over the International Bridge with their clinking dollars, The Triumph of the Emotions was the refectory of a convent, where pale women whose names had been long and noble ones of Spain ate simple fare, securely immured from sun and evil.

That world ended, and if any grey ghosts lingered they must have crossed themselves in pious horror at the bedlam which took its place. The walls were plastered in yellow and daubed with weird and gaudy paintings, spurious offspring of Rivera's revolutionary murals and the lascivious lithographs of a Texas saloon. A waxed floor was laid, tables and booths installed. Native musicians were set to mastering American jazz. The establishment prospered—for a time. To-day it has sunk doubtless to the category of a cheap cantina or has been put to other less lawful uses. Nothing endures on the border.

Kent Distant's eyes detected signs of this approaching degeneracy the night he escorted Janell Lincoln into the place. The festoons of paper and the imitation ivy which hung from the balcony and twined about the pillars were bedraggled and flyblown. There were cracks in the plaster. A vermilion and pink lady had lost a leg.

Although it was early—not much past seven-thirty—this was Saturday night and holiday season, so that most of the tables were occupied by groups of Americans in various stages of inebriation. A few enamel-faced women sat alone, smoking and scrutinizing each newcomer with jaded eyes. The odours of cooking and tobacco and perfume were heavy in the air.

"Greenwich Village," was Kent's comment.

He saw that his companion was determined to keep her illusions. "That's probably only on the surface, Kent. The guidebooks say that once you cross the Rio Grande you're in another civilization, centuries old. They can't be wrong."

He glanced down at her quizzically, thinking how young was the face beneath that *chic* little hat.

A waiter in a frayed evening-suit approached, bowed obsequiously, and at Kent's insistence guided them up the stairs to the balcony. It was Mr. Rennert's advice, he had explained to Janell on the way over. They wouldn't have unsteady dancers colliding with their table. There wouldn't be so much danger of becoming involved in a fracas.

"*El Triunfo de las Emociones.*" Janell read aloud the words at the top of the menu. "What a funny name for a cabaret."

"Yes, Mr. Rennert told me about that. It's a typical Mexican name for a *cantina*, a bar. But not for a place like this. It seems they took it from a travel book some American wrote. He saw it on a little *cantina* down in Cuernavaca. While he was getting material on Mexico from an automobile, Mr. Rennert said."

He lapsed into silence, staring at the card. "What's the matter, Kent?" Janell asked. "You seem nervous this evening."

"Sorry!" he said hastily. "I am a little nervous—about Dad."

"You haven't heard from him?"

"No." She probably would think it strange that he didn't go on and talk unreservedly about his feelings, as people she was accustomed to did. But it always cost him a wrench to do that, especially where his father was concerned. There was a part of one's self that ought never to be exposed. It was—well, sacred, in a way—in a way that white people could never comprehend. For in this attitude, as in few others, Kent's Indian blood differentiated him.

"What are we going to order?" he asked. "Mr. Rennert suggested we try venison. This is deer season and it's usually all right in these border restaurants."

Janell was bewildered by the menu. It was typewritten in Spanish and English, but many of the words were the same and meant nothing to her. *Enchiladas, tacos, tortillas* . . .

"I don't even see *chili con carne.*"

"You won't," he told her. "It's not Mexican at all. A German dish invented in San Antonio. That's what Mr. Rennert told me."

They decided on venison, with a random choice of Mexican accompaniments.

"I haven't told you," she said, "about our cruise, have I?"

"Your cruise? No."

"Father has a friend—a former patient of his—down at Point Isabel, who owns a yacht. He's up north for the holidays, and left word for Father to use the yacht if he wanted to. We decided to-day that we'd go on a little trip out in the Gulf. Be gone about a week."

"That's fine. When are you leaving?"

"To-morrow evening or Monday morning. Father wants to be sure that Professor Radisson is recovering."

"How is Radisson?"

"I'm not sure. Father spent a lot of time with him this afternoon. Something worried him, I think, and he didn't say much afterwards. He was aggravated, too, at Mr. Rennert."

"At Mr. Rennert?"

"Yes, Mr. Rennert's been appointed a deputy sheriff, you know, and—"

"A deputy sheriff? No, I didn't know that. To investigate these—these attacks?"

"Yes, and Father says it's gone to his head. He even went so far as to tell Father that he'd been criminally careless because the maid threw away the bullet he got out of Mr. Radisson's hand. Father was angry about it. That's what comes, he said, of giving a man a little bit of authority."

Kent's jaw set.

"I don't know anybody," he said stiffly, "who would be better qualified to use authority than Mr. Rennert. Now that he's in charge the mystery will be solved."

Both of them became absorbed in the deep bowls of Julienne soup which had been set before them.

The orchestra began to tune its instruments.

Janell glanced over the balcony railing and said, with obvious determination to change the subject: "There's an American who looks as though he's lost. That big one in white."

Kent's eyes followed hers. "That's Jarl Angerman. Works for Dr. Torday. I saw him with Mr. Rennert this morning. Mr. Rennert told me later who he was."

"Jarl Angerman!" She disregarded the platter of rice and eggs which the waiter had brought her.

Angerman stood for a moment at the edge of the dance floor, looking about him blankly. A little man in an evening-suit fluttered up to him, chattering. With some difficulty he got Angerman guided across the room to a vacant table which bore a reserved sign. Angerman moved with ponderous precision and sank heavily into a chair which was too small for him.

"I've heard Father speak of him," Janell said. "He hasn't any use for him. He's drunk, I suppose."

"I'm afraid so. Listen, Janell." Kent leaned toward her and spoke seriously. "Mr. Rennert gave me a regular lecture last night about Matamoros and these other border towns. He said it was all right for us to come here, because it's on a main street and near the radio station. He made me promise, though, that we wouldn't stay late and wouldn't venture on to any side streets There's the riffraff of two countries here, he says, and it's really dangerous after dark. He said if there was the least sign of trouble to get out and head for the bridge. So if I hustle you out in a hurry, you'll understand, won't you?"

"Of course. Father cautioned me, too. Oh, the cabaret must be beginning."

Kent glanced at his watch.

It was eight o'clock.

The lights were dimmed, and a spotlight pierced the thick clouds of smoke. Drums throbbed out, a violin wailed, and the seed-filled gourds that are called *maracas* hissed like angry rattlesnakes.

"*Ole!*" The shout went up from the orchestra, and a girl whirled upon the floor. She was tall and lithe and wore a low-cut bodice and full yellow skirt which spun about her bare brown legs.

"Marihuana," she began to sing in a low, drowsy voice, "sweet marihuana, listen to my plea."

The *tempo* quickened and she swayed, hands raised over her head, agile fingers clattering castanets.

"You alone can bring my lover back to me,
Even though I know it's only fantasy . . ."

She circled the edge of the floor, the spotlight following her. She slowed as she approached Angerman's table and fixed her eyes provocatively on his. He stared wide-eyed at her, his fingers gripped about an empty glass.

"Sweet marihuana . . ."

Exactly what happened then the couple on the balcony couldn't see. A man—in evening-suit, hence a waiter—passed between the dancer and Angerman. He stumbled. There was a crash of breaking dishes. The girl moved on hastily. In the smoky obscurity left by the shifting of the light confusion broke out. Black-coated men milled and shouted. In the midst of them stood Angerman's tall, white-clad figure. He was flailing about with his fists.

"Let's go, Janell."

"All right."

At the head of the stairs Kent thrust a bill into the hand of a waiter who was watching the mêlée below. He grasped the girl's arm and they sped toward the exit. As he pushed through the crowd which was gathering, Kent glanced once over his shoulder. The last thing he saw was the piston-like rise and fall of Angerman's white arms.

Berserk, he thought.

II

The lights of the International Bridge winked like will-o'-the-wisps that never got nearer. It wasn't so bad when the car was moving, but when they had to stop to allow traffic to pass at the intersections . . .

It was foolish, Kent told himself angrily, to act as he was doing; glancing warily at the dark alleys and darker doorways, where only the glow of cigarettes betrayed the presence of figures shrouded by *sarapes*; starting at every shrill cry from the old women who huddled over charcoal braziers, stirring unsavoury messes; getting nauseated by the odour of burning fat which pervaded the hot, stagnant air.

The girl at his side must have shared his feeling, for she sat close to him, and he thought that she trembled.

"We're all right now," he assured her. "Almost to the bridge."

He was sure now that she was trembling. "I don't like Mexico. It's not what I thought it would be. Like that bullfight yesterday."

"This isn't really Mexico. Only the dregs. They always come up at the border."

"But Brownsville and the cities on our side aren't like this."

"They used to be."

Their progress was slower still when they approached the busy section about the end of the bridge. The garish yellow light of the bazaars fell on crowds that moved sluggishly. They were caught in the Saturday night shifting of population, Matamoros seeking pleasure in the American city, Brownsville in the Mexican. A ceaseless ebb and flow of dark faces and white.

At the *garita* of the Mexican Customs a phlegmatic officer glanced perfunctorily into their car and waved them on. They were on the bridge, linked in an interminable chain which paralleled another similar one moving in the opposite direction. Along the railings at the sides jostled and eddied pedestrians in holiday spirits. Their ears were filled with din, shouts, the babble of talk, horns that demanded and begged and suggested passage, the intermittent popping of firecrackers. Their eyes smarted with flying sand.

Half-way across Kent cut round a saloon that seemed set on aggravating them by its slowness. This manoeuvre being successful, he tried it again—and made his mistake.

He found himself in the lane between the two lines of traffic, barred from re-entry into that on the right by the jam at the United States Customs. He glanced back and saw no break in the ranks. He didn't know what to do.

They were suspended over an ink-black gulf, where lonely lights smeared the surface of water and dotted wastes of flat sand.

Kent glanced curiously at the car which was aligned with his. It was a black saloon of unusual construction. There was a single seat in the front, where a woman, an American, sat at the wheel. The entire right side was taken up by a couch-like affair. The windows were open, and as they passed a lamppost Kent caught a glimpse of the man who sat far back among cushions. He wore no hat. His head had fallen forward and to the left, so that his chin rested on his chest and the right side of his face was turned to the light. He seemed to be staring blankly at nothing. Something was wrong with his face. . . .

The car moved forward and its interior was dark. "What is it?" Janell noticed the direction of Kent's gaze.

He laughed nervously. "A drunk, I suppose, in that car. A luxurious way to be taken home."

"Why, that's Dr. Torday's car! He had it made especially for him, so he could be taken back and forth from the broadcasting station. They say there are special shock-absorbers, so that he won't be jarred."

At the next light, close to the Customs, Kent craned his neck.

The man still stared fixedly. His face was stark white in the illumination, but streaked with something dark which ran from his right temple down over his cheek-bones and along his jaw.

Blood.

11
A CLOUD LIKE A MAN'S HAND

I

AT EIGHT O'CLOCK Rennert was rapping upon a door whose frosted glass panel bore the legend: Rolf Jester—Real Estate—Farm Loans and Mortgages.

He felt a full measure of relief only when he saw the letters merge with the approaching shadow of a man hastily putting big arms into a coat. The office was on the second floor, and had a window open upon a street which at this hour was unfrequented. Brilliantly lighted, it made a conspicuous rectangle in an otherwise dark façade. Rennert had paused upon the pavement opposite, sighted a crown of burnished red hair bent over a desk, and thought how easy murder could be.

Jester opened the door, and his welcoming smile expanded into a beam of delight. "Why, Hugh! Come in. Come in. I thought it was Darwin Wyllys."

Rennert walked past him and across the room. He jerked down the window and the blind, the turned and let some of his regard for this big-jointed, bighearted man harden his voice. "No need to make a target out of yourself, Rolf. I'm carrying a gun. If I had had a silencer on it two minutes ago I could have shot you through the head, got leisurely into my car, and driven off. In half an hour I'd be in bed or across the river in Mexico. No one the wiser. Savvy?"

Jester's puzzled look vanished and he frowned in quick concern. "Sit down, Hugh." His swivel-chair creaked with his weight as he tilted it far back. He clasped his hands at the nape of his neck and gave keen scrutiny to Rennert's face across the flat-topped desk. "What's wrong with you, old man?" he demanded kindly. "A touch of the sun to-day?"

Rennert pulled back his lapel.

The other's head jerked forward and he stared at the badge, then at Rennert. The corners of his mouth were suddenly compressed.

"Go ahead and laugh," Rennert said resignedly. "I can see you want to. But it's real. I didn't send in breakfast food labels for it."

Jester sobered. "I wasn't going to laugh, Hugh. But—are you actually a deputy sheriff?"

"Peter Bounty appointed me this afternoon."

"Tell me about it."

"I gave Wyllys your message. You've had no further word from him?"

"No. But he won't stay long. Then you and I can have the evening to ourselves." Jester grinned and scratched red hair. "Say, he seems to want to keep this business a secret. How in the hell do I go about chasing a deputy sheriff out of my office for a few minutes?"

Rennert smiled. "In this case, I don't think you can do it. It's partly to see Wyllys, separated from Angerman, that I came here to-night. He told me about purchasing the Campos *hacienda* for Angerman. Took it for granted that I knew. Just how do you figure in this deal, Rolf?"

Jester busied himself with the making of a cigarette, one of his earlier habits which he had never given up. "Well," he began, as his eyes measured the fall of tobacco from a cotton sack, "Wyllys came to me about six months ago and asked me to find out if the place was for sale. I wrote to old Manuel Campos, but he wouldn't consider selling. After his death, though, I had an idea that his son wouldn't want to be tied down. So I got in touch with Wyllys, found out that he was still in the market, and put the deal through. I met Carlos in Matamoros yesterday morning, before the bullfight, and got all the papers signed." He indicated a wire basket. "There they all are. A clear title. Angerman has full and immediate possession of the *hacienda*."

"Any strings attached?"

"None whatever."

"Did the death of Carlos have any effect on the transfer?"

"No, the papers had already been signed."

"But no one knew that?"

"No. Of course, Wyllys knew that I was going to see Carlos, but not just when."

"Did he make any explanation?"

"He said it was to be a sort of Christmas present to Angerman. He wasn't to know about it until the deal was clinched!" Jester hesitated. "There's one thing more, Hugh. Wyllys gave me the money partly in cash and partly in securities. The securities were originally in Mrs. Torday's name, I noticed. It's just a guess of mine, but I think that she was the actual purchaser, and didn't want to appear. I called Wyllys several times about the price. He was always vague and said he'd have to consult someone else. That's confidential, Hugh."

"Certainly. What do you know about Wyllys, Rolf? I can't get him fitted into things."

"I don't know much. He came down with the Tordays from Minnesota. I think he had some money of his own originally, but the last year or so Torday seems to have been supporting him. He does odd jobs for the Doc. Tried to manage the radio station when it was started, but made a failure of it. A weak sister, I'd call him." Jester glanced at his watch. "Are you sure he understood he was to meet me here at eight?"

"Yes, I made the time definite enough. Let's go on talking."

"All right. You might tell me why you're wearing that badge. I judge Pete Bounty has got you checking up on Torday."

"Among other things. My immediate object is to find out what I can about the Campos *hacienda* and about the party you took there. Is the ranch a valuable one? Oil or anything of that sort?"

"No. It's mountainous, but there's some good grazing land. Good farming land if it were irrigated."

"Give me some dope on this party."

"Well, they were just prospective customers, like I have on my hands every once in a while. The Lincolns, the Tordays and Wyllys came together. They'd been at a medical convention in San Antonio, and wanted to look over the Valley. David Distant was here. I'd been trying to sell him some land. Still am, in fact, but he won't make up his mind. Matt and Charles Bettis were from Kansas City; had some money they wanted to invest in a hotel. The Perkinses were an elderly couple from New Orleans. He was a retired banker, and they were considering coming to the Valley to live. That's the bunch."

Mentally Rennert checked over the list. "Now I want an account of your visit, Rolf. From the moment you arrived."

"That's a big order," Jester protested. "And God, it's hot in here! Let's take off our coats."

They did so, and Jester arranged an electric fan so that it would play over both of them. He hitched up his trousers, sat down and wedged a foot against an open drawer.

"You got there Saturday noon," Rennert began for him. "Who met you?"

"Carlos Campos and Angerman, in cars."

"What sort of a meeting took place between Angerman and the Tordays and Wyllys?"

"Well, Wyllys and Angerman seemed to be old friends. Mrs. Torday was a little reserved, but I could see that she was glad to see Angerman. He acted very stiff and formal."

"And Dr. Torday?"

Jester thought a moment, then shook his head. "I don't remember about him especially. Mrs. Torday introduced Angerman to him, like she did to all the rest of us."

"Go on."

Jester sighed and raised his fingers to his moustache. "We went to the house, where Manuel Campos welcomed us like a grandee, and we had a big lunch. When it got cooler that afternoon Carlos and Angerman took us on a tour of the *hacienda*. We had a late dinner that night, and afterwards sat around the patio. Talked and listened to the peons play guitars and sing. We went back to the Pullman to sleep. Campos wanted us to stay at the house, of course, but I thought that would be too much of an imposition. The next morning Carlos and Angerman came for us again, and took us to the house for breakfast. Then they had horses saddled and some of us went riding."

"I'd like to know," Rennert said, "who went riding. Also whether you stayed in a group or separated."

"Let's see." Jester cocked an eye at the ceiling. "We separated. David Distant and I went together, east of the house. Carlos, Wyllys, and the Bettis brothers went north. Mrs. Torday and Angerman rode off toward the west."

"In what direction was the switch?"

"West."

"How far from the house?"

"A quarter of a mile or more."

"Was it visible from the house?"

"No, there's a wall between." Jester waited, and, when no further question was forthcoming, went on: "We were supposed to have got back at twelve-thirty. Distant and I were a little late. He kept saying that we had plenty of time, and he had to stop and look at a bull-ring. But—"

"Hold on, Rolf. You say Distant stopped at a bull-ring. Why? Was he interested in bullfighting?"

"No, not that I know of. I don't know why he wanted to look at it. It was a small arena, enclosed in wood, that they used for rodeos and *novilladas*. Come to think about it, I wondered at the time. Distant had a funny smile on his face when he came out. He stood before the entrance and asked me if I had ever seen it before."

"Had you?"

"Yes, I'd seen it when I was at the *hacienda* before. I told him that. He frowned and suggested that I forget about it. He said Manuel Campos ought to burn it down because it was dangerous."

"Dangerous? Did he explain what he meant?"

"No, that's all he said. But he had something on his mind all the way back to the house."

"You must have had some inkling as to what he was thinking of, Rolf."

"I hadn't, Hugh."

"You weren't curious enough to ask him?"

Jester's voice was gently reproving as he said:

"You've been with me enough, Hugh, to know that I never try to get a fellow to confide in me if he doesn't want to. I'm not asking you to tell me more than you think best. And yet I'm pretty much in the dark as to what you're asking me these questions for."

"I'm sorry, Rolf. I'm taking advantage of your good nature, I know. But the truth is I'm groping in the dark myself—" Rennert's chin had sunk and he was rubbing his forehead with his fingertips, as if he would jog his brain out of its inertia. "Will you repeat Distant's exact words, if you can?"

"He said: 'If I were you, Mr. Jester, I think I would forget that I had seen that bull-ring. There's danger in it for our host. If I were in his place I would burn it to the ground.'"

II

Two minutes must have passed before Rennert spoke wearily: "I can't make sense out of it. Go on, will you, Rolf?"

Jester had been waiting patiently. "When we got back to the house," he resumed, "we found everybody there, ready to go. We took leave of Manuel Campos and went down to the Pullman to eat lunch. I insisted on that for two reasons. I didn't want to impose on his hospitality too much. And I knew how long-drawn-out Mexican meals are. I was afraid we'd miss the train if we waited. The cook had fixed sandwiches for us and the porter had taken them down to the car."

"The porter. I've been overlooking him. Do you know what time he came to the house?"

"No, but I had told him to get the food and have it ready to serve right after twelve-thirty. I suppose he got it about twelve. When we got to the railroad track we changed our minds. There was a little cave in a hill near by. Angerman thought it would be more pleasant to eat there than in the Pullman. So he took some of us there."

"You're sure it was Angerman's suggestion?"

"Yes, he and Mrs. Torday had ridden past there and had noticed it."

"But until then your plan had been to eat in the Pullman?"

"Yes."

"And was that plan generally known?"

"Oh, yes, I'd told the party about it the night before."

"How did it happen that all the group didn't go to the cave?"

"Well," Jester answered reluctantly, "there'd been some unpleasantness that morning. After breakfast, Lincoln, Torday, and Perkins strolled about the grounds. They found Angerman disciplining one of the peons. They came to me about it. I didn't know just what to do. It was none of my business, but I didn't think Manuel would stand for anything like that if he knew about it. So I went and told him. He expressed his regrets and said he'd look into the matter; reprimand Angerman if he thought it necessary. But the three men snubbed Angerman afterwards and made it plain they'd rather eat in a Pullman than in his company. It was an embarrassing situation, and I'm afraid I didn't handle it very well. Mrs. Torday did her best to ease things and came with us. But Dr. and Mrs. Lincoln, Torday, and the Perkinses left us." Jester stopped, and cleared his throat, glanced once more at his watch, and frowned. "Eight-forty. I guess Wyllys isn't coming."

Rennert made no answer. There was none to make. He said thoughtfully: "So, if the trouble about the peon had not arisen, there wouldn't have been anyone at all on the Pullman when the train struck it?"

"No, I suppose not."

"We've come to the wreck now."

"Yes. The train was due about two-thirteen. We got to the tracks just as it came in sight. We were going to wait until the Pullman was attached before we got on. We were telling Carlos and Radisson goodbye when—it happened." Jester winced. "It was so sudden that everybody was thrown into confusion, of course. Dr. Lincoln had come to the door of the Pullman and managed to swing himself to the ground just in the nick of time."

Rennert sat with half-closed eyes as he tried to visualize the scene—and to sort out all its implications.

"Rolf," he asked suddenly, "what kind of a woman was Mrs. Lincoln? I've never heard much about her."

"Well, I'll tell you." Jester had the aggressive tone which he always assumed when he was forced to speak ill of someone. "She was all right—but somewhat of a fool. The gushy sort. Tried to be literary. Maybe she was, *I* wouldn't know. She'd written the libretto for an opera, with the scene laid among the Aztecs. She was sending it round to a lot of big composers, trying to get them to write the music. She bored us by reading a lot of it aloud."

"Had she been in Mexico before?"

"No, but she'd read a book, by this fellow who wrote about the Conquest. What was his name?"

"Prescott?"

"Yes. That got her enthused and she wrote her poetry. One of the Spaniards in her story had red hair. So she made me sit on a damned hot wall so she could take my picture and see how my hair looked in the sun. Said she wanted inspiration." Jester (who always stoutly insisted his hair was brown) choked off further comment.

"Of course, Prescott himself was never in Mexico, yet managed to write about it well," Rennert said absently. "When did you and Mrs. Lincoln have your communion with the sun?"

"The afternoon we got there. Just about five o'clock."

"Where was the wall you sat on?"

"At the back of the house. It ran all the way round the grounds."

"What sort of a wall?"

"Just an ordinary one, made out of stones. About five feet high."

"Any coping?"

Rennert lighted another cigarette. "Where was Angerman at the time of the wreck?"

"He'd gone back to the house. Mrs. Lincoln had forgotten her kodak. She remembered it just before the train came in and Angerman volunteered to dash back after it."

"Had the original plan been for Angerman, Radisson and Carlos Campos to lunch with you on the Pullman?"

"Yes, that had been arranged the night before. We asked Manuel, too, but he didn't want to get out in the sun."

Rennert kept his gaze centred on the glowing end of the cigarette as he asked:

"Rolf, what do you remember about the sun that noon?"

"The sun? Why, I remember it was hot as hell, that's all."

Rennert's smile must have been exceedingly aggravating. "The entire group," he said, "was gathered at the *hacienda* when you and Distant returned shortly after twelve-thirty?"

"Yes."

"Were you all together up to the time you divided at the railroad track?"

"Yes. We were in different cars on our way to the track, but in sight of one another."

"And after Dr. Torday, the Lincolns and the Perkinses went to the Pullman?"

"We were all together. Wait a minute, though!"—Jester checked himself—"Angerman went out to gather wood for a fire. That was right after we got to the cave."

"How long was he gone?"

"Ten or fifteen minutes, something like that."

"Long enough to have gone to the switch?"

"Yes, he'd have had time. We were close to the switch."

"But not in sight of it?"

"No. But, Hugh," Jester broke out, "he wouldn't have had time to break it open, and to gather a big load of wood. Besides, we'd have heard the noise, if that's what you're driving at—and I can see it is; you're all wet."

"The switch might have been already broken, ready to turn. The wood already gathered, ready to pick up."

"But why would Angerman want to do it anyway?"

"Dr. Torday thinks he did it to get rid of him, so as he could marry Mrs. Torday."

Blood rushed to Jester's face.

"I don't believe that, Hugh. And I don't think you do either."

"I'm not saying whether I do or not. But we have to admit that it has been done."

"But Angerman couldn't have known that things would turn out as they did! That Torday would go to the Pullman and that he'd have a chance to change the switch before the train came."

"He may have trusted to luck that that's what would happen. That may have been why he suggested eating in the cave. Or—"

"What?"

"He may have changed the switch between twelve o'clock and twelve-thirty, then planned to eat with you folks on the Pullman and swing off it with Mrs. Torday—just as Dr. Lincoln did."

"Hold on! Why do you say 'twelve o'clock?' Why not any time that morning?"

"I went down to the railroad office this afternoon and got the time-table of the National Railways of Mexico which was in force that June. The Monterrey–Victoria section is a single track, remember. A south-bound train was scheduled to go through there at twelve-one every day. I presume it did. Do you happen to remember?"

"Yes," was the ready response. "I remember hearing it whistle while I was riding with Distant. That was the signal everyone had agreed on to start back to the house. I see, the switch must have been thrown after that or the south-bound train would have hit the Pullman."

"Besides, it was about that time the porter was absent from his post."

Jester was perspiring freely and running his finger between his neck and his collar. "But, Hugh," he exclaimed in exasperation more than anything else, "that would mean that Angerman and Mrs. Torday were in on it together. That they were going to let the train crash into a whole car-load of people just to kill one man. You've got to admit that's absurd."

"Someone changed the switch."

"The peon that Angerman whipped." Jester stared at him, almost in fright. "Do you mean to tell me you don't think he did it?"

Rennert considered his reply for a long time. "If I had to answer yes or no to that," he said wearily, "I'd have to flip a coin. It's the obvious thing to believe, all right. I wish I could convince myself—"

"Pete Bounty hasn't appointed you deputy just to find out who turned that switch, has he? He'd know that's out of his jurisdiction."

"No. I've gone at this in a roundabout way, Rolf. Bounty appointed me to learn who murdered Charles Bettis and Carlos Campos. Who tried to murder Torday and Radisson."

Jester snorted. "That's the fantastic plot that Juan Canard talked to me about. He came to the house this afternoon and asked me what I thought of it. I told him it was a lot of poppycock about the National Railways of Mexico trying to slaughter a bunch of witnesses. Why, everyone knows that Torday's case doesn't depend on our evidence."

"That's the trouble, Rolf. It leaves such few alternatives. It's possible that Torday has some enemy who doesn't know of how little value your evidence is. It's possible there's something in the testimony of you men that someone doesn't want brought out in court. There's another."

"Yes?"

Rennert drew his chair up to the desk and faced Jester. "The other is this: The much-discussed lawsuit of Torday's has nothing to do with this affair. Some individual has a motive for killing every one or certain ones who were present at the *hacienda* on that date. A motive that in some obscure way is connected with the left hand and the Christmas season." He went on to explain.

"And what is that motive?" Jester's voice sounded odd.

"I haven't the slightest idea."

"And why are you mixed up in it?"

"Well—"

"I'll tell you." Jester's eyes met and held Rennert's. His face was unaccustomedly serious. "Hugh, I'd like to tell you something about yourself. May I?"

"Shoot."

"You won't get sore if I'm frank?"

"Of course not."

"Well"—the blue-grey eyes were level and candid—"you've got one characteristic that I noticed as soon as I got acquainted with you. You probably don't realize it, but you do take an ungodly delight in dissecting people; looking for obscure motives. I think you let it get away with you sometimes. Furthermore—tell me when to stop—way down inside you're romantic as hell. I admit you've had some unusual experiences. But they're exceptions. You want and expect something strange or exciting to happen every day. When it doesn't, you use your imagination. That's what you're doing now. You've been wearing out the seat of your pants on those hotel chairs until you're bored—stale. You crave a diversion. So you blare into my office and bawl me out for sitting in front of an open window. You warn me that somebody's going to take a potshot at me. You need to do some hard work on that farm of yours, or to take up golf, or"—Jester's gaze fell momentarily to the framed portrait of Christine which faced him—"get married maybe." He grinned. "Got that digested?"

Rennert sat at his ease and studied Jester's homely earnest face through a haze of blue smoke. "Thank you, Rolf," he spoke lightly but with an underlying note of sincerity which the other could not mistake. "Stoutly said. Is there more?"

"Yes. Bruce Lincoln talked to Christine and me about going with him and his daughter on a little yacht trip out in the Gulf. Christine and I have made up our minds just this minute. We're going. And we're going to take you with us. You and I never have been out together on an excursion like that. We can have some fun, I know. It's just what you need. Pardon me." The telephone had rung.

Jester caught up the receiver and gave a brisk "Hello." His voice changed, and he asked: "Who? Oh, yes, he's here. Just a minute."

He clapped a hand over the mouthpiece. "For you, Hugh. It's Pete Bounty. He asked me if his deputy was here. I didn't think for a moment who he meant."

Rennert said, "Yes?" and was bantered by Bounty's lazy, pleasant voice, "Deputy Rennert?"

"Yes, Chief."

"Chief. Ahem! Very good. I called to see why you weren't attending to duty."

"I am, Chief. I expect I'm setting you a good example."

"Not unless you've been looking at a corpse, you're not."

"A corpse?" Rennert leaned heavily against the desk.

As he listened he stared down at the scratch pad upon which Jester's pencil was making idle markings while he waited. The big fingers began gradually to move the lead in spirals, broken by downward slashes, which took a definite shape before Rennert's eyes. A dark and bulging cloud, like an opening fist, which was spitting out jagged shafts of lightning. A hurricane cloud, which for this resident of the Magic Valley symbolized all the intangible fears which he had been trying so resolutely to deny.

Rennert said: "I'll be right down," hung up, and looked at Jester. His voice held no reproof or triumph at all.

"Bounty was speaking from the International Bridge. About half an hour ago the Customs men stopped Dr. Torday's car for an examination. Mrs. Torday was in it and Darwin Wyllys. Wyllys had been shot through the head while crossing the bridge."

12
INTERNATIONAL BRIDGE

I

NOT SINCE THE DAY that a revolutionary army occupied Matamoros and crowds swarmed to the Texas side of the Rio Grande for the vicarious thrill of being under gunfire, had Rennert seen so much confusion at the bridge. Solid ranks of automobiles filled the streets leading to it, their drivers exchanging good-natured persiflage with the perspiring police and members of the Border Patrol, who were trying to maintain a semblance of order. The explosion of fire-crackers made the scene all the more reminiscent of that other.

The gates, Rennert knew, had been closed.

He pushed and wriggled his way to the frame building which houses the United States Customs. Floodlights were on and in their hot insect-filled glare men, whose uniform Rennert had once worn, were making toilsome examination of luggage and passports, clearing the bridge. Duly thankful that such was not his job to-night, he walked towards the door.

"You might watch where you're going," complained a familiar pleasant voice.

Peter Bounty's chair was tilted back against the wall, his heels were caught on the lower rung. His hands were in his pockets and his shoulders were slouched. He wore a grey felt hat, pulled down over his forehead, but as he raised his face Rennert could see that his features were keener and more zestful. His lips were thinner and seemed about to break into a farcical smile.

132

There was a vacant chair beside him. "Sit down," he said. "I've saved a grandstand seat for you. A great show."

Rennert sat down. "You look as if you were enjoying it."

"I think maybe I am. Rennert, this was neatly done. Damned neatly done. And they're using all that energy out there looking for a gun that's six feet deep in the sands of the Rio Grande. The old Rio Grande that never gives up its secrets. I like the Mexican name for it, Rio Bravo." He trilled the r's. "The untamed, untamable river."

Bounty's vantage-point, Rennert saw, had been carefully chosen. They would be unnoticed here yet could scrutinize each pedestrian and each automobile which the Customs men let by.

Bounty had the faculty of adjusting his voice to a nicety to surrounding conditions, so that now it was a bland stream which poured effortlessly into Rennert's ears.

"I called you as soon as I got here. They told me at the hotel where to find you. Here's the dope from the Customs' men—the hard-working Customs' men who take everything in their stride. At eight-twenty—they're sure of the time—Torday's car drew up in front here. They know it and never examine it. Torday goes over every night in time for his seven-o'clock broadcast and comes back after his nine-o'clock one. Sometimes makes a trip home in between. They thought that's what he was doing to-night. But there was a woman at the wheel instead of Angerman, so they took a look inside. Torday has a built-in couch affair, but he wasn't on it. Another man was, a man who'd been shot. The woman was Mrs. Torday. She didn't scream or faint, but told a lucid story. She had met him at the radio station in Matamoros and was taking him to an appointment in Brownsville. She didn't know when he'd been shot. The traffic was heavy and she was occupied with her driving. But she was sure he was alive just before they reached the Mexican Customs. That was the last time she heard him speak."

"Did the Mexican officials verify the fact that he was alive when he passed them?"

"They regret very, very much, but they don't know one way or the other. They were busy, saw it was Torday's car, so just waved it on by. The Customs' doctor left his vaccines, the County doctor came. They conferred and said the man had been shot at fairly close range, twelve or fifteen feet maybe, with a small-calibre gun. Bullet went through his right temple and death must have been practically instantaneous. Further examination in progress. There's nothing at all impossible about the woman's story. Saturday night, holiday time, traffic unusually heavy, going and coming. The sides of the bridge crowded with pedestrians, too. So much noise you couldn't hear yourself think. Firecrackers popping steadily. It would have been the simplest thing in the world to plug the man from another car. Or to step up to his window while the traffic was jammed. A silencer was probably used. Even if it wasn't the sound might not have been noticed. Listen. That's a sample of what it will be like on that bridge when the gates are opened again."

They were silent for a moment, while firecrackers spat and cracked, clear and staccato above the din of horns and voices.

Bounty's hands fiddled with coins. "It was the first time," he said, "that I had ever seen Mrs. Torday. A good-looking woman."

"Yes," Rennert said, "she's a good-looking woman."

"Not a face to launch a thousand ships maybe, but a body to keep one from sailing away. You were right about banked fires."

"The Mexicans closed the gates on their side, I suppose, at the same time we did on ours?"

"Yes, a message was sent over from this office. Rennert, this chap Distant, who stays at your hotel. He's straight, you'd say?"

"Yes," Rennert looked at him quickly. "How's he mixed up in this?"

"He was driving on a line with Mrs. Torday when she stopped. They searched his car and let him go on. He was driving a hired car and had a girl with him—Dr. Lincoln's daughter. He explained that he'd lost his place in the procession and couldn't get back in. Said that he'd had a couple of glimpses in the Torday car, thought something was wrong with the passenger and was going to tell Mrs. Torday. He said he had seen no one near her car. You might talk to him."

"I'll do that. What became of Torday's automobile?"

"It's been taken away to be examined. I doubt whether it will have anything to tell. They called Torday at the radio station. He was brought over in another car, missed his nine-o'clock broadcast. Which means that thousands of listeners will go to bed with their day incomplete. I got here just after he did and heard his story, before he took his wife home. He says Darwin Wyllys was to have met someone in Brownsville at eight o'clock. That would be Rolf Jester?"

"Yes. I'll explain about that later."

"Mrs. Torday drove the doctor to his studio, then sent a man down to Tonatiuh to get Wyllys. He brought him to the station, where she took the wheel and started to take him to see Jester. It seems she is a better driver than he is. The plan was for her to leave him in Brownsville, where he was going to spend Sunday, then come back for Torday. Rennert, I watched Torday to-night. He wasn't grieved or shocked so much as scared. I didn't talk to him very long, and he didn't tell me what was on his mind. But we can guess, can't we?"

"I think we can. He suspected the bullet was meant for him, not Wyllys."

"Sure. No lights on inside the car; Wyllys in the same place Torday always rode; the time Torday frequently crosses the bridge; someone waiting." Bounty hoisted his shoulders in a shrug. "We talked about you, Rennert."

"About me?"

"Yes. He's calling a meeting at twelve o'clock noon to-morrow of all the men involved in this. Lincoln, Jester, Radisson, Bettis. Distant, if he gets here. The idea is to form sort of a league for self-defence. He wants you to be there."

Bounty was secretly amused by something, Rennert had no idea what. "Well," he said uncertainly, "I don't know. Did you tell him you had made me a deputy?"

"Yes, I told him. He persuaded me to let you attend his gathering. Orders now, deputy. Attend. You meet Torday at his house to-morrow at eleven-thirty. Use your own judgment as to what you do after you get there. But don't forget this: the first thing you're to do is to get a sealed envelope from Torday. You're to deliver that envelope to me, still sealed. Savvy?"

Rennert had turned about in his chair, but Bounty's face was suddenly shadowed by the brim of his hat.

"Just what," Rennert demanded, "is going on here?"

"Now, now, deputy, don't go questioning orders." Bounty found a match and chewed on it complacently. He indicated the last of the line which was passing the Customs' inspection. "This is about over with. Result just as expected. Every car, every pedestrian on the bridge, will have been searched for a gun that was chucked over the railing as soon as it was used. Or the owner may even have kept it and carried it off with him. Not one out of ten people were being searched to-night before this happened. If he was on foot he would have had an even better chance of getting off before the alarm was given than if he'd been in a car. But if he was in a car ahead, he could have got out while the traffic wasn't moving, walked back to the Torday car, shot his man, and driven on past the Customs as slick as you please. Or he may have been headed for the Mexican side."

"Has any record been kept of the people who were caught on the bridge?"

"Yes, on both sides. Close attention to passports, tourist cards and all that. The Mexicans are going through the motions, but they aren't really so interested because the body was found on the United States side of the line. Even if they did by any chance stop a man with a gun they would only be able to hold him for possession of it. Unless it could be proved that Wyllys was shot on the Mexican side, which is entirely possible. Then there wouldn't be any *corpus delicti*, because that would be in the United States. Wouldn't it make a nice international tangle if the gun had been fired a foot or so inside Mexico, but the man died in the United States? Or if the murderer had stood on the United States side, shot across the line, and then stepped over into Mexico? And the victim died in Mexico, but was carried across the line and found in the United States. Hell, we could go on like that all night. I suppose I'd better let you get to work."

"What did you have in mind?"

"You remember Juan Canard?"

"Yes."

"Well, he's inside, waiting on you. Says he wants to take you over into Matamoros and talk to you. He acts as if he were a buddy of yours."

"He came down for the story, I suppose?"

"He must have been within a few feet of the story when it happened."

II

"He was on the bridge?" Rennert asked quickly.

"Yes. His car's standing out there now. He doesn't know it's been searched"—Bounty winked—"but it has. I took a Customs man out and watched him go through it. Nothing there, of course. When I got here I found Canard fraternizing with everybody, interviewing the Tordays, and poking his nose into corners. Why don't you go with him? Do a little fraternizing yourself. You might learn something, who knows?"

"I shall. What do you know about the fellow, Bounty?"

"He's a local product who has had to come up against rather long odds. His mother migrated here from Monterrey soon after the Mexican Revolution broke out—in nineteen-ten or -eleven. Juan was born a few months later. She uses *Señora* with her name, but it has always been general knowledge in the Mexican quarter that she wasn't married. Their attitude toward things like that is more tolerant than ours. I don't know whether Juan ever knew who his father was or not. You can tell by looking at him that he's part American. He worked and went to school, won a lot of medals and some sort of scholarship. He studied journalism and got a job on the *Sun*." The sheriff slapped dust off his trouser legs. "He *would* be the ideal solution for our problem, wouldn't he? The ubiquitous reporter. But he's a good lad, to my mind, although a little forward sometimes. I can't see him in the role of murderer unless he's in the hire of the National Railways of Mexico. And that seems preposterous. Besides, we've agreed that they aren't concerned in this. Still, you said you saw Canard at the bullfight yesterday, didn't you?"

"Yes, he was in the *callejón* taking pictures. A mirror there would be on a level with the eyes of the *matador*. But one of his photographs was of Campos being flung into the air. That would mean that he would have had to manipulate a mirror and the camera at almost precisely the same time. To do either would require close concentration. I don't think he could have done it."

"You're sure he took the picture?"

"I didn't see any other photographer there. He might have got someone else to snap the camera while he held the mirror."

"An accomplice." Rennert sighed. He felt rather old and worn just then. "I'm discouraged. We aren't getting anywhere. Peter"—it was the first time he had used his companion's given name—"I'm convinced that we don't have an inkling of the motive for these crimes yet. Until we do, we're going to be running around in circles."

Bounty's manner was constrained. "Don't worry," he said in a low voice. "It'll turn out all right. You've been doing all you can. I was joking about your going with Canard to-night. There's no need of it. Go on home and go to bed. Or take in that movie you were talking about this afternoon."

"Oh, no; I really want to see Canard." Rennert started to rise. "How do you spend your Sundays?"

"Well, I admit I'm downright lazy on Sunday. I sleep late. Noon, maybe. Read the rest of the day. But if I can help you out, let me know."

"No, it's not that. I thought you might like to have dinner with me to-morrow night. At the hotel, about six. We can talk this business over. Or, if you prefer, we can forget it. I'd like to have you in either event. You're a bachelor, too, aren't you?"

"Yes." After a moment of silence Bounty looked at Rennert and said evenly: "The Jester Hotel is a rather swanky place on Sundays, isn't it? The Rotarians and their wives and the bridge club ladies eat there."

"I shouldn't call it swanky. Very informal. They do make a specialty of their Sunday dinners, though. That's why I thought you might like to come."

"I'm used to sitting on a stool at a cheap lunch counter. I don't eat with my knife exactly, but—"

"Don't be a damn fool."

The two men studied and understood each other.

Bounty's smile was slow and warm and satisfied.

"That's no way to talk to your superior officer while you're on duty," he complained. "I'll be there, Hugh."

As Rennert walked away he heard the low strains of *The Eyes of Texas:*

> The eyes of Texas are upon you
> 'Til Gabriel blows his horn!

13
BAR SINISTER

I

OUT OVER THE GULF a full moon was pushing its way through streamers of grey cloud. As Rennert walked toward the black roadster parked almost exactly in the centre of the lane reserved for southbound traffic, he contemplated the deserted, ill-lighted expanses of the bridge, and, below it, the dark void which was sluggishly moving water and sand. He was beginning to have an antipathy to sand, which so curiously in this case was always obtruding its presence when blood was spilled.

Afterwards, he was known to maintain, at incautious moments, that this impressionability of his towards the twin symbols of the bull-ring was nothing less than a premonition of the disclosure that was to come so soon. Which, of course, was absurd, he would promptly point out. Sand is everywhere along the Rio Grande.

Juan Canard opened the door of the car with Mexican courtesy, otherwise his manner was altogether American.

"My lucky night," he said, as he tossed away a cigarette. "I had come this far on my way to Matamoros when they closed the gates. I left the vehicle here and went to see what the excitement was." He hurried to the other side and slid behind the wheel. "Looks as if my ideas of yesterday afternoon weren't so far wrong after all, doesn't it?"

"Yes," Rennert agreed, "it does look that way."

"By the way"—it was said in sincere fashion—"I was glad to congratulate Mr. Bounty on his new deputy. He's smart, that man."

"Thanks."

Rennert had decided that he had better be uncommunicative for the present.

Theirs was the last car to leave the bridge. A note which Canard had secured from the United States Customs officials expedited their passage by the Mexican. A few minutes of dexterous driving took them past the halted north-bound procession. Rennert's head was none too steady by the time they threaded their way out of the hubbub and Canard turned to the right, down the street, he noticed, which led to the radio station.

Behind them rose the roar of starting motors and shifting gears as the gates were thrown open.

"Perhaps," Canard laughed, "I ought to tell you where I'm taking you. The Triumph of the Emotions. Any objections?"

"No."

"But you're wondering why I chose that place. Well, we're going there because I have a table reserved. I might as well be frank. I had invited another party to be there to-night. But I was late getting' started, and it's still later now. I doubt whether we'll find him. I doubt whether he ever came." Canard glanced at Rennert's face. "The date was with Jarl Angerman."

"Oh!"

"I made it before Dr. Torday had discharged him. He was to have met me as soon as he brought Torday over for the first broadcast. You understand why I say I don't think he bothered to keep it?"

"Yes, I understand. A friendly little *tête-à-tête?*"

"Of course, Mr. Rennert. In a gay, carefree atmosphere. Wine, women, song. I thought it might loosen his tongue."

"And now you're trying the same tactics on me?"

Canard shook his head sadly. "Not on you—again. I know you too well for that. Now, I'm taking you here simply because I hate to let this table go to waste. Especially when I'm not sure I can put it on my expense account."

Rennert was tempted to call a halt at the entrance of The Triumph of the Emotions. The night club was packed. Alcoholic stimulation had given voices and laughter hysterical pitch. The interior was banked with smoke.

But in a moment he was glad that he had let himself be led in. Canard's request to be conducted to the table which he had reserved for himself and a friend was met by a sharply inimical look on the face of the head waiter. The friend was big and blond? The Mexican was sorry, but that table had now been filled. There had been trouble with the big *rubio*. He kept his feet sticking out on the floor and one of the waiters had tripped over them. He had been told to keep his feet under the table. He had got mad. The police had been summoned. A shrug. If they wanted to see their friend they would find him in a cell at the Cárcel Municipal.

What time had this happened? Rennert wanted to know quickly, before the man could turn away.

About eight-five or eight-ten, was the reply. To his question as to how long previous to this the *rubio* had occupied his table Rennert got the usual indefinite Mexican answer. Ten or fifteen minutes was finally settled on as a good estimate.

His pockets lighter by several *pesos*, Rennert accompanied Canard back to the car.

The newspaper-man was excited. "Shall we drive by the gaol," he suggested, "and see if we can help Angerman?"

Rennert assented, bringing his mind back from an arrangement of time schedules. Allowing for discrepancies, there seemed to be no doubt that Angerman had been at The Triumph of the Emotions at the moment when that shot was fired on the bridge.

And Kent Distant had planned to take Miss Lincoln there. If the young man had been at the Customs office at eight-twenty, he must have made his departure from the night club about the time of the fracas There was a chance that he could confirm Angerman's alibi. . . .

"I want you to tell me," Rennert said as they got in the car, "why you were so interested in involving me in this case."

II

Canard's manner became more subdued. "That's what I wanted to explain to you to-night, Mr. Rennert. I had an idea Dr. Torday would tell you of our interview. I'll be frank. I've got to make some money. My mother has been sick for some time. The doctors have just said it's cancer. I'm going to send her to a hospital, and you know how much that costs."

Rennert wondered if a bit of defiance didn't creep into his voice.

"The two of us are alone in the world," he went on presently, "and I want her to have the best of care. Now I've been hoping for a rise in salary. I think I can get it if I convince the boss that I'm a wide-awake reporter. I'm looking for a story that will draw his attention. A scoop." He laughed. "I think I'm on the trail of that story. In fact I'm already making out headlines for it. *Reign of Terror in Valley Ended*. Not so good, is it? *Rennert Ends Reign of Terror in Valley*. It ought to have your name in it. Don't you think so?"

"No."

"Definitely?" Canard turned his head and regarded Rennert keenly.

"Definitely," Rennert said. "If there ever is a headline, and if there is a name in it, it's going to be Peter Bounty."

"You mean that, I suppose?"

"I mean it. But we're getting ahead of ourselves. I want to hear how you first thought of all this."

"Well, if you were looking down into the *callejón* of the bull-ring yesterday you saw me think of it. I was taking pictures and noticed Matt Bettis in the stands. That reminded me I was supposed to interview him about Dr. Torday's lawsuit. That got me to thinking that it was just a year ago that someone tried to run Torday off the highway and murder him. I was covering the police run then, and it was pretty general knowledge that Torday was more frightened than the circumstances called for. Some people thought he knew the identity of his assailant. It was right after that he hired Angerman as a bodyguard and started taking precautions about his estate.

"I was waiting then to snap a picture of Carlos Campos at the Moment of Truth. I knew he was to be one of Torday's witnesses. I went over the list. Matt Bettis. He had had a brother who was shot in a hunting accident. By whom no one ever knew. Campos went in with the sword, the horns got him, and I clicked the camera. In a few moments I heard about the mirror. Then my mind clicked. The Bettis fellow, Torday, Campos. But there wasn't time to consider the pros and cons of it. I had to get my pictures to the office. I bumped into you and Dr. Lincoln. Lincoln, another witness. You"— Canard made a gesture with his right hand—"a man with a lot of experience in the detective line. A man who had recently given up one job and come to live in the neighbourhood of Lincoln, Jester, Radisson and Bettis—I jumped to the conclusion that Torday had hired you. I really didn't believe you when you denied it. I didn't know whether to believe Torday or not when he denied it. But I thought if he was telling the truth, I'd advise him for his own good to make a deal with you. So I've gone ahead writing a rehash of the Torday neck-breaking episode—"

"You called on Professor Radisson this afternoon?"

"Yes, among the others. He was at home, I think, because his car was there, but he didn't answer the bell."

"Did you call him last night, at Dr. Lincoln's house?"

"Last night? Why, no." Canard waited a moment, then resumed. "As I say, I've gone ahead with a dull story, waiting for a chance to talk to you."

"It's Peter Bounty you'll have to talk to."

"I expected you to say that. My plan hasn't worked out just as I thought it would. But I think the results will be the same. Some- thing will be uncovered now that you're working on the case. I'm responsible, in a way, for getting you into it. Peter Bounty is a square-shooter. I'll have my scoop and earn my rise. Here's the gaol."

Their sojourn at the drab and fort-like building which is the Municipal Prison of the city of Matamoros was either satisfactory or unsatisfactory, Rennert wasn't sure which. They were met by guards with fixed bayonets, who only after long argument con- sented to summon a superior officer. A stodgy little man appeared and informed them waspishly that they could see no one at this hour of the night. He finally yielded to Rennert's blandishments enough to lead them into a grimy office, produce a ledger, and state that one Jarl Angerman had been confined to a cell at eight-thirty. The charge was disturbance of the peace. He would remain there until Monday morning, when the judge would hear his case and assess his fine.

Rennert looked back at the dismal glow of electric bulbs through barred windows and decided that the visit had been satisfactory, inasmuch as it proved conclusively that Angerman had an alibi for the time of Wyllys's murder. Although it left himself facing a wall which was almost blank.

"Mr. Rennert," Canard said thoughtfully as they drove away, "do you want—gratis and with no strings attached—some information which I don't think Peter Bounty had when he talked to you? It happened before he got to the bridge."

"Certainly, if you want to give it to me."

"The first question that Torday asked when he arrived was this: 'Has Jarl Angerman crossed the bridge to-night?' No one remembered. But it was plain that he suspected Angerman had meant to shoot him and had hit Wyllys instead. Now here's a little theory that you've probably already considered. It's not positive that Wyllys was shot on the bridge. The Mexican Customs men can't swear that he was alive when the Torday car passed them. To get from the radio station to the bridge that car would have to pass along the street where The Triumph of the Emotions is located. A very dark street in places. And Angerman turned up at The Triumph of the Emotions ahead of time. He raised a rough-house. He couldn't have found a better way to let everyone know he was there, or on his way to gaol, at eight-twenty."

"We have Mrs. Torday's statement."

Canard negotiated a difficult turn.

"Yes," he said, "you have Mrs. Torday's statement. That's all."

14
THE MARK OF THE BEAST

I

KENT DISTANT'S VOICE was unusually loud when he opened his door to Rennert's knock. "Come in, Mr. Rennert! My father's here. Was waiting on me when I got back from Matamoros." He closed the door and caught Rennert's elbow. "Dad, this is the man I've been telling you about. Mr. Hugh Rennert."

The height of the man who straightened from his task of unpacking a suitcase was a little less than Rennert's, his girth was a warning to the latter. His face was a brown full moon, although its shade was much lighter than that of many a white man after a few weeks of steady exposure to the Texas sun. It was rendered disharmonic only by slightly prominent cheek-bones and by a large mouth, which was widened now by a jovial smile. His black hair was thin and straight, his cheeks and jaw smooth and glabrous. His eyes were black, with the Mongoloid fold, and animated by friendliness as they rested on Rennert's.

"I am jealous of you, Mr. Rennert," he said as they shook hands. "I come here to see my boy and I find him talking of nothing but you. You have been taking good care of him, he tells me. I thank you." There was a peculiar but not unpleasant intonation to his voice which made it a bit difficult to understand.

Rennert was properly deprecatory about his services. "I suppose he told you that we had been worried about you."

"Yes"—Distant laughed happily—"but I came."

146

Kent, shoulder to shoulder with his father, was a foot the taller if not more. "He thinks that makes everything all right, Mr. Rennert. Do you know what he did? He went clear down to San Antonio to visit. Then over to Corpus Christi. He missed his train there and came on down on the 'bus. Otherwise he'd have got here at eleven-thirty-five last night. In time to spend Christmas with me. The last twenty-five minutes of it, that is. But sit down, Mr. Rennert."

"I haven't come for a visit, Kent. It's about bedtime, and I know your father's tired." Rennert sat on the edge of a chair. "Have you told him why we were worried?"

"Yes, I told him all I knew. And about to-night on the bridge. Have you heard about that, Mr. Rennert?"

"Yes, that's what I came to see you about." Rennert turned to the elder man. "I'm sorry, Mr. Distant, that we have to greet you with such unpleasantness. Do you mind if I monopolize Kent for a few minutes? I'm anxious to learn what he saw tonight."

"That is all right. I do not think he could go to bed happy unless he talked with you. I will listen."

"Now then, Kent," Rennert said, "let's hear everything that happened at The Triumph of the Emotions and on the bridge."

The young man told his story painstakingly. Rennert went over it with him in detail, questioning him particularly as to the time of Angerman's arrival. He leaned back, satisfied. The information was essentially the same as that which he had gained from the waiter in the night club.

He gave then to the father a short précis of the situation. "Does it suggest anything to your mind?" he asked. "The recurrence of these crimes at Christmas-time. The fact that three of these men have been left-handed."

Distant sat altogether passive, with his hands clasped against his stomach. Rennert found his attention centering on those hands, they were so small and graceful, almost bare of hairs. The man's feet, too, were small, shod in polished leather, and rested lightly upon the floor.

"No," Distant said gravely, "it does not mean anything to me, Mr. Rennert. But it is like a story that one begins in the middle. I will think about it." His voice was exceedingly pleasant when one became accustomed to it. He made little use of the stress accent, so that his phrases were entities rather than his words. He emphasized his gutturals, as Jarl Angerman did, and had difficulty with the letter "r," which he either dropped entirely or converted into an "l," like a Mexican.

"I'm under the impression," was Rennert's comment, "that you were present at the beginning of this story, on the Campos *hacienda*. You missed what followed. I don't suppose that during the past three and a half years you have ever suspected that an attempt had been made on your life?"

"No, Mr. Rennert." Distant seemed fairly amused by the idea.

"You visited here in the Valley once during that time, I believe?"

"Yes, in October. A year ago last fall."

"And nothing out of the way happened then?"

"No, nothing at all happened."

"I'm satisfied that this affair is definitely localized. I promised not to tarry, Mr. Distant. But let me ask you about one matter. I was talking with Mr. Jester to-night about the morning you and he went riding. He stated that on your return to the house you stopped at a small bull-ring. He was under the impression that something about it interested you. You asked him if he had ever seen it before. When he replied that he had observed the arena on a previous visit, you suggested that he forget about it. That it was a danger for your host. I should like very much to know what you meant by that."

"Oh, yes, that bull-ring." The Indian's eyes brightened. "I remember. I meant to explain to Mr. Jester later, when we were out of Mexico. I had seen a reproduction of a photograph of that arena— in a magazine. Mr. Jester had seen it too, but he did not recognize it. He had several copies on the train. We all read an article in it about Mexico. But I do not think the others noticed, when we got to the *hacienda*, that one of the pictures had been taken there."

Rennert was sitting forward again.

"What was the name of that article—and the author?"

Distant pursed his lips. "Let me see—"

"Was it 'The Last Trumpet,' by Simon Secondyne?"

"That was it! 'The Last Trumpet.'"

Tense, Rennert fumbled for a cigarette. "I recall now it must have been about that time the article appeared. The magazine was called *N.E.W.S.*, wasn't it?"

"That was it. North, East, West, South."

The flame of Rennert's match trembled a bit. "And the danger you spoke of?"

Distant hesitated. "The Mexican Government did not like that article. They barred the author from the country. I thought it was just as well that they did not know that one of the pictures for it had been taken on the Campos *hacienda*. There might be trouble."

"Did you learn anything about the author or when he had visited the *hacienda?*"

"No, I said nothing more about it."

"You say this article was read on the train. Did any of the party appear to know the author?"

"I do not think so."

Rennert glanced at his watch and rose hurriedly. "I'm going to ask you to excuse me now, Mr. Distant. I see I have just time to reach the Public Library before it closes. I want to read 'The Last Trumpet' again, if I can locate it."

"I hope that I have helped you, Mr. Rennert. It will be part payment to you for what you have done for my boy."

"At least you have given me a glimmer of light, Mr. Distant. I needed it." Rennert stood, hat in hand. "Was there by any chance another guest at the Campos *hacienda* at the time of your visit? Besides Professor Radisson, I mean."

Distant shook his head. "I do not think so."

"It was a large place, I understand. An individual could easily have remained out of sight—in his room, say—during the twenty-four hours you were there?"

"Yes, he could have done that."

Kent had been balancing himself on the balls of his feet, agog with interest. "But, Mr. Rennert, who would want to hide from the members of that party?"

"A man, perhaps, who wished to keep his presence in Mexico a secret from the authorities, to whom he was *persona non grata.*"

"Oh! You mean this Simon Secondyne?"

"Yes. Simon Secondyne."

II

One man still lingered at the checking desk of the Brownsville Public Library, although the reading rooms were being cleared of their occupants. His back was turned to the door, and the edge of the counter pressed against his stomach as he leaned over an open book. A middle-aged lady was busily recording the numbers of a stack of other volumes.

Rennert's face must have showed his surprise as he came to a halt before the solidly planted, protruding barrier of the man's rear and heard him say: "Do you mean to tell me that you haven't read this book, Miss Archer?"

The attendant smiled, shook her head and, without diminishing the speed of her pencil, eyed Rennert and the clock. "No, I haven't read it. There are so many books on Mexico, you know, that it's hard to keep up with all of them."

The man tilted his head to look up at her. "Now, Miss Archer," he protested, "you ought to know better than that. This has everything that anybody needs to know about Mexico. Everything. Writing about Mexico might as well have stopped with it."

"But it's a novel, isn't it?"

"Yes, it's a novel, but—"

That blue serge suit would *have* to go to the cleaner soon. The seat of the trousers was outlined by dust and streaked by what looked like red paint.

Rennert stepped up to the desk and asked: "What's the name of that novel, Peter?"

Bounty turned swiftly and for an instant let confusion pinken the tips of his ears. "Oh, hello, Ren—Hugh. I didn't know you were standing there."

"You had my approach blocked, so I had to eavesdrop." The book, Rennert saw, was Susan Smith's *The Glories of Venus*. He glanced at Bounty with understanding. "The one Mexican item," he said, "on my desert island list."

Miss Archer evidently thought it time to intervene. "Mr. Bounty," she told Rennert brightly, "is one of our most regular patrons. He's so versatile and his tastes are so catholic. I don't think we could close the library on Saturday nights unless he had been in for his week's supply of reading matter."

Rennert took the hint. "I'm very anxious, Miss Archer, to get a copy of a magazine called *N.E.W.S.* for three years ago last June, or thereabouts. I wonder if you could help me out? It's most important."

She hesitated and looked significantly at the clock.

Rennert smiled, and Bounty, accepting his cue, smiled too. Under this double battery of masculine persuasiveness, Miss Archer capitulated. "I'll see. *N.E.W.S.* I don't remember that magazine." She went to consult a card file.

"Don't go unless you're in a hurry, Peter," Rennert said in response to Bounty's inquiring glance. "I may have something to interest you."

Bounty stood on one foot. "I suppose you were sort of surprised to find me here."

"Maybe that works both ways."

"No, it would seem to anybody the most natural thing in the world for you to be in a library. But with me, a border sheriff, it's different. You can imagine the laugh I'd get if people knew I spent my time reading things like this." He indicated the green-and-orange volume before him.

"I understand now," Rennert said, "why you get along with Mexicans so well. Anyone who appreciates *The Glories of Venus* would."

"It expresses things they would if they could. Their attitude toward life and death. *Vacilada*. After seeing Wyllys's bloody body to-night I felt I needed something to steady me." Bounty turned pages with the true book-lover's excitement. "Remember this definition of *vacilada?* 'Life is the greatest insult that can be offered to a human being,'" he read, "'and yet if you will only accept that fact, you can manage to enjoy yourself thoroughly a great deal of the time.' Mexico, huh?"

"Um-huh," Rennert agreed. "Mexico."

Back came Miss Archer, bearing in triumph a dusty, dog's-eared magazine with a pale blue cover. "Magazines really are not supposed to be taken out of the library. And it's almost closing time."

Bounty was cajoling and managed to let his hand touch hers. "Aw, let him take it, Miss Archer. I'll see that he brings it back."

Miss Archer was flustered and adjusted her spectacles more firmly on the bridge of her nose. "Of course, if you say it's all right, Mr. Bounty."

Rennert was quick to pursue his advantage. He persuaded the lady to consult indices and files. He learned that *N.E.W.S.* had been a short-lived publication, quietly going the way of so many little magazines a few months after this issue. Nothing could be found to indicate that Simon Secondyne had written more than this one article, 'The Last Trumpet.'

At last Rennert gave it up, thanked her, and left the library with Bounty. They paused on the steps, and Bounty said: "There's a little hamburger joint down on the next corner, Hugh. I think I'll go get a bite. Come along and eat with common folks."

"I know the place, Peter. I eat there frequently. Let's go."

Bounty perched sideways in a booth and ate hamburgers that were fat and succulent with mustard and pickles and onions. He drank milk, and his face was contented. Only his eyes showed that he was listening to Rennert's words.

Rennert talked, ate sparingly, and thought how odd it was that there was nothing at all gross about the sight of the man across the little table, wedged into a tight little corner redolent of the kitchen and consuming so much food with so much gusto. A sleek and healthy young animal satisfying one kind of hunger as the man had sought fodder for another in the library. Odd, too, how he kept thinking of Bounty as young, although he was sure the latter's age approximated his own. What fountain of youth had he tapped? Rennert wondered.

Almost before he realized it, Rennert had given an account of most of his actions since leaving Bounty's office some seven hours earlier. The interviews with Radisson, Lincoln, Jester, Canard, Distant.

He finished and faced two more hamburgers and another glass of milk which had come at his companion's order. "No more," he said firmly. "There's a limit."

"Push 'em over here, then," Bounty said, his mouth full. "I'll attend to 'em. And I thought you liked hamburgers!"

Rennert complied. He also folded back the magazine to the article by Simon Secondyne, whose contents he had studied briefly while Miss Archer sought information for him.

"I think," he said, as he laid a finger on a page which bore two illustrations, "that this is the bull-ring at the Campos *hacienda*. I can't be sure, of course, until I ask Jester or Distant. But it's the only small arena. And you notice the C."

They were not particularly good photographs, since both had been overexposed in the bright sunlight, and one was marred on the lower left corner by the imprint of a grimy thumb. The first showed the exterior of a rude rural ring, with wooden sides like those of a stockade and an entrance gate over which had been branded a huge C; the other, an expanse of blood-soaked sand, whereupon a small black bull had collapsed to his knees. Over the animal stood a Mexican in peon garb, whose knife was about to administer the *golpe de gracia*—the *coup de grâce*—which the sword of an inexpert matador had failed to achieve. *The Mark of the Beast* was the caption, borrowed, doubtless, from Blasco Ibáñez's ideology: the real beast that roars on sunny afternoons in Hispanic countries is man, not the bull.

Bounty's jaws worked rhythmically as he regarded the page. "I remember reading this," he said indistinctly. "I never saw another bullfight."

"Any idea who this Simon Secondyne is? Or was?"

"Nope. Sounds like a *nom de plume*, doesn't it?" The sheriff drank milk and wiped his lips. "Hugh, let's see if I have this straight. You know—or are reasonably certain—that the man who wrote this article used a couple of pictures taken on the Campos *hacienda*. You know that Jester took copies of this magazine on his trip and that everybody on the party read them. You know that David Distant recognized the arena and advised Jester to keep mum about it so that the family wouldn't get into trouble. You know that Carlos Campos was killed in a bull-ring in Matamoros. Anything else?"

"That's all."

Bounty took another large bite and chewed as he flicked through the pages. He laid the magazine down and shifted his weight to one hip. "Then I'll swear, Hugh, I can't see how this is going to help us."

"Did you ever hear," Rennert asked him, "of a hunch?"

15
TONATIUH

I

A CONSCIENTIOUS SHEEP-DOG must have a hard time of it, Rennert reflected as he drove northward, unless his flock is a unit. Rennert's charges were scattered, intractable, and he was beginning to wonder whether to some of them he appeared in the role of guardian or wolf.

He paused at the entrance to Dr. Lincoln's driveway to scrutinize a scene which, save for the tarnished moonlight, matched that of the night before. The shingled house was lighted, but the building behind it was dark.

Rennert drove in and parked. The hour was late, he knew, but his call was not a social one. The garage doors were ajar, and he ascertained that Radisson's car was in place but that the saloon was not.

He crossed the grass to the front of the house, found the screen door latched, and rapped smartly upon the jamb. As he waited for a response he unbuttoned his coat and let his badge peep out. His mood was a rather bumptious one at that moment.

The porch light was turned on from within, and he found himself under the suspicious surveillance of an elderly Mexican woman, who was rendered shapeless by voluminous dark skirts.

"I'm looking for Dr. Lincoln. Can you tell me where he is?"

"No."

"Do you know when he will return?"

"No."

He couldn't decide whether the monosyllable held indifference or wariness.

"Is Professor Radisson in his apartment?"

She made no answer, but turned her head at a call from within: "Who is it, Maria?"

"Tell Miss Lincoln," he interposed, "that it's Mr. Rennert. I should like to see her for a moment if it's convenient."

The woman disappeared, returned, and unlocked the door. Rennert crossed the porch and entered the living-room.

Janell Lincoln came from the rear, fully dressed, but obviously flurried and hospitable only with an effort.

"Good evening, Mr. Rennert. You're looking for Father? He's not here. I think he'll be back tonight, but I don't know when."

"He's out on a call?"

"No." The girl hesitated. "He took Professor Radisson over to Tonatiuh, to the hospital there."

Rennert felt a surge of apprehension. "Mr. Radisson's condition got worse?"

"Yes, much worse. He was going to stay with us to-night, so Father could take care of him if he needed anything. But when Father changed the bandage he saw that the wound was in bad shape. Blood-poisoning had set in. He—he's going to have to amputate the hand, I think."

"To-night?"

"I think so."

"When did they leave?"

"About three-quarters of an hour ago."

"May I use your telephone, Miss Lincoln?"

"Certainly. It's in the study. I'll turn the light on for you." She preceded him down the hall and left him in the book-lined room which he had visited twenty-four hours before, and which he would not have left so docilely had he possessed then the authority which he had now.

The telephone was on the table beside the chair in which Radisson had sat. Rennert thumbed quickly through the directory until he found Bounty's number, with an address on a street, he noted incidentally, with which he was unfamiliar. He dialed.

His eyes made inventory of the surface of the table. Absorbent cotton, gauze, adhesive tape. Thin surgeon's scissors. A tin of boric acid, for use as dusting powder doubtless. In the wastebasket below, a discarded bandage.

Keeping the receiver to his ear, Rennert opened a drawer and secured a sheet of note-paper. He stooped, lifted the bandage with two fingers, and laid it on the paper. It consisted of a cotton pad, discoloured by blood and medicament; a coil of gauze, with strips of tape at the edges, which had served to circle the hand; a length of soft linen cloth, its outside soiled and smeared with red, which had been looped over the thumb and fastened about the wrist. An unpleasant sight. He folded the paper about the whole and put it in his pocket.

He glanced at the door, whipped out his handkerchief, wrapped it about the boric acid tin and thrust it into another pocket. Blood poisoning, of course, might very well have set in and done its deadly work in such a short time. Radisson had shown all the symptoms of it that afternoon. But Rennert wasn't satisfied. He wanted a chemist to examine these appurtenances to infection's progress.

Either Bounty had not had time to reach his home or had stopped somewhere. Rennert hung up.

He returned to the living-room and thanked Janell.

"Mr. Rennert"—she stopped him as he was about to leave—"I don't suppose I'll see you again until next summer. Father and I are driving down to Point Isabel to-morrow. From there we're going on a yacht cruise out in the Gulf. After that I'll be leaving for school. So I'll say good-bye now." She added indifferently, "You might tell Kent Distant the same thing for me. He left in such a hurry to-night that I forgot. I'll be too busy to-morrow to see him."

"All right, Miss Lincoln." Rennert was in a hurry to be off. "It's too bad the two of you couldn't have had more time together."

She tossed her head. "Oh, I think we spent quite enough time together."

Rennert indulged in a lifting of eyebrows. "Do I gather that Kent didn't make a hit?"

"Well, yes. In my opinion, he's an awful prig, Mr. Rennert."

II

Normally a slow and cautious driver, Rennert was reckless as he retraced his route to the bridge. He fumed and swore at stop signs until he remembered that he was no longer a law-abiding citizen, but a law-enforcing deputy sheriff. Going was easier after that.

The bridge would remain open until two, he ascertained as he passed. It was the first time that Matamoros had given him the feeling of being in a hostile land. Due, doubtless, to thoughts of Angerman, "in durance vile," and the knowledge that the same fate might await him were he to transgress any Mexican law.

He slowed down, but even so went astray in the maze of dark alleys which he had traversed with Angerman in the sunlight. Hot and dust-powdered, he emerged upon the road which led to Tonatiuh and sped over the flat desert floor.

Moonlight lay cool and milky over the sand, dappled by stagnant shadows that were depressions worn by wind and by weirdly moving shadows that were clouds scudding across the sky. Nothing inimical here, now that there was no sun, only vastness and loneliness and the hollow otherworldly sensation which comes to a man when he finds himself cut off suddenly from his kind.

A pallid yellow light burned in the shack by the gate of the sanatorium. Rennert pounded the horn. A man—a harder, larger, grimmer individual than the one who had been on duty that morning—came to the door and regarded him with unconcealed suspicion.

"What d'you want?"

Rennert wanted to see Dr. Bruce Lincoln. He was so firm about it that the other finally consented to telephone to the office for instructions. It was against the rules to open the gate at that hour of the night.

After an interminable period the Cerberus returned, with an assured insolence in his manner. "Sorry, buddy, but Doctor Lincoln can't be bothered now. Better run on back to town."

"Did you tell him who I was?"

"Yeah, I told him."

Rennert got out of the car. He had at last the satisfaction of being able to flash his badge without feeling melodramatic. "Get Dr. Lincoln on the wire," he said in as impressive a voice as he could summon. "I'll talk to him. It's official business."

The guard started to laugh but checked himself suddenly, doubtless at the consideration that the tables might be reversed one of these days and that this ordinary-looking man would be formidable in a session in the back room of the sheriff's office in Brownsville. "All right." He used a more respectful tone. "Come on in. I'm only carryin' out orders."

Rennert stood in a square wooden box which held a telephone, a split-bottom chair, and nothing else save the faces and limbs of film actresses.

He heard a curt "That you, Rennert?" against his ear. "Lincoln speaking. What is it you want?"

"To talk to you, Doctor."

"Heavens, Rennert! This is no time to talk. I'm extremely busy. If you have anything to say, see me to-morrow."

"Have you performed the operation on Professor Radisson yet?"

The silence lengthened until he thought the line had gone dead.

"I'm sorry to tell you, Rennert, that I did not have a chance to operate. Mr. Radisson died while the ether was being administered. About a quarter of an hour ago. His heart was in a worse condition than I thought. Besides, he was in an advanced state of blood-poisoning."

It was close to suffocation in that little box whose thin sides had been baked by the sun throughout the day. Insects swarmed about the unshaded bulb and crawled down Rennert's neck. The eyes of the man by the door were flinty, following his every move.

"You are sure it was blood-poisoning, Doctor?"

"I shouldn't have made that statement, Rennert, if I weren't sure."

"Nevertheless, you won't object if I examine the body?"

Lincoln's voice was suggestive of an efficient office, comfortable, equipped with electric fans and ice-water. "I do object. I don't like your tone at all, Rennert. Professor Radisson died in a private hospital in Mexico. I see no reason why I should allow a deputy sheriff of a Texas County any privileges in that hospital. Our organization runs smoothly. Everything is being taken care of. You and your methods would produce the results of the proverbial bull in a china closet. No, I cannot permit you to come inside our grounds—at least to-night."

"Do you intend to bring the body to Texas for burial?"

"I haven't had time to give the matter any thought." Rennert began to suspect that the other was enjoying this interchange. "Unless Radisson has relatives who insist that his remains be sent to the United States, I presume that the burial will be in Mexico. We make our own arrangements with the Tamaulipas authorities in such cases."

Rennert had recourse to all his will power to remain calm. "There are special circumstances, Doctor, that I will explain—"

But a click told him that Lincoln had dropped the receiver upon its hook.

He replaced his own with deliberation and turned to the man with the eyes of flint. "Please tell Dr. Lincoln," he said, "that I shall see him when he returns to Texas."

16
COUP DE GRÂCE

I

RENNERT WOKE with a start, to blink his eyes in the warm, dazzling sunlight which flooded the sheets. Through the open window drifted the drowsy hum of a countryside coming slowly to life while some Brownsville church sent the blithe peal of chimes to die away as the currents of air shifted, then to swell out again.

But it wasn't the chimes, he knew, that had awakened him. It was a sound from nearer at hand.

It was only a matter of seconds before a board creaked overhead, then another. A heavy individual—Matt Bettis, doubtless—was trying to walk noiselessly across the attic.

Rennert sat on the edge of the bed and thrust his feet into slippers, his arms into the sleeves of a dressing-gown. He wanted very much to go back to sleep.

At the rear of the hall a door closed softly, footsteps descended the short flight of stairs and came down the carpet.

Rennert opened his door to pick the morning paper from his threshold. "Hello, Bettis," he said.

Matt Bettis did not scowl, but his facial expression was unfriendly, as were his eyes as they focused on Rennert's face. He was in his shirt sleeves and carried the same plate and enameled pitcher which Rennert had seen on a previous occasion. "Hello."

"Nice morning, isn't it?"

"Nice enough."

"Would you mind stepping inside for a moment, Bettis? I want to ask you something."

The other hesitated, then walked into Rennert's room.

"Pardon the informality," Rennert said as he closed the door. "Won't you sit down?"

"No thanks."

"A cigarette?"

"No, thanks."

Rennert sat on the bed and lighted a cigarette. "I was reading an article in an old magazine last night," he remarked. "'The Last Trumpet' was the title. The author was Simon Secondyne. Ever read it?"

Bettis stared at him. His lips were slightly parted, and there was a faint twitching at the corners of his mouth. "Yes," he blurted. "I read it. Why?"

"I'd like to know something about the author. Can you tell me?"

Bettis was as poor a dissembler as Rennert had ever seen. There was no reason at all for his smile, and his adam's-apple betrayed the fact that he was swallowing agitatedly. "No," he said, "I don't know anything about him. Why should I?"

"His article was illustrated by two pictures which I think were taken on the Campos *hacienda*, Perhaps you can tell me." Rennert got to his feet, took the copy of *N.E.W.S.* from his table and showed his caller the two photographs in question. "Do you recognize them?"

Bettis gave them but a fleeting glance then raised his eyes to Rennert's. There was something sharply repellent about the cold shifting pupils in juxtaposition with the pubescent cheeks and the smiling lips.

"I'm not sure," he said, "whether I recognize them or not. I was only at the place once."

"You saw the Campos bull-ring, did you?"

"Maybe I did, and maybe I didn't. That's too long ago to remember. Why do you want to know?"

"Call it curiosity, if you want to. You recall the day of the train wreck at the *hacienda*, don't you?"

"Yes."

"The period between twelve and twelve-thirty noon?"

"Not specially."

"Better try to. Because I want to know where you were at that time."

Bettis's smile widened a little. Either assurance or bluff was coming to his aid. "That's right. You're a deputy sheriff now, aren't you? I was forgetting that, seeing you there in pyjamas. Why, I was riding a horse at the time you mention."

"With whom?"

"My brother."

"No one else?"

"No. Campos and Wyllys were with us, but Wyllys got sick and Campos took him back to the house."

"Did you ride near the railroad tracks?"

"No, we didn't go that way." Bettis turned towards the door.

"Was that you who called this meeting down at Torday's at noon to-day?"

"No, he called it himself."

"I suppose I'll see you there?"

"If you go, you will."

Rennert waited until Bettis had gone, then walked to the rear of the hall, climbed the stairs, and stood at the attic door, listening. When he heard no sounds from within he stooped and examined the lock. It was a recently patented one which, according to the advertisements, would defy any tampering.

Rennert smiled smugly, and went back to his room.

He searched through the drawers of his dresser until he found a small wash-leather case which contained a number of keys and thin steel instruments seemingly designed for no purpose at all. They were scarred, however, from years of usage. The luggage of more than one tourist had surrendered to their pressure and given up secrets from hidden compartments. This was a memento of the Customs Service which Rennert had carried away with him, with little thought that he would have a use for it.

Within three minutes he was in the attic. It was a large place, with dormer windows which let the sunlight flood over a heterogeneous collection of discarded furniture. A low cooing guided him to the eaves on the north. He stopped before five wicker cages, each of which contained a pigeon.

He knelt down and scrutinized them closely. They were olive-grey and black, with black bands on their wings. Their beaks were long, their eye wattles abnormally developed.

He glanced at the nearest window and saw that one of the panes had been removed.

Rennert was puzzled as he went downstairs again, locking the door behind him. He was wide awake, too, even before he stepped under his shower.

He wondered if Rolf Jester could explain the presence of those very special birds in his hotel.

II

With Rolf Jester's belated devotion to domesticity had come an attachment to the soil which made him spend his spare moments studying seed catalogues and pottering about yard and garden.

Rennert found him in disreputable corduroys and Stetson hat, trimming a privet hedge at the side of the house. At his feet sprawled an ancient brown and white spaniel, who followed her master's every motion with filmed but adoring eyes.

"Morning, Squire!" was Rennert's greeting as he brought the car to a stop.

"Howdy!" Jester put down the shears and came towards him. "Get out."

"Thanks. I only want to talk to you a while if you can spare the time."

"All you want."

The dog wobbled after Jester, nosed his trousers, then was so completely overcome by his proximity that she lay on her back and tried to kick her feet in the air like a puppy. Jester grinned, and

ruffled the skin on her throat with his toe. This sent her into par-
oxysms of delight.

"Can you tell me," Rennert asked, "why Matt Bettis keeps homing pigeons in the attic of the hotel?"

Jester propped a foot on the running-board, pushed the hat
back from his moist face, and stared at him incredulously. "Homing pigeons? Lord, no. Does he?"

"He does. You remember I told you yesterday I'd heard someone walking above me lately. I took the liberty of picking the lock
this morning. He has five pigeons there in cages. There's a hole in
the window for them to leave or enter by. I was hoping you might
be able to explain."

Jester shook his head, and his face became thoughtful. "You
don't think, do you, that he's doing any smuggling across the river?"

"That's the first thing I thought of. It's done so much along the
border. But if that's it, it's on a very small scale. And he can't have
been getting by with it for long. Everyone who tries it gets caught
sooner or later. It might be drugs, of course, for his own use. Did
you ever know of him using them?"

"No. He drinks and gambles a lot—that sort of thing—but I
never heard of him taking drugs."

"He doesn't look as if he did. You don't mind my keeping an
eye on that attic for a few days, Rolf?"

"Hell, no. But if you want to know about those pigeons let's go
down to the hotel now. I'll make him tell us what he uses 'em for."

"He'd merely say that they're pets or something of the sort. All
we'd accomplish would be to make him suspicious. Let's see what
develops. Get in and sit down, Rolf. I want to show you something."

When Jester was beside him Rennert pointed out the photographs in the Simon Secondyne article. "Recognize those?"

Jester studied them for a few moments, then exclaimed: "Why,
Hugh, this is the bull-ring on the Campos *hacienda!*" He turned
pages. "And this is the magazine you and Christine and I were talking about night before last. Where did you get it?"

Rennert told him of his interview with David Distant.

"Distant says you took several copies with you on that trip. Just as reading matter?"

"No. Manuel Campos had asked me to bring 'em."

Rennert glanced at him sharply.

"Why?"

"Well, that issue was prohibited in Mexico. He wrote and asked me if I could slip some in when I came. There wasn't any trouble because the Mexican officials hardly looked at our luggage on the Pullman. Afterwards I got the copies out and let the crowd read that article. There'd been so much talk about it."

"You don't know why Campos asked for so many?"

"No."

"What did he say when you handed them to him?"

"He just thanked me and paid for them. I didn't want to take the money, but he insisted. Said it wasn't his."

"Do you have any idea whom he was buying them for?"

"No, I don't."

"Did anyone on your party besides Distant go near that bull-ring or show any interest in it?"

Jester thought for a moment.

"Mrs. Lincoln did. I remember her strolling around the house and getting lyrical over the view. She thought the ring was a fort that they used as protection against bandits. Carlos explained what it was. She wanted me to go look at it with her, but I talked her out of the idea. I had to take a walk with her, though. That was when she made me blister myself on that wall"—his voice became gruff—"so she could see my hair in the sun. And, say, Hugh, that reminds me! While we were there I saw Charles Bettis go in that ring. I'd forgotten that."

"Charles Bettis. Had he been present when Mrs. Lincoln called attention to it?"

"Yes, I think so."

"Did he make any mention of it afterwards?"

"Not that I remember."

"Rolf, did the Campos family have frequent guests at their home?"

"Yes, they were always entertaining somebody or other. People would come and stay weeks at a time. Americans and Mexicans both. The hunting was good about there."

"Were there any other guests at the time you took your party?"

"No. Radisson was there, of course, but he was more or less of a permanent fixture."

"Rolf, I haven't told you yet. Radisson died last night." Rennert deleted from his account of the visit to Tonatiuh all references to Dr. Lincoln's attitude. Not from any lack of confidence in Jester, but because he knew that it was not in the latter's sanguine nature to harbour suspicion readily against such a neighbour as the tall physician.

He wondered, however, if some such thought did not cross the other's mind. "Hugh, Christine and I talked this whole thing over last night. I told her all you said at the office. I knew it'd be all right. We decided not to go on that cruise with the Lincolns. She was very firm about it, said I ought to stay here, take precautions of course, and help you in any way I can. She agreed with you that what happened on the *hacienda* that time was connected with what's going on now. She made me go over the whole story of our visit, to see if I couldn't remember something I hadn't told you. There was one thing. Under ordinary circumstances I wouldn't say anything about it. But Christine insisted I tell you. It was the night before the wreck. Mrs. Torday left the Pullman."

"Let's hear about it, Rolf."

"Well, I don't know what time it was—after midnight, I'm sure. Everybody was in his berth. I had gone to sleep, but I woke up when someone brushed against my curtain. I didn't think anything about it until I heard voices at the end of the car and the door being opened. I thought I'd better investigate. I got up and met the porter in the passage. I asked him what the trouble was. He tried to tell me that I was mistaken. But I started to raise hell with him and he admitted that one of the ladies had asked him to let her out. She said she wanted to take a walk, as she couldn't sleep. She'd given him a tip to leave the door open until she got back and say nothing about it. From his description I knew it was Mrs. Torday."

Jester was silent for a moment, frowning. "Hugh, I didn't know what to do. There wasn't any danger, of course, unless she wandered off and got lost. And I had an idea what she wanted to go out for. If that was the case, I was going to keep my mouth shut. So I went outside quietly and saw her walking away with Angerman in the direction of the house. He had a flashlight, and I could tell by his size, his riding breeches, and his boots who it was. I went back to bed." It was said a bit defiantly. "Far be it from me to interfere with anybody's private affairs."

"And that was all?"

"All except this. Somebody else left that Pullman a few minutes after Mrs. Torday did and came back before she did. I lay there dozing and heard him. But I didn't get up to investigate. And I'll tell you why. I thought it was Dr. Torday, who had missed his wife and was looking for her. I figured that if he wanted my help he could call me. And if there was going to be any family rumpus I'd better hug my pillow and stay out of it. But I didn't go back to sleep. In about half an hour this second person came back and got in a berth. But it wasn't Torday's berth. It was farther toward the front of the car. I waited until Mrs. Torday got back a few minutes later, then got up and laid the law down to the porter that he wasn't to let another soul out that night. I got a good night's sleep after that."

"You're positive it was Mrs. Torday who left first?"

"Yes. I peeped out of the curtains when she got back."

"But you have no idea who the second individual was?"

"No."

"You said it was a man. How did you know that?"

"Well, I judged it was by the way he walked heavy-like."

"You didn't ask the porter who it was?"

"No, I wasn't interested so long as I could get to sleep."

"You stated that this person's berth was between Torday's and the front of the car. Whose might it have been?"

"Let's see. I was about the middle of the Pullman. Beyond me were the Tordays, in opposite berths, then Dr. and Mrs. Lincoln, the same arrangement. Then Matt and Charles Bettis."

"So it must have been one of the last four?"

"Yes, I suppose so."

Rennert was interested, intensely so. "I gather that it was the dark of the moon that night?"

"Yes."

"Peter Bounty mentioned the fact that Charles Bettis was wearing a wrist-watch when he was killed. Did he have it on during that trip?"

"I swear, Hugh, I can't be sure. Seems to me he did."

"You couldn't possibly remember whether it had a luminous dial?"

Jester shook his head. "That's too much. But I do remember that the one he had on when he died was luminous. Because we looked at the hands."

"Good. Now, Rolf, I want you to gossip to me about Charles Bettis. What sort of a man he was. Something about your dealings with both the brothers."

"Well, I might as well be frank, Hugh, even if the fellow is dead. Charles Bettis was a rat, in my opinion. He was something like Matt, only smarter. Taller and better-looking. I never had much to do with him except in a business way. They had a little money, as I told you, that they wanted to invest in a hotel. I had that old farmhouse on my hands and knew it could be made into a residential hotel without much trouble. They offered to buy it from me on the installment plan: so much down and payments the first of every year. I had no other prospect, so I agreed. I was sorry afterwards, because the place didn't have a very good reputation the way they ran it. They made the first annual payment, but after Charles was killed Matt seemed to lose hold. Talked about leaving the Valley and going back to Kansas City. He didn't make his payment two years ago so I took over the place. I let Matt stay on as manager, however, on a salary, until he made up his mind what he wanted to do. He promised to make the hotel quiet and respectable. I was to get all the profit but give him credit for what he and Charles had already paid in. The first of the next year he surprised me by handing me ten thousand dollars. He told me yesterday that he'd be able to make the same payment this week. So it looks as if he were going to own the hotel after all."

"Do you have any idea where he gets the money?"

"No. Not out of his salary, I'm sure. Because he spends a lot. My guess is that he wins it in some sort of gambling."

"Let me go over this again, Rolf." Rennert made tally on his fingers. "Your party visits the Campos *hacienda* in June. You return and the Bettises take over the hotel. They pay you the first of the year. The following Christmas Charles is shot, and Matt defaults on a payment the next week. The first of the next year—one year ago Friday, that is—Matt pays you ten thousand dollars. He plans to give you the same amount within the next five days. I have that right?"

"Yes."

Rennert sighed with relief. "Rolf, I think that dispels the phantom of Christmas."

"The phantom of Christmas?"

"Yes. These crimes have been committed at the Christmas season, not for any esoteric reason, but simply because Christmas precedes New Year."

Jester's face was perplexed. "You mean Matt Bettis has been doing them—to get the money he gives me?"

"I'm not sure yet, Rolf. I'm not trying to act mysterious. It's just that I don't have the puzzle put together yet. I think I have all the pieces—you've given me most of them—but I can't make them fit." Rennert consulted his watch. "I have to see Torday at eleven-thirty. You'll be there at noon?"

"I suppose so." Jester climbed out of the car. "I told him I would when he called me last night. I don't know exactly what he wants, but I thought I ought to co-operate."

He leaned over and patted the dog's head. The touch of his hand gave her such uncontrollable delight that she capered and tumbled, then lay exhausted upon the grass.

Jester's eyes weren't clear as he stood and gazed at her. "Poor thing. I've had her all her life. We've got old together. Her teeth are gone and I have to feed her with a spoon, like a baby. There's something wrong with her that the veterinary can't diagnose. A pain in some place, and she can't tell us where it is. I'm not going to see her tormented with any more treatments. I'm going to shoot her—when I get up nerve enough to do it."

Strangely enough, Rennert remained calm as the pieces of the puzzle slid smoothly into place and he faced a perfect design.

He started his motor, then, prompted by the warm welling of gratitude for Jester, called: "Rolf, let me give you some advice: get another manager for your hotel as soon as possible."

"Then Matt Bettis—"

"Matt Bettis is going to be behind bars if I can possibly put him there."

17
THE SHADOWLESS HOUR

I

THIS NOON the Venetian blinds were lowered against the sun and in the penumbral coolness Dr. Torday was an old man. A sick old man whose sunken eyes were dull from gazing on some special horror of his own.

For the first time Rennert felt a tinge of pity for the occupant of the wheel-chair which faced his straight-backed one. The prospect of a lifetime to be spent in a straight-jacket such as that was enough to breed venom in any man.

"How are you feeling this morning, Doctor?"

Torday smiled faintly, as if pleased by the solicitude in Rennert's voice. "My worst," he said, "my worst. I never rise before twelve o'clock. Before that time I can neither smoke nor drink—not even coffee. I must follow a rigid diet. So I prefer to sleep. Today I have been awake since daylight. May I ring for something for you?"

"Don't, please."

"I've told the cook to prepare eggnog for us at twelve. You will take that, I hope?"

"Yes. Before we go any further, I should like to remind you of an envelope which Mr. Bounty instructed me to get from you."

Torday's smile was sardonic now. "I might have known you wouldn't forget that. Here it is; take it." He transferred a sealed manila envelope from the table to Rennert's outstretched hand.

"Thank you."

172

"There's no occasion for thanks," the other remarked drily. "I'm sorry, in a way, that you didn't see fit to come to an agreement with me directly. But perhaps this arrangement is better." He asked suddenly: "Do you have a poker face, Rennert? Or don't you know what's in that envelope you just put in your pocket?"

"I have no idea what's in it. I'm merely acting for Mr. Bounty."

Torday's amusement found vent in a low chuckle, which increased in volume until it was a ringing peal of laughter. "I didn't know you were so innocent, Rennert. No doubt you believe in Santa Claus. And trust to the ravens to bring manna. No wonder Peter Bounty has taken you under his wing. You don't know him very well, do you?"

"I think I do," Rennert said stiffly.

"Let's see. I couldn't convince you that he's an extortionist, could I? Could I?" The questions darted at him.

It astonished Rennert to find that he couldn't laugh at such an incredible assertion, couldn't rise to spirited defence of the man whom he trusted implicitly. There was a cold numbness in the regions of his heart which made breathing difficult. "I don't think you could," was the best he could do.

Torday's laughter rose again. "You'll see! You'll see that I'm right. But I bear no grudge against him now that I find he has a sense of humour. Making you his agent! I couldn't understand why he insisted that the envelope be sealed. I spoke too hastily to Bounty at the bridge last night. I rather think I respect the man for his audacity. Tell him that, will you?"

"I shall." Rennert got a grip on himself. "Have you heard, Doctor, that Professor Radisson died last night at Tonatiuh?"

"Yes, yes." Torday seemed fretful at the changing of the subject. "Dr. Lincoln called me this morning and told me of it. I'm sorry. For every reason, of course. Especially sorry that it should have happened at Tonatiuh. Death is bad for the place. But it was unavoidable, I judge."

"Did he make any reference to my telephone conversation with him?"

"He said you had been down there and had wanted to turn the place inside out." Torday's eyes met his with a bit of impudence.

"If you had entered into an agreement with me, Rennert, as I wanted you to, you would have had a perfect right to do as you wish at Tonatiuh. But you preferred to range yourself beside Peter Bounty. So it's well you learned that outside his little bailiwick he's an ordinary mortal and can't help you." He gestured with a hand. "But no matter. We won't quibble. I dare say Lincoln was a trifle brusque last night. He's always getting his pinfeathers ruffled. What was it you wanted?"

"I wanted to examine Radisson's body."

"Why?"

"I don't think I'll answer that question, Doctor."

"Heavens and earth!" Torday said irritably. "Now you're ruffled. I suppose, if we don't bring the body back to Texas and let you look at it, nasty rumours will be going around about the management of our hospital."

"I can't say as to that." Rennert was almost indifferent. "I shan't be responsible for any rumours, if that's what is worrying you."

"Oh, they start! They always start somehow. I'll have the body brought in and turned over to you. It will relieve us of responsibility. Does that satisfy you?"

"I made no demand, Doctor."

"Let's dismiss the matter. I'm tired bandying words. Let's decide what we're going to do to-day. I thought it best to lay the whole case before these men. Make it clear to them where their danger lies. They can be on their guard against Jarl Angerman. They may be able to give us—pardon, I mean you—evidence which will facilitate an arrest. If not, it will be a question of *sauve qui peut.*"

"Angerman has an alibi for the time last night when Mrs. Torday was driving between the two Customs offices," Rennert explained. "So, you see, if she is correct and her brother was alive when she passed on to the bridge, we must look for another culprit."

The little remaining colour drained from the invalid's face as he listened. His left hand went to the wooden box on the table, took out an ivory cigarette-holder; then, as if suddenly mindful that indulgence in nicotine was yet forbidden, replaced it.

"I was so sure it was Jarl," he mused. "So soon after what happened yesterday afternoon. I thought he shot Darwin by mistake. But this leaves us facing the unknown. Are you certain you haven't overlooked something?"

"There's only the possibility that Mrs. Torday was in error, that the shooting occurred in Matamoros. Would it be convenient for her to talk to me a moment?"

"I think so." Torday tapped a bell. "We must make sure. We must. We can't have this uncertainty." His fingers beat an impatient tattoo until the maid came. "Ask Mrs. Torday to come here," he ordered. "Mr. Rennert is with me."

The firmness of Mrs. Torday's carriage must have been dictated by pride. She wore no make-up, and a simple black dress enhanced the whiteness of her composed face. When she gave Rennert her hand, he was struck by the coldness of it.

"Irene," her husband said, "we've been talking about last night on the bridge. Are you sure Darwin was alive when you passed the Mexican Customs?"

Her gaze was perfectly level. "Yes, I am sure. Why do you ask?"

"Mr. Rennert suggested he might have been shot in Matamoros instead of on the bridge."

She turned her head swiftly.

"I am ready to give my oath, Mr. Rennert, that Darwin spoke to me while we were stopped in front of the Mexican Customs office. He said: 'Give 'em the haughty look, Sis, and shoot on by.' Is that sufficient?"

"It is, Mrs. Torday. You understand why I wanted to make sure. There was so much noise and confusion. One could so easily have been mistaken."

"I know. But I wasn't."

"Did you see anyone you knew on that bridge?"

"No one." Her eyes held his. "You have some reason for asking, Mr. Rennert? What is it?"

Rennert forestalled Torday's attempt to speak. "To prove that at least one man could not have murdered your brother, Mrs.

Torday. To give him an unquestionable alibi. I am referring to Jarl Angerman."

There was no controlling the sudden brightness which sprang into her eyes or the spots of colour which appeared on her cheeks. She twined her fingers. "I knew that Jarl did not do it. But now—it's proven?"

"Yes."

Torday's dry laugh broke their interchange. "Jarl's alibi is a good one, Irene. There's no doubting that. He was on a drunken carousal last night. When you were crossing the bridge he was in a dive in Matamoros, chasing a chorus girl. He got in a brawl and they threw him in gaol. He's there now, and I dare say those clothes of his aren't so white."

She drew herself up and looked at him with unconcealed contempt. "Jarl is responsible to no one for his actions," she said steadily. "To no one at all." She turned to Rennert. "Is there anything else? If not, I'll ask you to excuse me."

"That is all, Mrs. Torday. Thank you." There was a great deal more, of course, but that would have to wait for a more propitious occasion.

When she had gone Rennert addressed Torday: "I must ask you some questions, Doctor, before the others arrive. They may appear pointless. They may actually be pointless. I notice that you are left-handed. Has that fact ever played any important part in your life? At the time of your accident or in the years since, has it had any significance for you or for others?"

There was no doubt in Rennert's mind that the other's perplexity was genuine, as he raised the hand in question, bent it back and forth and regarded it.

"Mr. Rennert, if you had asked me that yesterday, when I first met you, I should have thought you were trying to impress me by abstruseness. I know you too well for that now. I suppose when I was a child my sinistrality was of some importance. I believe it affects children in different ways. Some consider it a mark of distinction, like the ability to wriggle their ears. Others are rather ashamed of it. It might even develop into an inferiority complex.

But as far as I can recall, it never made any difference to me. Certainly, during the years you speak of, it has meant nothing." His eyes came to Rennert's face and sharpened a bit. "I remember reading in the paper that Carlos Campos was left-handed. Does that have any bearing on your question?"

"Yes. Charles Bettis, too, was left-handed."

"He was? I didn't know that. Odd. The left hand. The hand sinister. But we mustn't let ourselves run after will-o'-the-wisps, Mr. Rennert."

"I know," Rennert replied patiently. "Now another—"

"Just a minute!" A movement of the white, delicate hand stopped him. "It has just occurred to me. Jarl Angerman is ambidexterous. The man lives for physical perfection. He trained himself long ago to the use of both hands."

"You spoke of that yesterday." Rennert glanced at his watch. "Another matter. Do you remember an article called 'The Last Trumpet' in the magazine *N.E.W.S.?* Mr. Jester had copies with him on your trip to the *hacienda*."

"'The Last Trumpet.' No; I don't recall it."

"It concerned bullfighting in part." Rennert watched him. "The author was Simon Secondyne."

"Simon Secondyne. Unusual name. But if I ever saw or heard it, it has slipped my mind."

"Two more questions, Doctor," Rennert hurried on. All he was doing now was testing the chain which he had constructed, assuring himself of its solidity. "Did you leave the Pullman the night before your accident?"

"Leave it? Why, no. I remember I slept soundly all night. I took a sedative before I went to my berth. That and the fresh mountain air put me to sleep at once."

"And the next day. Between twelve o'clock noon and twelve-thirty. Do you remember where you were?"

"Twelve and twelve-thirty." Torday raised a hand to his forehead. "Let me think. I believe I was in one of the bedrooms of the *hacienda* about that time. Yes, in Professor Radisson's room. With Darwin Wyllys. He had gone riding and had come back feeling ill.

I was a bit worried about his condition and sat with him until the others returned and we went to the Pullman. He had a narrow escape, I think, from sunstroke."

At the front of the house a bell pealed softly. Rennert relaxed and lighted a cigarette. "You retained no special memory of the sun at that hour, then?"

"Of the sun?" Torday's eyes were on the door. "No, I can't say that I did. It seemed to be beating straight down."

"It was," Rennert said as he rose.

II

The door had opened on noiseless hinges and the maid was saying: "Here is Mr. Jester, Doctor."

Rolf was self-conscious as he greeted Torday, and stumbled through words of condolence for Wyllys's death.

His host thanked him perfunctorily and with obvious impatience. His spirits were rising. "How fitting it is, Mr. Jester, that you should arrive with the hour of noon! I was just telling Mr. Rennert that I must keep to a diet in the mornings. But at noon comes release. I can revel in the pleasures of the palate. And you symbolize conviviality so perfectly, Jester. The joy of living. You look as if you had never been sick a day in your life. Ah, see what follows in your wake!"

The little Mexican was wheeling in a tea-wagon on which reposed an immense cut-glass bowl brimful of eggnog, stiffly frothed, its surface gilded by spices.

The bell rang again and she hurried out, leaving the refreshments between Torday's left side and Rennert.

"Will you do the honours, Rennert?" Torday asked. "You'll find cigarettes in the bar by the window." As Rennert went to get them, he continued with growing exuberance, "I thought we might need both stimulation and nourishment today, Jester. And eggnog is the traditional drink for Christmas in the South, I've learned. We'll hope it makes our Christmas a more merry one than it has been so far. Good afternoon, Mr. Bettis."

Rennert returned and laid the box of cigarettes beside the bowl just as Bettis came in.

The hotel manager bobbed his head at Rennert and at Jester as he went toward Torday. "Hello, Doctor," he said shortly. "What's the idea of this meeting?"

"How are you, Bettis? It has been some time since I've seen you. I shall explain as soon as we are all assembled."

"Who's going to be here?" There was a pugnaciousness about Bettis's manner as he stood planted directly in front of Torday.

Just for an instant the latter's eyes were eloquent of dislike. He looked down then, delved again into the carved box and brought out the ivory holder. "Dr. Lincoln and Mr. Distant are still to come. There will be only six of us instead of seven. Our number is decreasing rapidly."

"What do you mean?"

"I was referring to Professor Radisson's death. There's the bell again. We shall soon be ready."

Rennert had been intent on Bettis's face as he received the news. The quick backward jerk of the head, the startled eyes, the gulping of the throat told all that was necessary.

"You will be interested to know," Rennert said to him, "that Mr. Radisson died of blood-poisoning last night."

Bettis fell back a step, and his hand sought the top of a chair. He looked down at the floor.

There was a moment of strained silence, during which they heard Dr. Lincoln's voice in the hall. "You don't need to come with me. I know the way."

The physician entered hurriedly and included them all in a nod, "Good afternoon, gentlemen." His eyes met Rennert's for a fraction of a second. "Good afternoon, Mr. Rennert."

"Good afternoon, Doctor."

Torday waved a hand in the direction of the wagon. "Let's be informal and help ourselves. Mr. Distant will forgive us, I hope, if we don't wait for him any longer."

There ensued the usual period of confusion and delay, while each man urged another to precede him. Rennert, for whom such pother was a source of unreasonable irritation, set to work unceremoniously and ladled out the eggnog. When he had filled five cups he carried one to Torday, who took it in his left hand.

"Thank you, Rennert. Will you give me a cigarette, too?"

"Certainly. I beg your pardon."

Rennert brought the box and held it while Torday took a cigarette and inserted it into the holder. He struck a match and left the cripple inhaling deeply and gratefully.

He turned to find the others standing in a row, cups in their hands. Rolf Jester, elbow to elbow with himself. Bettis, Lincoln.

Torday cleared his throat, wrinkled the skin about his mouth as if he could restrain himself no longer, raised his cup.

"Gentlemen, your health!"

He drank deeply.

And died.

18
THE MOMENT OF TRUTH

I

TORDAY DRANK AND DIED. The event had for Rennert just that suddenness.

There was a matter of seconds when an agonized cry lingered in the air, when the man's chin was dropping towards his chest, when—simultaneously—his left hand slid down over his shirt front, emptying the cup, and the right let the cigarette sink into the cream and gold liquid and sizzle out.

Then Torday was staring in the blank finality of death at the lower rung of the nearest chair, while the thick eggnog spread slowly. . . .

In two swift steps Dr. Lincoln was at his side, bending over him, examining pulse and heart and eyes.

A thud drew Rennert's attention to the others. Matt Bettis's cup had fallen from fingers which seemed to have become nerveless. The man's face was stupid from shock and his eyes bulged behind the moist lenses of his spectacles. Rolf Jester was gripping the handle of his cup so tightly that the tendons stood out whitely on his tanned skin. Perspiration beaded his face and his breath was coming and going stertorously.

"God, Hugh, God!" he murmured in monotone. Lincoln's voice was deepened by strain: "He's dead."

He straightened and gingerly applied to the end of his tongue a finger which he had dipped into the eggnog.

Rennert placed his cup carefully on the top of the wagon, waited a moment, and asked: "Can you tell the cause, Doctor?"

Lincoln shook his head, brought out a handkerchief and wiped his hands, while his gaze went to the cut-glass bowl.

"Did any of the rest of you touch that eggnog?" he demanded sharply.

The four of them looked at one another, checking the negative motions of their heads.

"Then," Dr. Lincoln said, "you have politeness to thank for your lives. The politeness that made you wait for Torday. Otherwise—" He shrugged expressively.

Rennert stepped to the telephone on the table by Torday's side, picked up the receiver, and faced them as he dialed.

"I'm going to ask each one of you to remain exactly where he is. Please oblige me and we'll get this over quickly."

It was several moments before a sleepy voice answered, none too amiably: "Hello."

"Peter?"

"Yes." The tone changed. "That you, Hugh?"

"Yes. I'm at Dr. Torday's house. He has just died. Can you come? And notify the county doctor."

"It's murder?"

"Yes, it's murder, Peter."

Bounty swore unintelligibly. "I'll be there as soon as I can get my clothes on. You're holding the fort all right?"

"I'm holding it."

Rennert hung up and looked from one to another of the three men, who had all been striving to keep their eyes averted from the wheel-chair. He took a deep breath and thought of himself as girding up his loins.

"I'm sure," he said, "that you gentlemen will see how necessary it is that I search you. If poison was brought into this room the container will still be here. Now"—he tried to smile agreeably— "who wants to be first?"

For a moment no one spoke, and he was reminded of the scene in the Matamoros bull-ring when the police had made a similar but less polite pronouncement. . . .

"I fail to see anything of the sort," Dr. Lincoln said frigidly. "You know very well that you were standing by that eggnog when I came in, Rennert. You know that I did not approach it before Torday drank. And I assure you that I have no ability at sleight of hand."

"The same goes for me," Bettis put in. "We know you've got a tin badge and a gun—"

Rennert began to lose patience, partially because his nerves were on edge from uncertainty. The whole theory which he had been building up so painstakingly seemed about to topple. . . .

It was Rolf Jester, of course, who came to his support by stepping forward, extending his arms and saying, in a tone intended for the others:

"We know exactly why you're doing this, Rennert, and that it is for our own protection. You had your back turned for about a minute when you went to get those cigarettes. I couldn't have slipped anything into that bowl without Torday seeing me, but he can't swear to it now. I insist that you search me. And I think these fellows had better do the same."

Rennert searched him swiftly but thoroughly, knowing that any concession to friendship would render the man's gesture a pointless one. Unseen by the others, he gave Jester an approbatory pressure on the small of the back.

"Thanks, Rolf. There's no need for you to stay any longer."

"Maybe you want me to help you? I'll be glad to, if you say so."

"No. I can handle this without any trouble. Run along. Now, Doctor."

Lincoln submitted without further protest, but his manner was one of outraged dignity.

Rennert asked as his light fingers sped at their task:

"Did you get my message last night, Doctor?"

"Yes. I hope you'll listen to reason, Rennert—"

"Let's not talk now. I shall notify when to appear at the sheriff's office."

"What for?"

"For questioning. You may go now."

"Do I have your permission," the physician asked as he drew himself up to his full height and buttoned his coat, "to notify Mrs. Torday of her husband's death? It's customary."

Rennert had heard the bell and was giving part of his attention to the door, part to Bettis, who had lighted a cigarette.

"So I was aware, Doctor. I shall appreciate it if you will break the news to Mrs. Torday. I hope you can prevail on her to remain in her room for the present. Either Mr. Bounty or I—"

"Good afternoon!" David Distant greeted them in high good humour. "I am so sorry to be late. Have I missed anything?"

II

The Indian came into the room and extended a hand to Lincoln, who was standing so that he blocked the view of the wheelchair. "I am so glad to see you again, Doctor. I have been looking forward—"

The physician had released his hand after a brief pressure and stepped aside, with a nod in the direction of Torday.

"You've missed a murder. Someone poisoned the eggnog that we were about to drink. You're fortunate you *didn't* come earlier. Mr. Rennert here might think you guilty."

Distant's face did not lose at once the wide smile which gave it moonlike proportions. The smile stayed incongruously while the emotion which had stamped it there fled. His eyes were sharp, more than a little wary, as they traveled from one face to another and stopped on Rennert's.

"Mr. Rennert would not make that mistake," he said gravely.

"I shouldn't say that he's altogether infallible," Dr. Lincoln threw back as he went through the doorway.

Distant's eyes had not faltered in their scrutiny of Rennert's.

"Do you want me to go or to stay here, Mr. Rennert?"

"I think it would be better if you left, Distant. I'll see you at the hotel later."

"Yes, we will hope that our next meeting will be more pleasant." With a polite bow the Indian was gone.

Rennert turned to Bettis.

"Sorry to make you wait," he said in a pleasant tone.

Deliberately Bettis dropped his cigarette to the rug and ground it out with his toe.

"This is much better," he said with satisfaction, as his narrowed eyes took Rennert's measure. "Just the two of us alone. I've got a gun too and I can draw it as quick as you can yours. This is the chance I've been wanting. To talk to you. I'm damned tired of having you prying into my affairs, you stuffed busybody. You're not going to lay a hand on me. Understand? I'll punch that smirk off your face—"

Rennert didn't hit him on the chin, but directly below it.

Bettis grunted and went down. With him went a feather which had become dislodged from somewhere about his clothing. A tiny olive-grey and white feather crossed by a black band, it eddied about for an instant, then settled to the floor by Torday's slippered feet.

Rennert knelt down to examine the man. He had not intended to put so much force into the blow.

"Not bad for an amateur! Not bad." Peter Bounty came buoyantly into the room. "Maybe a fraction of an inch off, but good enough. I was really surprised. I had no idea you packed such a wallop."

Rennert had risen. "I suppose I shouldn't have done that, Peter."

Bounty stood beside him, hands in his pockets, and gave a crooked sideways grin. "Shouldn't have done it? I'd like to know why not! I saw it. The guy had it coming to him. He doesn't know how lucky he is you didn't give it to him with the muzzle of your gun. I told you I'd stand by you, didn't I, whatever you did?"

"Yes, but—"

"But nothing. Forget about it. He'll come to in a minute. Tell me what happened to Torday. I never moved so fast in my life. Came in the kitchen door."

Bounty fished in his pocket, found a partially chewed match, and resumed mastication of it as Rennert talked. He looked as if he needed a shave, a cold shower and coffee. His tie had been knot-ted too hastily and one of his shoes was unlaced. He repressed a yawn as he listened to what Rennert had to say about a murderer and his motive.

"No proof," he repeated Rennert's words. "I suppose it's about time we were getting some. I told the maid and the cook to stay in the kitchen. I'll go talk to 'em while you interview Mrs. Torday. She's probably in her boudoir. I wouldn't be able to keep my mind on my business there." He watched Bettis as the latter stirred and tried to sit up. "I've got a couple of the boys outside. I'll have one of them take this down to gaol and lock it up. O.K.?"

"There's not much proof against him."

Bounty drew a pair of handcuffs from his pocket and lounged forward.

"Resisted an officer, didn't he? That will hold him until I can have a little heart to heart talk with him. Maybe he'll decide to be a good boy and tell me all about it, who knows?"

The narrow toe of his shoe prodded here and there, curiously, as if this were some strange and blubbery creature cast upon a seashore—and Rennert knew that if Bettis were at all wise he would hold nothing back from this soft-spoken sheriff of a border county. . . .

Bounty stooped and snapped the cuffs on Bettis's wrists.

Rennert found himself confronted by the same broad expanse of blue serge. Thin and glossy. Dustier than the night before. Still streaked by red . . .

"Hold that position, Peter!" Rennert called sharply as he went nearer. He lifted the tails of the coat, scrutinized their edges, then gave his attention to the taut cloth of the seat of the trousers.

"It only goes to prove," Bounty talked away to himself, his hands on his knees, "that you never can tell about a man. Really, I was dumbfounded—"

"Turn round, Peter."

Bounty straightened and turned, shaking his head sadly.

"Just imagine such a predicament! The most embarrassing moment of my life—"

"Where have you sat in red paint lately, Peter?"

"Red paint?" An uncertain blue was dominant in Bounty's eyes now. "I didn't know I had."

"Those are the same trousers you wore yesterday?"

"Yes, I didn't take time to change this morning. I have another pair," he hastened to impress on Rennert.

"That paint wasn't there when I visited your office yesterday afternoon. It was when you were in the Public Library last night. Think back now and tell me where you got it."

"I sit in so many places. You're not trying to kid me, Hugh?"

"I was never more serious in my life."

"How would the International Bridge do?"

"Exactly what I hoped you'd say. Tell me about it."

"It was while I was watching that Customs fellow search Juan Canard's car. I leaned against the railing. There was a placard of some sort there. Where a Mexican had set up a tamale stand, I think. I knocked it off, I remember, and it fell in the river—"

"In the river!" Rennert clicked his tongue. "That's unfortunate for you, Peter. Because it means you're going to have to remain on your feet until you get those trousers off. You may pass down in the history of Texas as the only sheriff who ever carried evidence against a murderer on the seat of his pants."

19
SUN ON CAPRICORN

I

MRS. TORDAY received Rennert in an upstairs sitting-room, a large and airy place which was a blend of green and ivory. She was dry-eyed, her manner was controlled, but he knew that she was in imperative need of some vent for her pent-up emotions. He analysed her as a simple woman of great physical stamina, whose weeping would be hysterical if short lived, whose demonstrations of anger or of affection would be gusts. Rennert sat none too easily in his chair.

"I can tell you nothing about the preparation of that eggnog," she stated in reply to his question. "Dr. Torday asked Mrs. Mootz, our cook, to have it ready to serve promptly at twelve. She made it in the kitchen, I judge, as she always does. She has been with us for years, since soon after we came to the Valley. It would be ridiculous to suspect her of being a party to any conspiracy against Dr. Torday. Anita Rodriguez, the maid, is a simple little soul who has worked here for six months or so. My same remark applies to her."

"Who else has access to the house, Mrs. Torday?"

"There's a nurse who cared for Dr. Torday. She is away for the holidays, however. Three men act as gardeners and chauffeurs—guards, as well. They scarcely ever come into the house. Dr. Torday treated them all well, paid them good wages. They will all lose by his death." She was silent for a moment, pressing her palms together, before she looked straight at Rennert and said: "There's no need to tell you that up until yesterday Jarl Angerman came here every day."

"I know."

Before he could continue she rose with a swift and involuntary shudder of despair, and walked to a wide window which overlooked the lawn on the south. She flung back the curtains and let the sun pour over her.

Rennert waited a moment. "Will you talk to me quite frankly, Mrs. Torday? About Jarl Angerman?"

"Yes, but I can't while we're sitting so sedately. As if we were waiting for tea to be served. Come and stand with me here, Mr. Rennert—in the sun. It will make things easier to explain." When he stood beside her she took his arm and kneaded it with her fingers. "I want to assure myself that you are a man of flesh and blood. Not just an officer of the law who is getting his job done as soon as possible. Because I trust you, Mr. Rennert. And I need your help."

"I know you do." Rennert was uncomfortable. "Can't you think of me as a friend?"

"Yes. Tell me. You meant what you said about Jarl having an alibi for last night—while I was on the bridge?"

"I did."

"But people will tell you that I lied to protect Jarl. They will say that he shot Darwin by mistake for Dr. Torday. That I let him kill my own brother and said nothing. That he and I poisoned my husband because he stood between us. But it's not true, Mr. Rennert! I swear it. By that crucifix."

His eyes followed hers to a cross of carved dark wood which was the sole adornment of an ivory wall. "I believe you, Mrs. Torday," he said.

Her hand was a vice, surprisingly strong, upon his arm.

"Thank you. Because so much of what people say is true. Jarl and I do love each other. We always have. And we were too stupid—both of us—to know it until it was too late. Darwin's and my father was a university professor. We weren't rich at all, but that didn't matter in such a community. It was my father's position, his academic standing that counted. One autumn a farm boy came

to live with us. A million years ago that was. He stayed in the base-
ment, made the fires, tended the yard. His name was Jarl Angerman. A big, earnest, good-natured fellow. He was Darwin's age,
they were in the same classes. They studied together, and I would
help them sometimes. Jarl hadn't had a good start in school. He
would get discouraged. I always tried to cheer him up." Her laugh
was almost natural. "I suppose it would sound trite, Mr. Rennert
to say that we were like brother and sister. But it's true."

"True things are usually trite."

"And the rest of it is the same. I was studying voice and had
ambitions for a career. But we didn't have money enough for foreign study and I felt frustrated. I found out later I couldn't sing at
all, but I didn't know it then. I met Paul Torday. A fashionable
practitioner who had traveled and who was just old enough to be
distinguished. I liked him. Because, Mr. Rennert"—her voice sank—
"he was attractive before his accident. That changed him into another man. We were married and I was thrilled to think he was my
husband. It wasn't until I told Jarl goodbye that I realized the mistake I'd made. It shocked me, but I went away and told myself that
I wasn't going to let it affect my life. Jarl went back to the farm,
then drifted off. But I kept hearing of him through Darwin. That's
how I knew he was working on that Mexican ranch. But there's no
need to go into that, is there?"

"There is, Mrs. Torday. You can help me by talking of that visit."

"I will then, of course. Paul had been wanting to establish a
health resort somewhere in the south. We came to San Antonio
with Dr. and Mrs. Lincoln, then on down to the Valley. Darwin was
with us. He had written to Jarl asking him to meet us here. Jarl
wouldn't do it. Darwin didn't know why, but I did. I felt I had to
see Jarl. We might never be so close to each other again. Paul and
Dr. Lincoln were talking about Mr. Jester's excursion. When I
found that it included the *hacienda* where Jarl worked, I urged
them to go. Poor Jarl. He was embarrassed, miserable and happy
all at the same time while we were there. Paul didn't care for out-
door life, so I spent hours with Jarl. Riding with him. Reminiscing

and hearing him talk about his work. He loved Mexico and the people with whom he was associated. And then—the wreck."

"There are some questions, Mrs. Torday, which I am very anxious to ask. One concerns the flogging of a peon a few hours before your departure. Is it true that—"

"Of course it's true!" she exclaimed impatiently. "But it wasn't the brutal thing that Paul always made it out. Jarl told me about it that morning while we were riding. One of the workers was notorious for mistreating animals. Jarl was in a constant state of indignation about it. He had tried to get the owner of the place to discharge the man, but never could. Finally, Jarl took it on himself to stop it. He told the fellow that the next time he heard of his abuse of an animal he was going to give him the same punishment. That morning he found him beating a horse. Jarl asked someone who saw it how many times he had struck the animal. He dragged the man into a shed then, and carried out his promise. He didn't hurt him, though, only frightened him thoroughly. The broken whip was the one the man had used, not Jarl. Paul knew the truth about the affair, but he always discoloured it. He knew, too, the truth about Jarl and me. And he took a delight in tormenting Jarl, who would endure anything so long as he could be near me. I had been responsible for Jarl coming here—a year ago—when Paul wanted someone to manage his affairs and act as bodyguard. I got Darwin to suggest Jarl. But it was a horrible mistake."

"When you realized that you decided to purchase the Campos *hacienda* for Angerman?"

"Yes, I knew how he loved it and would have gone back if it hadn't been for me. I had enough money to buy it. I had Darwin attend to the transaction, so that my name wouldn't appear. I was going to persuade Jarl that he would be happier owning his own property in Mexico than serving my husband. And I was going to tell him that I would be happier, knowing that he was waiting for me there. Mr. Rennert, he knows nothing about what has been happening, does he? He's in that Mexican gaol. Can't you get him out this afternoon?"

"I doubt it, Mrs. Torday. But he will be released in the morning. And I plan to see him at once. I was going to ask him a question, but you can answer it as well. Did you leave the Pullman the night before your husband's accident?"

She nodded.

"You met Angerman?"

She turned her head to look at him. "Yes, I met Jarl. We walked part of the way up to the house, then back. That is all."

"Were you aware that someone left that Pullman after you?"

"Yes, I remember. We heard someone walking behind us. We stepped out of the road until he passed. It was Mr. Bettis. Not the one who has the hotel now, but his brother. He had a flashlight, so I recognized him."

"Did you see him return?"

"Yes, he was walking much faster—almost running."

"He had had time to go to the house?"

"Oh, yes, plenty of time. We wondered what he had been doing. Jarl asked me if we had any thieves in our party."

Rennert disengaged her arm. "There were people in that party, Mrs. Torday, who were a great deal more dangerous than thieves."

II

Rennert found Peter Bounty standing in a white-tiled kitchen, consuming bacon and eggs while he conversed amicably with Mrs. Mootz.

Mrs. Mootz, large-framed, silver-haired, had a moist, kindly face and grey eyes which were alight with approval of Peter Bounty, of Peter Bounty's friendliness, of Peter Bounty's appetite and the justice which he was doing to her cooking.

Rennert heard her say: "I know you're joking, Mr. Bounty. Maybe if I brought you a rocking-chair you'd like that?"

Bounty grinned.

"Come in, Hugh," he called out, "and meet Mrs. Mootz. The best cook in Brownsville. Maybe she'll fix you a bite if you sit down.

I've been trying to convince her that I always eat standing up. This is Mr. Rennert, Mrs. Mootz. Deputy and friend of mine."

Mrs. Mootz beamed.

"Indeed, I will fix you anything you want, Mr. Rennert, It's an honour to do anything for Mr. Bounty or his friends. I said when he was running for office that what we needed was a sheriff who wasn't stuck-up and who'd treat everybody alike. I remember he stopped one of his speeches to give my little grandson a piece of candy. Just as nice as could be. Sit right down here, Mr. Rennert."

"Thank you, Mrs. Mootz. I won't eat anything." Rennert perched on a stool and glanced inquiringly at Bounty.

The latter poured thick cream into his coffee, added two tea-spoonfuls of sugar and began to stir it.

"Mrs. Mootz," he suggested, "I think Mr. Rennert would like to hear about the eggnog. Tell him just what you told me, won't you?"

"Well, it was this way," she responded with alacrity. "Dr. Torday told me to have that eggnog ready at twelve sharp. I began fixing it about eleven-thirty. I made it just like I always do, and I know there was nothing wrong with it. And besides, like I swore up and down to Mr. Bounty, I tasted it more than once. And after the last time I tasted it, I only added one jigger of rum. Because Dr. Torday liked it strong. There it is."

She pointed dramatically to a bottle on the sink. It was of West Indian Negrita rum, and almost full.

"I'd used up the other bottle," she went on, "so I had to open that one. The seal hadn't been broken, of that I'm sure. That bottle was one of half a dozen that Dr. Lincoln gave Dr. Torday for Christmas. It's been right on a shelf ever since. Now nobody came in this kitchen while I was working. At twelve o'clock, Anita—that's the maid—came in and wheeled out the wagon with the eggnog and the cups. She left the door open, and I know she took it straight along the hall to the study. Mr. Bounty talked to her, and she said there wasn't anybody there and that she didn't put anything at all in it. Mr. Bounty understood right away what the trouble was. It was some of this bad rum that comes from Jamaica and those places." (Here, unseen by her, Bounty managed to wink at Rennert.) "It's made under such unsanitary conditions. I hope it'll be a lesson to people to be careful what they buy from foreign countries. Let me give you some more coffee, Mr. Bounty."

Bounty sighed.

"I must go to work, Mrs. Mootz," he said. "Maybe I'll come back. I'll take this rum with me and have it tested." He brought out a handkerchief and carefully picked up the bottle. "Thanks a lot for the meal."

"I'm so glad you liked it, Mr. Bounty. Be sure now and send me some of your cards when it's time for you to stand for re-election. It'll give them to all my friends."

Bounty assured her that he would appreciate her support, and went with Rennert along the hall towards the study.

Rennert's face doubtless looked rather severe (as it usually did when his thoughts were busy), for the sheriff was apologetic.

"I hadn't had any breakfast, Hugh, and I was hungry," he explained. "I really haven't wasted any time. The county doctor has been here and carted away the body for a P.M. Bettis is sitting in a cell by now, nursing his jaw. I got the city chemist on the 'phone. He promised to examine the eggnog or anything else I brought him this afternoon." Bounty closed the door. "I thought I'd look this bottle over for finger-prints, just on the chance, then give it to him too. I'm sure Mrs. Mootz (darn, those were good eggs!) was telling the truth. Also little Anita, who's inclined to be flirtatious, in case you know anyone who is interested. So it looks as if it had to be the rum. Unless Mrs. Torday told you something?"

"Mrs. Torday only confirmed what I already knew."

Rennert's eyes were roaming over the scene. The tea-wagon with its glass bowl—the scattered cups—the empty wheel-chair, with the black silk scarf over one arm—the table littered with papers and smoking equipment—the floor. "You won't forget to give the chemist those trousers of yours?" he spoke abstractedly. "And that bandage which I have in my room. I'm counting on them being exhibits A and B. And"—he stepped forward and bent over—"I think this will be C."

Bounty stared at the object which Rennert handed him.

"Well, I'll be damned!" he ejaculated softly. "You think Torday was killed with that?"

"I'm willing to bet," Rennert said, "that he was."

III

Jarl Angerman's height might have served as a measuring-rod in the construction of his cell in the Cárcel Municipal of Matamoros. As he lay full-length upon an iron cot clamped to the concrete floor, his head touched one wall while his feet projected over the end-rest almost to the opposite one. Had the cot been placed the other way, his body would have covered almost exactly the distance between the wall below the narrow barred window and the door by which Rennert entered.

When the *carcelero* had turned the key in the lock, he reminded, "*Diez minutos, señor, na más*," and stumped off down the corridor. Rennert stood for a moment, thinking the prisoner was asleep. Through the rusty iron bars squeezed the meagre light of a sun declining on the farther tropic. The place had the aguish dampness of old adobe, and the odour of an open drain struck him an almost physical blow.

Angerman turned his head and gave Rennert a stare which was so apathetic as to lack recognition. His eyes were bloodshot and dull, with dark violet pouches below them. His cheeks and jaw bristled with blond stubble. The right side of his mouth was swollen and contused and still retained caked blood. There was blood on his rumpled clothing.

"Hello, Angerman!" Rennert was brisk and cheerful. "They finally let me in to see you. I brought you some food that may be an improvement on *frijoles*. You're not the first friend I've visited in a Mexican gaol." He laid his package on the uncovered mattress by Angerman's side.

"Thanks. Sit down."

Angerman moved his feet and Rennert lowered himself to a precarious and uncomfortable seat on the corner of the cot.

He lighted a cigarette, to combat the smell, and said: "I hear you had quite a party at The Triumph of the Emotions last night."

Angerman's face wore no expression as he stared at the ceiling.

"I don't want to talk about it."

"We won't then. They've given me only ten minutes anyway. But don't feel too remorseful. Everyone has to break loose occasionally. Have you heard of Darwin Wyllys's death?"

"Yes, I heard them talking about it in the patio this morning, while we were being finger-printed."

"His sister need never know now that he was a drug addict."

Angerman's lips tightened, and he was silent for a moment.

"I thought," he said, "that you understood about yesterday morning—at Tonatiuh."

"One glance at Wyllys was enough to tell me. I knew, as soon as I considered the situation, why you wanted to be left alone with him. He was bargaining with you for an injection, wasn't he?"

The other nodded.

"Was he after drugs at the bull-ring?"

Another nod. "There are always men there selling them. He got some morphine and did not want me to know it. But he gave it to me when I asked him. He was a good fellow, Mr. Rennert, but he was weak. I did what I could for him. Dr. Torday would not have let him have any if he had known. I was breaking Darwin of the habit gradually."

"How many cigarette-holders," Rennert asked quietly, "did you carve for Mrs. Torday to give her husband as a Christmas present?"

Angerman's head turned abruptly, and his blue eyes were bleak and non-committal as they regarded Rennert.

"Four," he answered cautiously.

"You did the work at your house at Tonatiuh?"

"Yes."

"What people visited your house while those holders were there?"

"There was Darwin, he came every day," the response was mechanical. "Professor Radisson stayed with me one day last week."

"There was no one else?"

"I think Dr. Lincoln came to see Mr. Radisson once while I was not there."

Outside, the *calcelero* clinked keys and Rennert got to his feet. "I think," he said, "that we shall find one of those holders was poisoned. It served its purpose in killing Dr. Torday."

Angerman sat upright. "Dr. Torday!" he echoed hoarsely. "He is dead?"

"He died at noon to-day."

"You have arrested his murderer?"

"No."

"Why not?" Angerman didn't care at all, of course. His eyes were on the barred window and the far-away winter sunlight, and their bleakness was melting.

"Because," Rennert said, "I can't."

20
THE CRIMINAL AND HIS MOTIVE

I

PETER BOUNTY wore blue serge at dinner. But his suit, Rennert noted without appearing to do so, was a new one and in every respect impeccable. It rested with natural ease upon the erect frame of a man whose regular habitat might have been the dining-room of the Hotel Jester. More than one pair of feminine eyes lingered on the polished and handsome occupant of the chair opposite Rennert's—and returned. Rennert was amused and elated and perhaps envious.

By tacit agreement the two of them avoided during the meal the subject of the affair which had drawn them into association. Reference to it came after their table had been honoured by a visit from J. B. Sizemore, the pompous president of the Chamber of Commerce, who, Rennert was well aware, had more than once spoken openly of Cameron County's need for a "streamlined" sheriff. Sizemore was effusive in his greeting of Bounty, called him "Peter," and invited him and Mr. Rennert to attend the Chamber's annual smoker. He had heard that Peter knew some good stories. Could he prevail on Peter to appear on the programme?

Peter let himself be prevailed upon and, when Sizemore had billowed on, glanced at Rennert in time to detect the twinkle of amusement in the latter's eyes. "You damned proselytizer!" he swore at him softly. "What are you trying to do—civilize me?"

Rennert knew that the sheriff was immensely gratified at the reception which had been accorded him here, so he said with a bit of maliciousness: "I see your knuckles are skinned."

Bounty quickly lowered his right hand from sight, then brought it back.

"Yes," he admitted as he gazed at it, "they do seem to be a little damaged. I was over in that orange grove this afternoon late. You know, the one between your house and the highway that you were too scrupulous to take from Torday. Nice bunch of trees there."

"Very nice. Did you try to climb one?"

"No." Bounty looked straight at him. "I wanted to have a talk with a fellow so I took him among the oranges, where we'd be close to Nature and not be disturbed. My object was to tell him what I thought of him, but I found I couldn't put it into words. So I took off my coat and hat, my sheriff's badge and gun, and temporarily resigned from office. I think he realized that I didn't like him."

"It was Matt Bettis, I judge."

"Yes. Any—er—criticism, Hugh? I wasn't acting as sheriff, re-member."

"No criticism at all, Peter. May I ask what happened to Bettis afterwards?"

"I told him there were 'buses leaving town every few hours. I suggested that he get on one and be outside Cameron County by midnight. I hinted that we didn't want to see him here again, ever. We don't, do we, Hugh?"

"We don't as far as I'm concerned. Rolf Jester has taken charge here at the hotel, I notice, and things seem to be running along smoothly. Did Bettis make any kind of a confession?"

"Sure. He knew we could never make a charge against him stick, now that Radisson is dead. Everything was just as you had it worked out. Matt and his brother read that article 'The Last Trumpet' on the train. At the *hacienda* Charles (Matt lays the blame on him) recognized the bull-ring as the one which had been photographed for the magazine. He tried to find out, just from curiosity, who Simon Secondyne was. No one knew. He got to thinking it over and decided it must be Radisson's pseudonym. The copies of *N.E.W.S.* that Campos asked Jester to bring were meant for Radisson, who had probably not been able to see a published copy. Campos himself was a friend of the professor's, so would keep still.

"That night Charles left the Pullman and went up to the house. He stood at Radisson's window and called him. Told him he knew he was Simon Secondyne and asked him how he'd like his information to get to the Mexican authorities. Radisson denied it. Then Bettis reminded him that the Campos bull-ring could be identified in the illustration. Also that he had left a thumb-mark on the photograph. That would prove he had taken the picture at least. The Mexican Government would need no more proof to expel him from the country. Radisson gave Bettis all the money he had on hand in exchange for his promise to keep still."

"Bettis, like almost every blackmailer, broke his promise."

"Matt swears that Charles had no intention of going any farther. But after they got to Brownsville they needed money to make payments on this hotel. Charles saw Radisson in Brownsville the next Christmas, found out where he was staying and telephoned him from a telephone-box, disguised his voice, and told him he needed ten thousand dollars. Radisson had better leave that sum in a specified place or he'd never get back into Mexico. Charles collected the money and saw how easy it would be to keep this up regularly. The next fall he wrote to Radisson and told him to be in Brownsville at Christmas-time with ten thousand dollars more. Bettis called him when he got there and ordered him to go to another spot in the country. There he'd find five homing pigeons in cages. Radisson was to put two one-thousand dollar bills in the quills which each bird had fastened to its wings, then turn them loose. There was no chance of following them across country, of course, so Radisson never knew where they went. After Charles's death Matt decided to keep the blackmail game going. He called Radisson on Christmas night and told him to have the money ready tomorrow. He planned to take the pigeons out to-night, call Radisson again in the morning and tell him where to find them." Bounty shook his head dolefully. "Wonder where Bettis will be in the morning?"

Rennert was recalling his conversation of the afternoon before.

"I was positive," he murmured, "that Radisson was telling the truth when he said he didn't know who had telephoned him at

Lincoln's house. That he wished he did know. The rest of his story was a fabrication, but that much was most emphatically true." He glanced at his companion's empty coffee-cup. "Why don't we go over to my house, smoke our cigars and talk about shoes and ships and sealing-wax?"

"Well," Bounty mimicked Rennert's tone of the day before, "why don't we? Though you have to answer some questions before we get on to shoes and things. Juan Canard is coming to the office in the morning and I want to be perfectly sure of my ground. You're adamant about letting your name appear?"

"Adamant."

"Well, thanks. That's all I can say."

"That's enough."

In the lobby they came upon Kent Distant, who was sitting in a chair, smoking and glancing at the door. He got up when they approached and Rennert introduced him to Bounty.

"Kent," Rennert said, "Janell Lincoln asked me to tell you good-bye. She's going away on a cruise, then back to school."

"Janell? Oh, yes. Thank you, Mr. Rennert."

"You don't seem exactly dejected."

"Well, I'll tell you, Mr. Rennert," the young man was confidential. "Janell is a sweet little girl, of course, but—I suppose I oughtn't to say this—but she's too much of a prig for us ever to be very good friends." He glanced uncertainly from one of the men to the other. "I'm waiting for Dad again. He went to mail some letters and was to have met me here fifteen minutes ago."

"You don't need to worry about him any more, Kent. The case is finished. I'll tell you and your father about it as soon as I have an opportunity."

"Finished!" Rennert didn't know until he heard that exclamation how worried the fellow had been. "Who was the murderer?"

"Professor Radisson."

"Radisson! Why, it doesn't seem possible, Mr. Rennert. Everyone said he was such a scholar and so wrapped up in his work."

"That's exactly the reason he committed murder, Kent."

II

Rennert and Peter Bounty sat on the flagstone terrace of Rennert's house and watched cigar smoke dissolve into moonlight. Their chairs were huge and soft and designed for lazy men.

"I want you to tell me," Bounty said, "how you built up your case against Radisson."

"*Our* case," Rennert corrected. "Radisson attracted my attention the night I drove past his house and found he had been shot. According to his story, he had just started to put a cigarette between his lips with his left hand when the bullet struck that hand. Now what would happen in such an event? The cigarette would fall, of course. Yet there was no cigarette on the ground where the blood had flowed. There was no trace of the match which he said he had tossed away with his right hand. There might conceivably be an explanation for their disappearance. Someone might have come along before I did and picked them up. But it didn't seem likely in such a short interval of time. My conclusion was that Radisson had not been smoking that cigarette. Why, I asked myself, should he lie about it? In order to lend credence to his story of having been fired at by someone in a car. A glowing cigarette would make an excellent target. Either he knew who had shot him and was trying to conceal this, or—he had shot himself. But why do either, I didn't know."

"You suspected that he was shielding Lincoln, didn't you?"

"Yes, out of fear, perhaps. Especially the next day when Lincoln told me that the bullet had been thrown away. I even suspected Lincoln of poisoning the wound in some way, when I learned that Radisson's condition was getting worse. I remembered that Lincoln had had a mirror in his pocket at the bullfight. I didn't think he could have used it to flash the sun in Campos's eyes, but it was possible. However, I couldn't see, even dimly, any motive which I could pin on him."

"His wife," Bounty reminded.

"That was only in connection with the wreck. Changing the switch and swinging off the train at the last moment would have been such an excellent way of ridding himself of her. But that, I knew, wouldn't account for all that had been happening since. When I went to your office I was inclined to think the motive lay somewhere in Torday's affairs. Then I learned of the Secondyne article and saw the left thumb-print on the photograph. It clicked then. Radisson was Secondyne. He had tried to shoot off the thumb by which he could be identified. There's no possible means by which the friction ridges of the skin can be altered. Neither cutting nor burning will do, because the pattern reappears as soon as the wound heals."

"I know. I've read it in the manuals of crime detection."

"So perhaps had Radisson. If he wanted to avoid having his thumb-print compared with that on the picture he had recourse to the only method possible. Last night, on my way home, my objects were two. To obtain a print of Radisson's left thumb and to make sure that the medicine being used on his wound was *bona fide*. The discarded bandage which I found in Lincoln's house would serve both purposes, I hoped. Blood or ointment might have taken a clear impression on the cloth. If not, iodine crystals would easily bring out the print."

"Then you didn't make headway with that bandage because of the paint on the outside?"

"No, I thought nothing of the paint at the time. The next morning I found the pigeons in the attic, and Rolf Jester told me of the payments which the Bettis brothers made on the hotel the first of every year. Blackmail seemed the logical way to account for their possession of the money. Rolf spoke then of his dog, which was suffering from some ailment which the veterinary couldn't diagnose. Not being able to locate the specific trouble, Rolf was going to cure every possible cause of suffering by inflicting death. That was exactly what Radisson was doing. A blackmailer had gone from the Pullman to his room that night and levied toll. Radisson knew only that he was a left-handed man. He felt sure that it was one of the group on the Pullman, therefore he tried to make a clean sweep of everyone who could be guilty. Cutting the Gordian knot, as it were."

"Matt Bettis claimed that he didn't know how Radisson could have found out the blackmailer was left-handed."

"I think my guess about the wrist-watch with the luminous dial was correct. It was a dark night and when Charles Bettis stood at Radisson's window he doubtless took care to disguise his face and voice. But when Radisson handed him the money he must have noticed that the other took it with his left hand and that on the right wrist he wore a wrist-watch. Hence he was left-handed. Radisson must have spent a miserable night, knowing that his secret was the property of someone else and facing the prospect of repeated extortions. The next morning he must have looked over the group, trying in vain to pick out the man he had talked to the night before. There wasn't much opportunity, because most of them went riding. He thought then of the switch, the Pullman, the two-thirteen train. About twelve he saw the porter come to the house. Which meant that in all likelihood no one would be near the tracks. The south-bound train had passed, so he broke open the switch and changed it. Did you see the impossibility in his alibi for noon?"

"I can't see it, Hugh. You told me that he couldn't sit in the shade of a wall at noon on June twentieth. Why not?"

"That *hacienda* was near the Tropic of Cancer, remember. That date only missed the summer solstice by twenty-four hours. So at noon the sun would be directly overhead and a wall would cast no shadow. The shadowless hour, the Mexicans call it."

"Head of the class, Hugh. But why make up that story about listening to a record? Why didn't he just say he was in his room alone?"

"Because Dr. Torday and Darwin Wyllys were there. They doubtless knew that he had gone outdoors. He may have gone to some pains to give himself an excuse to be away from the house. I thought at the time that he was very prompt with that alibi. After that talk with Rolf I was convinced of Radisson's guilt. Every Christmas his blackmailer called on him for money. Every Christmas he tried to avoid payment by killing his persecutor. He got the right one the first time, but Matt Bettis carried on. The only other left-handed man among the visitors was Torday. So he centred his attention on Torday the next year. Sooner or later it was sure to occur to him that Carlos Campos might have been the one to whom

he gave the money the first time. Carlos might be going secretly to
Brownsville in order to collect the blackmail. So Radisson got a
seat in the sun at the bullfight and dispatched Carlos. I thought it
odd that he attended the fight, since even from the box I could see
that he disliked what took place. Whether or not he was the first one
to throw away his mirror, we'll never know. My guess is that he was."

Rennert tossed the end of his cigar into the night.

"This noon, when Torday died, I was bothered. I was satisfied
that Radisson had murdered the others, but there was a possibility that another person had done away with Torday. Therefore my
insistence on a search of those present. I visualized Torday's actions just before he expired. He took a few draws upon the cigarette. He cleared his throat and wrinkled the skin about his mouth.
Then he drank. So the cigarette or the holder might have contained
the poison. But the cigarette came from a box which was custom-
arily passed to guests. So I decided on the holder. You told me only
that the chemist found potassium ferrocyanide inside. Did he have
anything more to say?"

Bounty's cigar had gone out, but he was still fondling it between his lips. "I was afraid you were going to ask me that. He had
a lot more to say, but I didn't understand it all. It seems the heat
decomposed the potassium ferrocyanide with which the inside of
the holder had been coated and liberated hydrocyanic acid. A very
small quantity would produce almost instantaneous death. And the
eggnog which Torday swallowed immediately would disguise the
taste. I don't suppose we'll ever know how Radisson got hold of
the stuff."

"In Mexico, doubtless. He poisoned one of the holders that
Angerman was making, knowing that sooner or later it would do its
work. It wasn't until this noon that Torday selected the deadly one."

"But, Hugh, wouldn't Radisson know that this would throw
suspicion on Angerman and Mrs. Torday? You told me he claimed
to be Angerman's friend."

"I think his knowledge that he had implicated an innocent man
accounted in large part for his warm defense of Angerman. His
conscience must have been troubling him. He probably reasoned

that it would be difficult to prove that Angerman himself had inserted the poison in the holder, that a clever lawyer could argue there were plenty of opportunities after the holders reached Torday. On the other hand, Radisson had gone so far that the life of one more person would probably make little difference to him."

Rennert was silent for a moment, thinking that Bounty had something to say. Whatever it was that was bothering the sheriff, he didn't see fit to put it into words yet.

"I'm glad," Rennert went on, "that things turned out as they did. In the first place, we had after all very little valid evidence against Radisson. The paint on the bandage which he was wearing on Saturday night matched that on the seat of the trousers which you had on at the same time. You could swear that yours came from the bridge. Therefore, Radisson had been on the bridge and got off before the gates were closed. By the way, I'm satisfied that he shot Wyllys in mistake for Torday. We could prove that his left thumb made the mark on the Simon Secondyne photograph. We could have made Matt Bettis admit to the blackmailing, thus proving that Radisson had a motive for all these murders. We could prove that he had the opportunity, that's about all. We would have had to restrict ourselves to what took place in the United States. There's poetic justice, too, in the fact that Radisson died by his own hand, as it were. Blood-poisoning from the wound which he had inflicted on himself after receiving another call from Bettis and learning that his murder of Campos had been in vain."

"You think the hospital at Tonatiuh wasn't at fault? That story about him dying under the ether sounded rather glib to me."

"We'll give them the benefit of the doubt. But when I have an operation it won't be down at Tonatiuh."

"What was your real purpose in dashing down there last night?"

"I wasn't quite sure about Lincoln. And I wanted to get that left thumb of Radisson's after it was amputated. He might claim that any finger-prints we put forward in evidence were made by someone else. We couldn't have proved conclusively that any single article in his house had been used by him alone. I wasn't sure what sort of an impression could begot from that bandage."

"What I'm gladdest of," Bounty laughed, "was that those pants of mine didn't have to go into court. I've been thinking all afternoon of the razzing I'd have suffered. May I ask what happened at that interview with Lincoln in my office? You noticed I was careful to leave the two of you alone."

Rennert smiled. "I'm afraid, Peter, that all I accomplished was to inflate the old ego a little bit by leaning back in that soft chair of yours, acting dignified and making Lincoln answer my questions. He swore he had no idea Radisson was guilty. He did admit that the wound showed indications of having been made at close range. When I frowned at that, he made haste to say that if he'd been sure he would have told me. We shook hands and parted good friends, at least on the surface."

Bounty's chuckle was deep. "Wearing a badge does have its advantages, doesn't it?" He sat forward suddenly with an air of determination. "I wish I'd known this Radisson. Then the whole thing might be clearer to me. In the first place, why did he ever write that article?"

Rennert shook his head.

"We'll probably never know. He may have done it merely to make some extra money. Perhaps as a sort of *tour de force*. My guess would be that he wrote it in the white heat of indignation after witnessing a particularly cruel spectacle somewhere in Mexico."

"Well, I'm going to say the same thing young Distant did back at the hotel. It doesn't seem possible that a scholar would commit wholesale murder just to keep from being shut out of Mexico."

Rennert stared into the moonlight for a long time before he made any reply. "Peter," he said slowly, "it doesn't seem possible to men like you and me. But we're vastly different from Radisson. We're conditioned by society. Murder to us is the worst of crimes. Murder for any motive. Radisson lived alone a great part of the time and doubtless came to think of himself almost as a law unto himself. Living in Mexico, too, makes human life seem cheaper. But those are minor considerations. Radisson had one all-absorbing interest, his work. It was his monomania. He had no personal motive at all, I'm positive. He didn't think of this blackmailer as threatening him, but the continuation of his studies. He knew that if he didn't complete these no one ever would. These Indian dialects are dying out rapidly; if they are ever recorded, it must be at once. So little time, he said to me once, and so much to do. His attempt to wipe out the entire group on the Pullman was doubtless the result of an impulse. Thereafter he could justify his actions by telling himself that a gambler like Bettis, a quack such as he thought Torday to be, a Mexican bullfighter were of little importance as compared to the monumental work which he would leave to civilization. If he had enough of the fanatic in him, he may have thought of them as sacrifices to the cause of knowledge. Other men have done so."

Rennert lighted a cigarette. It helped him talk. And he wanted to talk.

"Peter, sometimes I envy men like Radisson, who have found a lifework that's greater than they. Scientists in their laboratories. Writers who have tasted what Kipling called 'that fatal facile drink.' Crusaders even. If I knew I had to die to-night, I'm afraid my regret would boil down to the fact that I'd miss to-morrow morning's breakfast and the smoke that follows it. Sleeping and sitting here in a comfortable chair. Books, I suppose, as an incidental."

Bounty was so far back in his chair that his face could scarcely be seen. "I know. I know exactly. I think I feel that envy more than you do, Hugh. Because I do more eating and sleeping than you—defiantly."

For a long time no word passed between them. "I think," Rennert said, "that it was that shrimp we had for dinner."

"Yes," Bounty agreed, "I'm sure it was the shrimp."

Rennert took the deputy sheriff's badge from the pocket to which he had consigned it. He laid it on the arm of Bounty's chair with the words: "I was about to forget to return that."

Bounty gazed at it and his voice was low and quick.

"Keep it, Hugh. I'll have a vacancy on the regular force the first of the year."

"I can't, Peter. You know that. There's no need to go into my reasons, is there?"

"No," Bounty said reluctantly as he put away the shield. "No, hell, no. I understand."

"I was about to forget something else. That envelope you told me to get from Torday." Rennert held it out.

Bounty made no motion to take it.

"That"—he spoke with satisfaction—"is something you *are* going to keep. Open it and look over what's inside."

Rennert tore the flap, struck a match, and ran his eyes down the sheet of paper which was within. It was a deed, duly signed and attested, whereby Paul Torday conveyed to Hugh Rennert a section of land in Cameron County. It was that section which extended between Rennert's house and the highway.

Rennert looked at Bounty.

"How come, Peter?"

"How come?" Bounty countered airily. "That's your pay cheque. Didn't think I'd let my men work without pay, did you?"

"Peter," Rennert said sternly, "Torday called you an extortionist this noon. Why?"

Bounty lay back peacefully and closed his eyes. "Why ask so many questions, Hugh? You bother me. Torday wanted you to solve this case. I told him you were my deputy and you weren't getting any pay. I didn't know whether I was going to let you do it or not. Of course if someone were to pay you, give you an orange grove for example, then it would be different. I'd see that you solved it in quick order. So Torday volunteered to furnish the pay. Oh, quite readily. I was going to register that deed for you, so you wouldn't get scrupulous and tear it up. But now that Torday's gone and the case is solved, there's no reason why you shouldn't keep it, is there?"

"Well," Rennert folded the paper and put it carefully into his pocket, "we'll hope Torday's ghost isn't out in that moonlight."

www.ingramcontent.com/pod-product-compliance
Lightning Source LLC
Chambersburg PA
CBHW020646260626
47157CB00008B/2923